IT'S GOOD
FOR THE SOUL

"Don't worry about confessing. You'd be surprised what people have told me. Remember, it used to be my job to get people to tell me their deepest, darkest secrets. . . ."

He winced. "Ouch!"

"No. No. I didn't mean it that way." She didn't want to think about the Daily Mail. She didn't want to remember she'd once thought of him as the-evil-boss-from-hell. She didn't want to remember she'd once planned to do whatever it took to get back her job. Tonight she wanted it to be just Rebecca and David, with no expectations. No promises. Just the honesty of desire beating between them.

She touched his thigh and their eyes met. She shifted closer, reacting to the invitation on his face. "Let's agree, David. Tonight, nothing about the Daily Mail will taint the celebration."

"Daily Mail? Never heard of it . . ."

TALK OF
THE TOWN

SHERRILL BODINE

FOREVER

NEW YORK   BOSTON

Copyright © 2008 by Sherrill Bodine
All rights reserved. Except as permitted under the U.S. Copyright Act of 1976, no part of this publication may be reproduced, distributed, or transmitted in any form or by any means, or stored in a database or retrieval system, without the prior written permission of the publisher.

Cover design by Melody Cassen
Cover photo by Gen Nishino/Getty
Book design by Giorgetta Bell McRee

Forever
Hachette Book Group
237 Park Avenue
New York, NY 10017
Visit our Web site at www.HachetteBookGroup.com

Forever is an imprint of Grand Central Publishing. The Forever name and logo is a trademark of Hachette Book Group, Inc.

Printed in the United States of America

First Printing: December 2008

10 9 8 7 6 5 4 3 2 1

*I dedicate this book with loving gratitude
to Chicago's real queen of gossip, Ann Gerber,
who, with great wit, so generously shared her expertise.
I literally could not have written this without you,
my dear friend.*

Acknowledgments

I love you, Chicago!
The entire city and the vast number of people who make
it such a great place to live inspire me.

Special thanks must go—

to my husband, John, who continues to be the hero of
my story in Chicago, just as he has been in all the varied
places we have cohabitated with our charming children

to my critique group—Cheryl Jefferson, Jude Mandell,
Patricia Rosemoor, and Rosemary Paulas—for gently but
firmly suggesting how I could make this book better and
patting me on the head when I obeyed their orders

to Susanna Homan of "Susanna's Night Out" in the *Chicago Sun-Times,* for telling me all her war stories

to my literary agent, Danielle Egan-Miller, for welcoming me back into the fold and insisting I write about life
in my favorite city.

P.S. I'm also quite fond of New York City. I especially
adore Grand Central Publishing for wanting me to write
books for them, and I *adore* my editor, Michele Bidel-
spach, for refusing to accept anything except my best
work; obviously, we're a perfect match—we're the same
diminutive height, and we both love *Project Runway* and
chocolate!

TALK OF
THE TOWN

THE CHICAGO DAILY MAIL
WEDNESDAY EDITION

Rebecca Covington's World

Darlings, you know I tell you absolutely everything! This bit of diet news is so bizarre that at first I threw it in the wastebasket. But hey—I promised you. The newest, sickest diet is the Last Hope Diet. You drink only Diet Coke and eat Kleenex. Yes, eat Kleenex! Does it have fiber? Don't even think about it.

Catty Comments

Sshh . . . it's a secret, *but* . . .

Who is the high-profile, wealthy, this-close-to-ruining-his-career, married politician who has been seen ringing the chimes of a hot lady friend in a Gold Coast high-rise? He pretends he's a pizza delivery guy and carries the big quilted heating bag. What might it contain? Diamonds? Pearls? Perhaps even a giant pepperoni pizza? Although he wears dark sunglasses and a cap pulled over his thick locks, *nothing* can disguise his killer smile. Or those oh-so-kissable lips.

Chapter 1

Some Monday mornings start out so well.

The cab Rebecca stepped into had her picture advertising "Rebecca Covington's World," in the *Chicago Daily Mail,* plastered across the back of the front seat.

She squinted at the ad. How long had it been since she'd done a new press photo? Her blond hair was so much lighter and shorter now . . . her face thinner . . . *older.*

"You're lookin' good, Miss Covington. Wife loves your columns," shouted the delightful cabdriver.

Before she looked up at the charming man, she remembered to widen her eyes to smooth out the dreaded lines on her forehead, just as Harry had instructed.

"Thank you," she cooed to the cabbie. "You've made my day." Of course, she gave him a huge tip when she alighted in front of the Chicago Daily Mail building.

Feeling wonderful, and looking forward to seeing Pauline Alper, BFF since they bonded over their divorces only two years apart and shed enough tears together to raise the water level in Lake Michigan, Rebecca swished through the doors and into the small lobby.

Pauline looked up from behind the reception desk, saw

Rebecca, burst into loud sobs, and buried her wet face in two fistfuls of pink Kleenex.

Shocked by Pauline's tears instead of her usual warm welcome, Rebecca rushed across the lobby to offer her shoulder to cry upon. "Pauline, tell me everything."

Instead of being comforted, Pauline jumped up, crying even louder, and ran to the "For Staff Only" restroom.

Her heart pounding, terrified at what could be so wrong, Rebecca raced after Pauline and stood outside the locked stall. "Sweetheart, it isn't your girls, is it?" The thought of any harm coming to Pauline's daughters, Patty and Polly, caused tears to burn in her eyes.

"No," came Pauline's muffled reply, followed by a cacophony of fresh sobs.

Weak with relief, Rebecca collapsed against the cool metal door. "Thank God! Then whatever it is can be fixed. I saw you with the box of pink Kleenex on your desk. You didn't try that ridiculous Kleenex diet and become violently ill, did you?"

"No," Pauline hiccupped.

"Good. Then please come out so I can help you. You're crying so hard you really will make yourself sick."

"I can't stop . . . I'm . . . so . . . so . . . sad," Pauline wailed between sobs.

"Sweetheart, you're hyperventilating!" Rebecca's voice rose in alarm. She'd never forgotten the day Pauline fainted in her living room after a bout of prolonged crying over the divorce wars. "Please stop."

"I . . . can't . . . ," Pauline gasped.

Drastic action must be taken.

"Keep breathing, sweetheart!" Rebecca kicked off her black Brian Atwood stilettos. Hiked up her black Carolina Herrera skirt until the top of her pantyhose showed.

Not caring if the expensive Wolford fishnets got bigger holes, she dropped to her hands and knees onto the cold, hard, black and white tile floor. "Pauline, keep breathing and tell me what's wrong," she called through the opening at the bottom of the stall.

An instant later, from beneath the door Pauline peered back, her green eyes swollen nearly shut from weeping. "Rebecca, get up! That's . . . your . . . favorite designer outfit. You'll . . . you'll . . . ruin . . . ruin your beautiful clothes," she sobbed anew.

"Sweetheart, I will get up. But you're really scaring me." Rebecca held Pauline's red-rimmed eyes in a steady gaze. "Remember our pledge to always be there for each other. This is one of those moments, but this bathroom floor is no place to have a heart-to-heart. Please splash gallons of cold water on your face and come to my office. I'll shut the door, bring out the chocolate like always, and we'll talk for as long as you need. Promise you'll come up with me."

Pauline heaved a long, ragged sigh and nodded. "I promise. Oh, please don't . . . hurt yourself getting up."

"I'm fine," Rebecca lied while struggling to her feet. Ignoring the little twinges of pain in her abused knees, she slid back into her shoes. She washed her hands for a good five minutes, all the while staring at the locked stall door, willing it to open. When that didn't work she called through it again. "Are you all right? I'm sure I have enough Leonidas chocolates to handle this emergency. Ready to go up, sweetheart?"

"Not yet . . . please go on . . . I promise . . . I'll be there . . . soon," Pauline called back in a soft, breathless voice.

Rebecca hated to leave, but she sensed Pauline wanted a little privacy. "All right. I'll be in my office waiting for you."

Knowing Pauline would keep her promise, Rebecca climbed up the short flight of stairs to the *Daily Mail* offices. On the wide landing, the din of voices and noise from the newsroom seeped through the closed glass double doors. Even now in the throes of such powerful angst over Pauline, Rebecca felt a wave of gratitude for having escaped from there so long ago. In the newsroom she'd been just another reporter. She loved being Rebecca Covington, Chicago's most notorious gossip columnist. She loved that she belonged in the quiet executive hallway. Now, if she was having a really bad day, she could shut her door and hide for a few minutes to perfect her confident front for the world.

Her stilettos clicked musically on the tile floor as she hurried to her office, where she'd hide Pauline for as long as it took to calm her down and find out what was wrong. At the end of the short hall, Tim Porter's secretary, Maybella, glanced up from her desk and quickly looked back down, but not before Rebecca spied a smirk on her glossy fuchsia lips.

Something is up.

When Tim stepped out of his office and planted himself in front of her, she knew from the stricken look on his face that something wasn't just up. Something was drastically wrong.

"No!" Rebecca gasped, clasping her alligator bag to her heaving bosom. "Not you, too! What's happened?"

Gently, he ushered her into his office. "Sit down, Rebecca. I have something to tell you."

The aura of doom surrounding him could mean only one thing. She flung herself into the chair before her knees buckled from the shock. "Tim, I can't *believe* you've been fired! You're the finest managing editor in the newspaper business. How could they do this? You have two boys in college and a wife making a life's work of restoring your crumbling mansion in Lake Forest." Devastated for him, she leaned forward to clasp his hand. "How can I help?"

He took a file from his tidy desk and laid it on her lap. "Sign these papers."

She flipped open the file and squinted down at the small, blurry print. She tried holding the papers at arm's length to read. "Darling, if it's that you want me to cosign for a loan, I must tell you my credit isn't any better than yours."

"Here, try these," he said, holding out a pair of reading glasses from his own shirt pocket.

She placed the glasses on her nose, and the letters loomed larger before her eyes.

An unpleasant numbness, like when she slept on her leg wrong, spread through every limb. "These are termination papers. With *my* name on them." Not believing her eyes, refusing to accept it, she kept staring at him. "Is this some kind of joke?"

His face turned a deep crimson. "Damn it, Rebecca. It's your own fault. You shouldn't have run the blind item about that politician. Didn't you double-check your sources? Who was it?"

A rush of scalding anger brought feeling back into her body. Tim didn't need to know that the paper's very own security guard, who moonlighted at several Gold Coast condos, was her most reliable source. Until now. She couldn't believe he had gotten it *so* wrong this time. Something wasn't ringing true. "You know I never divulge my sources!" she snapped, not liking where this was going.

"Well, you might have to divulge it this time in court," he snapped back. "The item struck a nerve with our junior senator, who is damn well connected. He's been in California for weeks trying to reconcile with his wife. He hasn't been anywhere near any Gold Coast condo. He's threatening to sue."

"So what?" She shrugged, relief making her smile. Now she was on safe, familiar ground. "The last time someone threatened to sue, circulation skyrocketed and I received a generous bonus. Tim, darling, you know I'm the queen of naughty gossip in Chicago. That's what sells papers. That's what you pay me to do."

"Not anymore."

She felt the earth shift beneath her in a strange, silent shudder. It started at her toes and rushed up to her brain, just as it had ten years ago when she'd gone home sick from work and walked into her condo to find her husband, Peter, in their bed performing oral sex on his young executive assistant.

Then, like now, every sense deserted her except sight.

She saw Tim's lips moving, but no sound reached her.

She closed her eyes, believing that when she opened them it would all turn out to be a terrible nightmare.

But it didn't work this time, either.

"Rebecca, did you hear me?" She heard Tim shout as his beady eyes nearly popped out of their sockets. "Your position has been filled by Shannon Forrester from the women's page."

"That's utterly ridiculous!" she shouted back, all her senses restored to full furious force. "*I'm* the gossip columnist for the *Daily Mail*. It's been my identity for fifteen years. I'm not giving it up to anyone!"

Tim shook his head. "I'm sorry, Rebecca, but you don't have a choice. The blind item fiasco in your column brought it to a head faster than I wanted. Regardless of how we feel, there are changes coming under the new owner. He has evaluated the staff and feels Shannon will keep up with the youth market and bring a fresh perspective to the paper. Younger. Sassier. Sexier."

Not caring how many wrinkles she made in her face, Rebecca sneered at him in disgust. "It's ridiculous to think no one over forty has *sexy, sassy* fun! What is going on? I asked you if the rumors were true about the paper being bought and you told me no. How could you lie to me?"

Tim recoiled. "I'm sorry, but I'm not at liberty to discuss anything but your termination."

Wounded to her core by his cavalier treatment, tears choked the back of her throat. She rose majestically onto her wobbly legs. "I'd always hoped that should the worst happen, I'd built relationships along the way so my friends would stand by me."

Tim slumped down onto the edge of his desk. "Rebecca, give me a break. My job could be on the line if you don't cooperate."

His dejected voice and posture caused her to feel a flicker of pity. She doused it with righteous indignation. "I won't be discarded like last year's fashion mistake, Tim. This is blatant age discrimination. I have two more years left on my contract. I'm not leaving without a fight. I'm calling my lawyer." Becoming more furious by the second, she made the ultimate threat. "Then I'm calling Charlie Bartholomew at the *Chicago Journal and Courier.*"

At mention of Charlie, all color drained from Tim's face. The nasty rivalry between the two papers was the stuff of urban legend. It had sucked dry more than one managing editor.

"Rebecca, you're trying to kill me," he groaned. "I can't afford a messy legal battle with you right on the heels of the takeover. It's bad PR for all of us. God knows what that bastard Charlie might do if he gets wind of this too soon. He could screw up this deal. He'd like nothing better."

She lifted her chin in defiance and glared at him. "Then give me my column back."

"I can't do that. But I've been authorized to offer you another job." He stood and slid his fingers around his shirt collar to loosen it. Perspiration glistened on his wide, red forehead above his suddenly glassy-looking eyes. "Your salary will remain the same for the duration of your contract. However, the only place for you on the paper is writing a twice-weekly recipe column for the Home and Food section."

Her blood felt like it was freezing in her veins and she hid her trembling hands in her lap. She'd felt this same icy helplessness in her condo bedroom, when she realized her identity as Peter's wife was erased. Hollow with pain from yet another rejection, she'd turned on her heels and quietly walked out the door. Sometimes she fantasized about what she should have done all those years ago. She should have screamed or thrown a shoe at her miserable cheating husband. Better yet, she should have pulled out every follicle of hair *she'd paid* to have transplanted along his receding hairline. The moment of truth was at hand. Had she learned nothing? Would she allow herself to be replaced by a younger woman again?

Anger and pride roared through her in one loud answer. *No! This time I'll dig in my stilettos and fight for what I want.* "I accept the job."

Tim sighed like a balloon deflating. "Thank you, Rebecca. You'll be working under Kate Carmichael. She's a good egg."

"She's also a Pulitzer Prize winner and a *real* professional." With a last disdainful look at Tim, who deserved every drop of her disgust, she swung away to the door, determined to let no one see how much this blow had stunned her. "I'll clean out my office and move to the Home section."

"Rebecca . . ." His voice stopped her, but her fierce pride wouldn't let her give him the courtesy of looking back.

"Shannon has already moved into your office."

Rebecca took a deep, steadying breath to calm her raging anger so he wouldn't see it. Then she glanced over her shoulder to smile sweetly at him. "Only temporarily, Tim. Only temporarily."

With her head held high, and ignoring Tim's smirking secretary, who had never been one of her fans, Rebecca forced herself to stroll slowly toward the brown cardboard box with her personal mementos sticking out the top. It was sitting forlornly outside her former office.

She couldn't believe how badly she'd misjudged Shannon's ambitions. Rebecca had believed her when she confessed her goal was to be a *serious* journalist. She'd even helped Shannon with a few in-depth features on society in Chicago and commiserated with her when one of Shannon's pet goldfish had been found belly-up in the small aquarium she kept on her desk.

Rebecca gazed into her beloved sanctuary, ready to confront Shannon, but she was hidden by the high-backed, ergonomically correct chair, which was turned away from the open door.

Everything else appeared the same. The much-coveted window, the oversized desk, and the large-screen computer monitor. But now next to the computer where her silver canister of Leonidas chocolates should be, there was a tiny aquarium with two goldfish and, beside it, a clear glass plate of edamame.

She'd always admired how Shannon embraced healthy eating, and she vowed every morning she would do the same, until inevitably she gave in to her passion for a chocolate-filled croissant. Now it seemed ridiculous to prefer soybeans to chocolate. Shannon would need those endorphins to survive Chicago's society beat.

Rebecca shook her head to clear it of the very thought of someone else doing her job. Shannon would quickly realize she didn't have the life experience to write Rebecca's column, and so would the mysterious, obviously ignorant, new owner. Then Rebecca would be right back where she belonged.

The chair swiveled around and there was Shannon, dead-black hair falling straight around her pale oval face. Did Rebecca see surprise in her slightly bulgy blue eyes?

"Rebecca, I didn't know you were here," Shannon gasped in her soft, saccharine voice and made the little movement with her mouth that somehow always made her appear sympathetic.

Now that she knew Shannon was such a backstabber, Rebecca wouldn't be surprised if the girl practiced the expression in front of a mirror. The ugly thought that Shannon could have had something to do with the false lead flit across her mind.

"Shannon, I'm amazed that you'd settle for this position. I wouldn't think it was *serious* enough for you."

A self-satisfied smile curving her lips, Shannon

shrugged. "Circumstances change. I don't know what else to say, except good-bye and best of luck to you."

If her iron will to always appear in control hadn't clamped down like a vise, Rebecca would have given in to her burning desire to toss Shannon's skinny butt out of *her* chair. Instead, she smiled back so hard her face ached. "No need to say good-bye. I'll be right through the newsroom and around the corner in the Home and Food section."

Hoping her calm facade was still in place, Rebecca swept up the box and turned to walk away. Out of the corner of her eye she caught Shannon hastily picking up the phone. If she was calling Tim or the mysterious new owner so they could plot their next move to get rid of her, they should save their breaths.

Let them do their worst—this time I'm not going anywhere.

She held her box of office treasures like a shield. On top, the picture of her with Harrison Ford, taken when he was in town shooting *The Fugitive,* stared back at her.

So we both looked a little younger in those days. But damn it, we still look good today. If I wasn't in the media where they judge my age in dog years, I'd be considered in my prime.

She felt a remarkable connection with her aging hero. Both their careers might be down at the moment, but certainly they weren't *finished.*

With a vow to win whatever battles with Shannon and The-New-Evil-Boss-from-Hell lay ahead, she clutched the picture of Harrison to her breasts, pushed open the glass double doors to the newsroom, and walked defiantly back into chaos.

Chapter 2

On the ball field in Ellen Sumner Park, Juan Cortez's leadoff was too aggressive at second base. "Back a step, buddy, back a step," David Sumner muttered to himself while pacing in front of his Little League team.

At home plate, Pedro got fisted with an inside fastball that blooped over the first baseman's head and down the right-field line. Short on power but long on speed, he legged it into a double.

Juan did a header into third base, and David cheered along with the team when the umpire yelled, "Safe!"

David's cell phone vibrated against his thigh and he yanked it out of his pocket. "This better be good, Louise. We're down two in the bottom of the seventh."

"David, it's Tim Porter. Your secretary gave me this number when I told her it was important."

"Make it quick." David made a mental note to let Tim know this time was only for the kids he coached. Only half listening to Tim, David watched little Miguellia place the helmet over her regular hat because it was too big for her.

"Rebecca Covington took the job in the Home section. There won't be an age discrimination suit." Tim finally had his attention.

David felt a jolt of relief, and then it was lost in his concern for Miguellia, head down, dragging the bat behind her, moving toward home plate.

He tried to focus on Tim for one minute. "Rebecca Covington has pride. She won't give up her column that easily. She'll take the money for a while, but this isn't over. Keep me informed. Thanks. Gotta go."

David watched Miguellia take a warm-up swing. He ached inside, as it looked as though the bat was swinging her. After digging in, Miguellia took a wild hack with everything she had, missing the ball by a foot when the pitch was over her head.

David signaled the umpire for a time-out and motioned Miguellia off to the side, where no one else could hear them. He knelt and smiled at her. "How you doing?"

"Coach, we need a home run to win," Miguellia said, eyes downcast.

"Don't try to win the game in one swing. Just try to make good contact. That's all we need, and you can do it."

When he saw a grin spread over Miguellia's tiny face, David stood and gave her a gentle pat on top of her helmet. "Go get it."

Among the sprinkling of parents watching from around the field, David saw Miguellia's dad give him a thumbs-up. Beyond the spectators, kids and adults were playing in the Boundless Playground, accessible to all regardless of their special challenges.

He knew Ellen would have loved this park that he'd

funded and named in her honor. He could almost hear her voice cheering on little Miguellia . . . just like sometimes he could still hear and feel her cheering him on.

Chaos!

Stepping inside the newsroom doors, Rebecca was hit by a tidal wave of ringing phones, scraping chairs, rustling papers, shouted curses, and murmuring voices. She swayed to a halt and stared down the room, lined on both sides by dozens of cluttered desks.

It all blurred together, except for the central aisle, which appeared to be narrowing dangerously into a black hole right before her eyes.

I can't go back here!

She gave herself a mental kick in the butt.

Stop whining, you coward. Remember who you are.

She took two deep yoga breaths, silently chanting the mantra she'd lived by since her tenth birthday, when she looked up the word *narcissistic,* after she heard her granny shouting it at her parents.

It wasn't my fault my parents were so self-absorbed I lived more at Granny's than with them.

Another breath and the mantra she'd added later.

It wasn't my fault Peter turned out to be such a jerk.

One last deep yoga breath for her new mantra.

I will not be defeated by an ambitious girl or a new boss who doesn't know what the hell he's doing.

She vowed to save herself like she'd always done and show a brave face to the world, in the hopes that the facade would fool both them and herself into believing it.

Rose Murphy, a young writer from Tempo, glanced up

over the pile of papers on her desk, which was crowned by a sign that read "Creative Minds Are Seldom Tidy," and saw Rebecca. Rose's shy smile but frankly curious stare left Rebecca no choice. If she wished to maintain her dignity, she would glide gracefully forward, like heroines always did.

Head held high, stomach sucked in, she smiled gently at all who gazed up at her and kept walking. The corner that led to the small alcove housing the Home section loomed only a few feet ahead.

Just as she turned it, Joe Richards, the ancient, irreverent sports columnist, raised his Cubs baseball-cap-clad head from his chest, where he habitually napped the day away, and bellowed after her, "Give 'em hell, Becca!"

Rebecca could have wept over Joe's show of support, but she caught sight of Pauline and Kate, her new boss, waiting beside an empty desk. The last thing she wanted was for Pauline to start hyperventilating again. Her face was still the same shade as her natural brilliant red hair.

A rush of protective love for Pauline, like older sisters surely must feel for younger siblings, strengthened Rebecca's resolve. She turned on her brightest, aren't-we-having-a-fabulous-time smile.

"Rebecca . . . I've . . . put your messages on your . . . new desk," Pauline gulped and blew her nose into pink Kleenex.

"Sweetheart, everything will be fine. I'm looking forward to working with Kate for a while."

Blinking wet, spiky lashes, Pauline looked back and forth between Kate and Rebecca until obviously satisfied enough to nod. "Okay, if you say so. Oh, and Dr. Harry Grant wants you to call him at home as soon as possible. He's worried about you. And Cathy Post from Three

Thousand Communications called five times. She wants the scoop."

Rebecca thumped the box onto the desk, perched beside it, and laughed as convincingly as possible through the tight dread constricting her chest. "Did *everyone* know except me?"

Kate held out a copy of *Crain's*. "Today's issue has a story on the *Daily Mail* acquisition."

"Did they spell my name correctly?" Rebecca asked, still trying to be funny, for everyone's sake—including her own.

Kate didn't appear amused. She shook her head. "They only mention that the paper has been acquired by an unknown buyer. Very hush-hush. However, they do speculate that there will be personnel changes."

"Personnel changes," Pauline echoed and straightened her hunched shoulders. "I suppose I'd best get back to the switchboard. Are you sure you'll be all right, Rebecca?"

"I'm absolutely wonderful." Reaching into the cardboard box, Rebecca pulled out the silver canister. "Here, I promised you chocolate. Take two. Remember the small ovals are the caramels. Your favorites." She kept smiling while Pauline slipped two chocolates into her pocket and Kate took one.

Rebecca held her painful forced smile until Pauline was safely away. Then she collapsed in a heap against the cardboard box and glanced up to find Kate watching her like a benevolent schoolteacher.

She stiffened her spine and tried to recapture her fake grin, but her face hurt too much. "I'm fine. Really, I am," she lied to her new boss.

"You don't need to pretend for me. We should talk in my office," Kate said in her crisp, matter-of-fact way.

They stepped around the short gray partition separating Kate's barely adequate cubbyhole office from Rebecca's lone desk, situated in what was essentially a short hallway.

Afraid her facade was cracking around the edges, Rebecca carefully sat firmly on the small, hard chair. "Kate, I promise not to become hysterical. If you have any information that might shed light on what just happened to me, I'd really like to hear it."

Leaning against the file cabinet, Kate gazed down at her with clear brown eyes. "Here is what I know. Our owner, Perry Communications, suffered a year-end loss of four hundred million after it had to slash the value of its stock. The PC board voted to pull the news megalith back to its media foundations in an effort to stop any further corporate crumbling. The *Chicago Daily Mail* is one of the crumbs someone picked up. There will be others."

Grateful for Kate's no-nonsense approach instead of sympathy, Rebecca nodded. "Thank you. Brilliant and concise." She glanced at the Pulitzer for business writing on Kate's desk. "The owners of *Wealth Weekly* were fools to let you get away from them."

A flicker of a smile curled Kate's narrow lips. "I thought so at the time. They wanted younger, hungrier writers. A similar situation to what just happened here to you."

Drawn to Kate, Rebecca leaned forward. "Isn't it *unbelievable* when it happens?"

Unblinking, Kate stared her straight in the eyes. "I didn't believe it at first. It took a breakdown and four months in a hospital to come to grips with it. Now Prozac makes it possible for me to happily edit the stress-free Home section. But you knew all this, didn't you?"

There wasn't a hint of self-pity in Kate's voice, but her pain hit Rebecca right between the eyes. Of course Rebecca knew, but she had forgotten. It had been the talk of the media community when the brilliant Kate Carmichael came out of forced retirement to edit the *Daily Mail*'s lowly Home section. But she hadn't known until this instant that Kate was hiding her real feelings, just like Rebecca did. "I'm sorry to have brought it up, Kate. I'm an insensitive, selfish bitch to have forgotten."

Kate shook her head, folding her arms across her neat but utterly shapeless black jacket. "You're not a bitch. Or insensitive. Which is why you've been successful for so long. Now may I ask what you plan to do? Nothing as drastic as what I did, I hope?"

Deeply touched by Kate's unexpected kindness, Rebecca stood with new determination. "I plan to do an outstanding job for you until I get my column back. But right now I feel the overwhelming need to get out of here. I think better when I'm shopping. Do you mind?"

Kate's surprisingly robust laughter soothed Rebecca's bruised ego. "You will be punching no time clock for me. Tomorrow we can discuss your two food columns for the week. If you have time, you might begin researching recipes. Meanwhile, please go improve the retail economy. The latest numbers are dismal."

Intrigued, and very grateful, Rebecca gazed back at Kate, already working at her desk. Her snow-white short hair and apple-cheeked complexion complemented her black suit, but the outfit did nothing for her figure. Really, with such great legs and nice shoulders, Kate could look wonderful in the right clothes. Rebecca vowed to immediately help her with all fashion choices. Shopping for two would be doubly therapeutic. When Kate looked better, she'd feel better. Sometimes new clothes helped hide the cracks when the facade was crumbling. Like now.

Rebecca slipped down the back stairs to the side door to avoid anyone who might be lurking in the lobby.

She walked out onto the sidewalk and nearly tripped over Cathy Post, who was leaning against the building while talking on two cell phones at the same time.

Seriously not wanting to inflict her private pity party on anyone else, Rebecca tried to duck back inside the door.

Cathy spotted her, "Rebecca!" She dropped one phone into her voluminous slouchy black bag and pulled out an open Diet Coke in one sweeping movement. "Rebecca, you were my friend before; you're my friend now. The grand opening of Allen's Restaurant to benefit the Chicago Academy for the Arts is in three weeks. I want you there as my guest. Bring a date or anyone you want. You need to be seen around town."

Once Cathy finally stopped for breath, Rebecca got a word in. "Thank you, darling. I appreciate your support."

"Not everyone will be on your side. I am. I can't blackball Shannon from PR events, because it wouldn't be fair to my clients, who are paying me a lot of money to promote them." Cathy stopped for another breath and another gulp of Diet Coke.

Rebecca wished she could disagree about Shannon, but her sense of fair play wouldn't let her. "You're right. It would be totally unethical."

"I knew you'd understand. You know my business travels on the favor economy. Over the years, you've done me more favors than I can count. Now, what can I do for you?"

Rebecca plastered on her pat smile and shook her head. "Thank you, darling. I'm fine. Really, I am."

"Do you want me to find out whatever I can about the new owner of the paper?"

Stunned by how much she wanted to know who he was, Rebecca gasped. "Could you?"

"By dinner tonight I will have spoken to five people who will give me all the information you need. I'll call you."

When both of Cathy's phones rang at once, Rebecca blew her a kiss and strolled toward Oak Street.

By the time she got there, she'd wiped away the two tears that had welled up despite her best efforts not to show her feelings. Really, she hadn't expected such an outpouring of support, first from Kate and now from Cathy. It helped her formulate a plan for how to handle this temporary setback. She'd find out who bought the paper and help him understand he'd made a colossal mistake in replacing her.

Feeling more herself, she walked up the short flight of stairs to Très Treat. The small, low-ceilinged shop was stark. The legendary linens needed no lavish displays.

She looked around for the manager, Jessica, who had sent her a lovely note after Rebecca wrote a fabulous column about their linens being simply the finest gift to truly impress.

She heard Jessica's voice before she spotted her in the corner, talking to an older woman.

". . . believe she's out shopping after getting fired. I heard the new owner thinks she's too old for the job. I'm not surprised."

Hearing enough to feel slightly ill, Rebecca backed up

to escape and hit her heel against the leg of a display table. The clatter caused both women to turn and stare at her.

Plastering on her best PR smile, she grabbed up the closest two pillow covers and swept toward the corner. "There you are, Jessica. I simply *must* have these."

Instead of Jessica rushing to assist her, like she always had before, the older saleswoman took the linens from Rebecca's hands. "Let me help you."

Feeling even sicker, Rebecca realized she didn't know the price of her impulse purchase. Idly tapping the toe of her stiletto, she feigned boredom, hoping they couldn't see her panic at how much her pride was costing her. She glanced over at Jessica, who immediately scurried off into a back room.

"That will be three hundred and eighty dollars apiece. Plus tax. Are you still interested?" the sales associate asked solemnly.

"Of course." Determined not to show a flicker of her burning shock, she whipped out her Visa card.

A few minutes later the saleswoman returned. Her face devoid of emotion, she handed the card back. "I'm sorry. Do you have another card?"

Rebecca felt rooted to the floor by embarrassment. *How late did I send that payment?*

Her devilish pride won again. "Here, try this one." She pulled out her second credit card, the one she used only for *extreme emergencies,* because the interest rate was criminally high. The horrible thought it might not still be active crossed her mind, but surely she'd had her quota of rejections today.

"I'm sorry. This card has also been declined." The saleswoman inched the pillow covers closer to her side of the counter.

Rebecca eyed the linens with loathing. *Let the damn store keep them.* Again her pride reared its fierce head. *No. I can't let them see me sweat.*

"I'm sure the problem is in your system." She opened her checkbook. "I'll write a check."

"I'll have to okay it with the manager." The poor embarrassed woman bolted into the back room.

Almost immediately, Jessica was forced to appear. She didn't look happy, and she absolutely refused to meet Rebecca's eyes. "You may write a check, but we need to see your driver's license."

The ugly truth hit Rebecca over the head. She might spin it any way she wanted, but not everyone would be supporting her. The ping of disappointment hurt more than a little, but she refused to show it. She shot the manager a haughty look and pulled out her driver's license. "Please hurry," she said, trying to sound as confident as she'd been when she first walked in here. "I'm late for an important meeting at the newspaper office."

Moments later, bruised but unbowed, Rebecca swept out the door, swinging a Très Treat bag stamped with their slogan, "Our Linens Dress the Beds of the World's Rich and Famous."

These seriously priceless linens weren't going to be used until she was *in bed* with someone rich and famous. Or someone she was so absolutely mad about she might marry him.

Determined to continue her charade of "everything is marvelous," she continued to stroll down Oak Street. She stopped to admire a dress in the window at Luca Luca but dared not go in, for fear she'd spend *next* month's mortgage payment, too.

When Simone, the manager, spotted Rebecca looking

in the window, she rushed to fling open the door. "Tell me it's not true. You are not leaving the paper."

Rebecca laughed as convincingly as she could muster. "Really, how do these rumors get started? Of course I'm not leaving the paper. How could they possibly get along without me?" She knew she'd succeeded when Simone nodded and smiled.

"That's what I told everyone on the street." Simone glanced meaningfully at her snooty neighbors. "Your column is the only reason I read the paper."

Wanting to break the news gently, Rebecca leaned closer. "Can you keep a secret? Seriously, you can't breathe this to anyone."

Simone's dark eyes lit with interest and she tilted her head forward to catch every word. "Yes, I promise."

"I won't be writing my column for a short while, because I'm on special assignment. The new owner is going to revamp the paper, starting with the Home section. It's going to be absolutely marvelous! Kate Carmichael, the editor, is a brilliant Pulitzer winner. Together, we're going to do things that will revolutionize the whole concept of home and food."

Simone looked stunned, which is how Rebecca felt at realizing how easily she could spin the truth. But Simone also appeared to be a trifle skeptical.

Eager to convince her and the world that everything was truly divine, Rebecca dove deeper into her fantasy. "Yes, there's talk of several TV spots. Perhaps even our own network show. Which is why I'm out shopping for Kate's new wardrobe." *That* was the grain of truth in everything she'd said, just like the stories in most of the tabloids had at least one fact correct.

Apparently buying Rebecca's version of the story,

Simone pushed the door to the shop open wider. "We would love to dress both of you."

"Thank you, darling. I personally love everything in your store. But Kate has a slightly different style. I'm going to stroll down to Prada for a peek."

"But you will allow us to dress you?" Simone insisted.

"Absolutely! Must run now." Rebecca put a finger to her lips. "Remember, not a word to anyone."

As always when Rebecca didn't behave well, guilt made her feel positively wicked.

It will serve me right if my nose is growing longer and longer with the lies I'm spreading all over Oak Street.

When she felt this rotten, there was only one person to turn to for a cure. Her best friend, Harry, who actually *had* made her nose shorter.

She sent him a text message as she walked past Prada's windows. Three minutes later he replied: "I'm home."

As fast as she could move in her four-inch heels, Rebecca ran to Harry's beautiful old stone town house on the Gold Coast.

When she opened the black wrought-iron gate to his tiny front garden, Harry walked out onto his front porch. His face was all chiseled concern, like Rupert Everett in *My Best Friend's Wedding*. Since several of his patients gushed how much he looked like Rupert, Harry had helped the resemblance along by adopting the same haircut and debonair style.

Just like Julia Roberts in the movie, Rebecca launched herself into *her* best friend's outstretched arms. "Harry, I've lost my mind," she sobbed.

"No, sweet pea. You've only lost your job."

His strong arms were so comforting she turned into an instant weakling and meekly let him lead her into the living room. They snuggled into the huge cream leather couch in front of the black marble fireplace, where he'd placed a tangle of branches, ready for the first frosty night in September.

Her sigh caught in her throat, and she tried to cover it but gave up. Harry she trusted. "I'm totally out of control. I've been telling lies all over town. And I spent eight hundred dollars on a pair of *pillowcases!*"

"What's the thread count?"

She sat up to look into his amused face. "It's not funny. I'm serious. I'm a mess. No one wants me. Tim and our evil new owner want me to slink off so Shannon can take over my job. It's too much like Peter leaving me for that infant Cassandra. Remember, he wanted me to slink off, too, while he reversed his vasectomy for *her*."

Totally absorbed in self-pity, she wallowed in tears, letting them drip down her cheeks. "Now Shannon has my three and one-half pages on Wednesday and one and one-half pages on Sunday. Peter has a wife and Angelina, the most adorable eight-year-old daughter in the world. And all I have is two recipes a week." She flung herself back onto his chest to sob with gusto.

He patted her back, making cooing sounds, until she calmed down enough to hiccup and sigh. "Thank you. I needed that. I feel better now."

"Sweet pea, I know there are problems in being over forty in the entertainment world. However, it's bliss compared to being an aging gay man." He held her at arm's length to study her ravaged face. "I could do your eyes again. Or maybe a lift. But you really don't—"

"I don't want a face-lift. I need a life-lift."

He forced her to meet his narrow gray gaze. "If there's a silver lining, you always find it. You always cry if I

cry. Then you cheer me up. Now it's my turn. What can
I do?"

"Get me out of this mess!" she demanded and tried
to laugh. "I hate to ask, but I seriously do need help. I
haven't owned a cookbook since my divorce. Peter took
those, too. Maybe that's why Tim offered me the job,
thinking I'd refuse because I'm so rusty in the kitchen.
But I plan to do an *outstanding* job for my wonderful new
boss, so I must have recipes."

"Come with me."

He pulled her into his immaculate kitchen, where
everything was picture-perfect, from the sparkling clean
Viking stove to the gleaming copper pots hanging over
the antique oak butcher block.

Like always, stress made her ravenous. She eyed his
refrigerator. "Harry, what do you have to eat?"

"I promise to feed you soon. First, look." With a
flourish, he flung open a cabinet door to reveal a shelf of
cookbooks. Then he opened another cabinet and another,
all displaying perfectly arranged cookbooks lined up like
little soldiers. "Remember how many boxes there were
when I inherited my great aunt Harriet's library last year?
All these cookbooks were in the last three boxes I didn't
unpack until later." He ran his long surgeon's fingers
over the bindings. "I've arranged them all by courses.
It relaxes me to read them and plan the perfect dining
experience."

She shook her head and studied him, looking for stress
fractures. "Harry, I've known you for twenty years.
You've never cooked one gourmet meal for me."

"I've never actually cooked anything from these
books." He shrugged his wide shoulders. "But recently
I've been fantasizing about it. I need a new hobby, since

I haven't had sex in years." Grinning, he answered the ringing phone at his elbow.

"Dr. Harry Grant here," he boomed out. Then he laughed in his warm, charming, confident way that convinced women to put their faces and bodies in his capable hands. "What a pleasant surprise, Cathy. Yes, Rebecca is here. Just a moment, please."

Eager for possible Evil-Boss-from-Hell news, she grabbed the phone and paced around the butcher block. "Cathy, darling, how in the world did you track me down here?"

"My assistant saw you shopping on Oak Street. I'm in a meeting at the Pump Room and saw you run past the windows. I tried to catch you, but you were already turning onto Astor."

Uh-oh. Those Oak Street lies are already coming back to haunt me. She needed to know how bad it was going to be to plot her defense. "By the way, have you heard any more rumors concerning my changed situation?"

"You mean about revolutionizing the concept of food and home? I've told everyone you'd put your own stamp on the Home section. So, yeah, you will be revolutionizing it."

In awe of Cathy's brilliant PR spin, Rebecca stopped pacing to lean one hip into the sturdy butcher block. "What an excellent interpretation of my comments. Do you have anything on the new owner?"

"His name is David Alan Sumner. He's DAS Media's CEO and owner. Just turned forty-nine. Widower for five years. Twin sons. Ryan, a vet. Michael, a marine biologist. He started out in communications. Started buying failing newspapers and TV stations and making them profitable. He cashed in big on reality programming.

Remember *Defeating Your Demons* and *Celebrity Bingo*? His. Along with dozens of others. He's forming his own small network. Not unlike how FOX used to be. He's been called the ethical Rupert Murdock. I'm hoping to snag him for the Allen's opening. Rumor has it he'll be in town by then. That's it so far."

A little giddy at being able to at least put a name on the Evil One, Rebecca laughed. "Cathy, I owe you. Thanks. I'll talk to you soon."

Harry raised his arched brows. "Well? Good news?"

"Maybe a silver lining. David Alan Sumner sounds married to his work, like most CEOs I know. Now I have to figure out a way to dazzle him with my brilliance so he becomes dough in my hands and gives me back my column." She pulled *Martha Stewart's Hors d'Oeuvres Handbook* from the cabinet. "This is perfect. Martha was down and out just like me not so long ago, and look at her now."

Looking positively enthralled, Harry turned the pages of the cookbook. "Excellent idea to start with hors d'oeuvres. You should build the perfect meal over several columns. I particularly like the look of the lobster and mushroom quesadillas."

Rebecca gazed down at the beautiful color photograph he held out. "It looks yummy. I want to do a good job for Kate until I get my *real* job back."

The next morning, when Kate studied the color photograph of the quesadillas, she nodded. "I agree it looks delicious. Recipe sounds reasonable. Now, how do you plan to change it?"

Rebecca stared at her in confusion. What did she mean, *change* it?

A deep furrow appeared between Kate's eyes. "You do understand that our policy is that you can't simply copy someone's recipe. You must experiment with it. Improve or change it in some way. You must make it yours, Rebecca."

Rebecca laughed a little too loud. *Of course I didn't know.* "Of course I know what must be done." She clutched the cookbook to her bosom. "I'm off this very minute to experiment. I'll arrange for the staff photographer to shoot this afternoon. I'll have my copy in ahead of deadline for you to edit."

Kate settled back in her chair. "Rebecca, I don't need to edit your work. I trust you to do your usual excellent job."

"Thank you, Kate." Holding her falsely confident smile, Rebecca stepped out of the cubbyhole.

The moment she was alone, she threw the offending cookbook on the desk and collapsed onto her chair. *Of course I'll do my best for you, Kate. But how?*

Panic urged her to call Harry, but she forced herself to wait until she heard Kate talking on the phone. Glancing around, she cupped her hand around the receiver so no one could overhear. She got his voice mail but still whispered, "Harry, I'm going to use my key and get into your place. I have to actually cook. My stove's been broken for six months. See you later."

She made one quick stop at home to change into a Juicy Couture cashmere sweat suit for the ordeal ahead. Then it was on to her now-crucial visit to that bastion of gourmet and healthy grocery shopping, Whole Foods. Once in the store's wide aisles, she kept consulting her cookbook. Taking Martha's advice to buy one cooked lobster tail for the recipe, rather than buying a small whole lobster and cooking it herself, seemed to be a good idea. To be on the safe side, she bought two. In the end she doubled all the ingredients. Plus she bought frozen flour tortillas that could be cut in half for a miniature look.

What seemed like hours later, she staggered into Harry's immaculate kitchen, ladened with grocery bags.

Her tension headache started the instant she placed the medium skillet brushed with olive oil over high heat. As Martha instructed, she waited until the skillet warmed before throwing in the mushrooms. When they colored slightly, she removed them. The recipe said to sprinkle with salt and pepper to taste and set aside. She tried one, and it tasted delicious. She heaved a huge sigh of relief and flexed her shoulders.

Really, this isn't so difficult. She felt so pleased with her efforts she decided this would be an excellent place to add her special touch.

Chocolate makes everything taste better. She dug out the Leonidas milk chocolate bar she kept in her tote for emergencies. It smelled so delicious she nibbled on a corner before using the rest to make her own version of *mole* sauce.

Humming contentedly, she drizzled it over the mushrooms and then popped one into her mouth.

Poison! She gagged, spitting the noxious fungus into the sink. Water didn't help the hideous aftertaste. Desperate, she popped open a bottle of champagne and guzzled a glass and then another, until the ghastly taste in her mouth dissipated at last.

She eyed the disgusting mushrooms. *Who knew they'd be the only food on the planet that doesn't taste better covered with chocolate!*

Hopefully, once she added the ricotta cheese, lobster, and spinach leaves, no one would be the wiser.

Until today she'd always loved mushrooms. Now she wasn't so sure. They slipped out of the damn tortilla layers, which refused to stick together the way they were supposed to. They bounced off the counter, and when she tried to catch them before they splattered on the floor, the cast-iron skillet overheated. Mushrooms were everywhere, like Tribbles in *Star Trek,* and soon the smell of burned tortillas and all the ingredients oozing out of them filled the room.

The smoke detector's tiny beep sounded like a siren in her aching head. Smoke poured up around her, making her eyes burn. Grabbing a kitchen chair, she climbed onto the wicker seat. Stretched to her full five feet two and one-half inches, plus three-inch wedges, she was almost able to brush the tips of her fingers against the bleeping alarm. With a do-or-die upward lunge, she slapped the plastic cover. It popped off and hit her on the head.

"Damn it!" Rearing back, rubbing her throbbing temple, she felt the chair totter beneath her.

"My God!" Harry bellowed from the open door before rushing to her rescue. "Get down before you kill yourself!"

Totally remorseful, she clutched his hand while he gazed around the wreckage of his once-pristine kitchen. "I'm sorry, Harry." If the smoke weren't already making her eyes water, she'd be shedding real tears.

He kissed her sticky hand and sighed. "Let's get to work, sweet pea."

With Harry's help, Rebecca started over with mushrooms sautéed in all the champagne she hadn't already consumed. After consulting a recipe he'd been lusting over, Harry substituted Maytag blue cheese for the ricotta.

Only minutes before the photographer was scheduled

to arrive, they both stared down at the finished product. "It looks all right, doesn't it?" she asked, hoping for encouragement.

"Yes. But shouldn't we taste it?"

Stoically resisting her cowardly urge to encourage him to go first, she cut off a small piece. Determined to swallow it no matter how bad it tasted, she bit into the quesadilla. The delicious combination of lobster, mushrooms, and bleu cheese melted in her mouth.

"It's delicious. Here, have a bite."

Chewing, Harry's eyes rolled in ecstasy. "Divine. Worth every calorie."

Best of all, it would photograph beautifully for Wednesday's edition.

CHICAGO DAILY MAIL
WEDNESDAY FOOD

LOBSTER AND MUSHROOM
QUESADILLAS

1 teaspoon olive oil
8 ounces white button mushrooms, wiped clean, very
    thinly sliced
1 stick butter
½ cup champagne
Kosher salt and freshly ground black pepper
12 miniature flour tortillas
12 ounces bleu cheese
2½ cups baby spinach
1 10-ounce cooked lobster tail, cut into ½-inch pieces
¼ cup fresh tarragon

Heat a medium skillet brushed with olive oil over medium-high heat until warm. Sauté mushrooms in butter and champagne. Sprinkle with salt and pepper to taste and set aside.

To assemble: Arrange half of the flour tortillas on a baking sheet. Spread 2 teaspoons of bleu cheese onto each. Place a spinach leaf on top of cheese. Cover with slices of the reserved mushrooms, 2 pieces of lobster, and 3 tarragon leaves. Add a small dollop of cheese and season with salt and pepper to taste. Cover the filling with a second tortilla. Press down so that the layers stick together. Repeat with the remaining tortillas. Cover the tortillas with plastic wrap or a damp towel to prevent them from drying out.

Heat a dry cast-iron skillet over medium heat until very warm, 1 to 2 minutes. Working in batches, cook the quesadillas until the cheese is melted and they are warm throughout, about 1½ minutes per side. Cover with foil and keep warm in a 200-degree oven. Repeat with the remaining quesadillas. Serve warm.

Chapter 3

David's Lear jet climbed steadily up through the cumulus clouds hanging over New York and streaked through a clear, shimmering blue sky.

He turned away from the window, rested his head against the leather seat, and closed his eyes. A part of him was weary of the nomadic life he'd led the last five years, but mostly he loved the challenge of building the media empire he and Ellen had dreamed about. The thought brought such bittersweet nostalgia he opened his eyes to break the reverie. The best way to stop the memories was to focus on business.

He read today's edition of the *Three River Review,* the first small newspaper he and Ellen had acquired, in upstate New York, and went through the other three DAS-owned papers, ending with Wednesday's *Chicago Daily Mail.*

He checked his watch and called Tim Porter at home.

Tim's husky, slow "Hello" made David glance at his watch again. Sometimes he forgot not everyone rose at dawn.

"Sorry, Tim. Forgot it's early there. Wanted to talk to you about today's edition. Shannon's new column hit the right note. It's exactly on target for where I'm heading with the paper."

"Great. I'll tell her at the office this morning."

Tim was silent, and in those moments David knew the managing editor was nervous. David had watched him at all the meetings before the takeover. Had noticed Tim's giveaway, the long pauses before he brought up something that might cause problems for him or the deal.

"What did you think of Rebecca's first food column, David?" Tim asked.

David flicked through the pages and looked again at the recipe for lobster quesadillas. "Ordinary stuff. Let's see if she comes up with anything better. Is she giving you problems?"

"No. No. She's being a real pro, like she's always been." Tim's voice sounded stronger now.

"Good. I'll be in touch," David said absently and hung up the phone. Easing deeper into his seat, his eyes narrowed on the simple food column. It was nothing more than a throwaway recipe, but he'd just learned something about his managing editor. Obviously, Tim hadn't wanted to demote Rebecca when David ordered it, even though he hadn't argued against it. David liked team players, who understood when change, whether you liked it or not, was good business. Nothing personal.

David smiled, remembering Rebecca's file. Maybe she'd truly surprise him and turn out to be a team player, after all.

~~*~~

On Wednesday morning, Rebecca walked into Kate's office, looking for approval about her column. She hadn't had to worry about an editor being pleased since she left the newsroom years ago. Strange how eager she felt for Kate to like it.

Kate peered up over her half-glasses and nodded. "A fine job, Rebecca. I liked the addition of the bleu cheese and champagne. It's exactly what I asked you to do."

Her confidence restored, Rebecca strolled toward Tim's office to receive his richly deserved accolades. She was still hurt by how cavalierly he'd dismissed her, but she'd decided to forgive him. Actually, she needed to console him about "Shannon Shares with Her Friends." As soon as the paper arrived this morning she'd read her competition, and any infinitesimal fear she'd had about Shannon possibly deserving her job vanished. The column was laughable in all the wrong places, besides containing at least two pictures that should have had "X ratings" for tacky. But what *had* surprised her was a picture of George Crosby, of all people, surrounded by friends in the bar at Gibson's. It had looked like it was shot by an artist.

George looked just as sweetly hunky in the photo as he had when Rebecca met him at a Health and Career Fair in the roughest inner-city high school where they were both volunteering for the day. It had been lust at first sight and a playful good time together ever since. Seeing his picture reminded her that she hadn't returned his last two phone calls.

Rebecca arrived at Tim's office just as Shannon was leaving. Paralyzed with disbelief, Rebecca froze in the open doorway. Why were Shannon and Tim positively glowing?

Smiling, Shannon gave Tim a coy little wave and floated toward Rebecca. "Your column was so . . . revolutionary," she whispered in passing.

Refusing to acknowledge her rush of embarrassment or allow Shannon a flicker of satisfaction for her zinger, Rebecca pretended not to hear. She strolled in and placed her meager one page on Tim's desk. "What do you think?"

He frowned down at it. "The picture is great. My wife said the quesadillas looked good enough to eat. Maybe it will inspire her to actually use the new kitchen." He laughed and looked up expectantly for Rebecca to join in.

She mustered a weak smile. "Do you know what the new owner thought about my first food column?"

"Rebecca, you know I love your work. Always have. Always will." Tim glanced around like the room was bugged before leaning closer. "He thought it was standard stuff. Ordinary. He wants the paper to be more hip. Edgy. Why don't you try kicking it up a little? Give it the old Rebecca Covington touch."

The phone rang before she could remind Tim in no uncertain terms that according to the new boss, the *old* Rebecca wasn't good enough now.

"Yes, Shannon." Tim rolled his eyes and shrugged. "No, no, I'm not busy. Yes. Absolutely. Yes. That's right . . . he loved your column . . . thought it was exactly on the mark. Yes . . . yes, I think so . . ."

Tim dismissed her with a grimace and a wave. Rebecca had no choice but to gather up the newspaper page and walk out. All the way back to the Home section she rolled her *ordinary* column tighter and tighter between her clenched fists.

So, Evil One . . . boss from hell . . . you want my special touch? You're going to get it!

She placed her poor shredded column beside her computer, sat down, and stared at her screen.

Part of her wanted to tell them all to go to hell, pack up, and stalk off with dignity. The other part refused to surrender.

Staring at her screen saver of a glorious rose-colored sunset, she struggled between her common sense and her pride. Usually her Midwest common sense won out, but she had a healthy ability to rationalize. Tim *had* given her a direct order to add the "old Rebecca Covington" touch. Really, he had ordered her to do it, she told herself over and over again.

To obey his request, like she had Kate's, she would change the spinach vichyssoise for Sunday's Food section.

She shuddered at the thought of another ordeal in Harry's kitchen, but she'd promised to pay for all damages from now on.

She knew her Sunday column would either dazzle David Alan Sumner with her edgy brilliance or this time he'd fire her for good.

Chapter 4

At dawn, when David hit the gym in his condo building, the Sunday editions of his papers hadn't arrived.

An hour later, finished with his workout and showered, he came back upstairs to find the bundle of newspapers at his door. As he did every morning that he happened to be in this austere penthouse he facetiously called home, he poured himself a cup of coffee and sat down to read, saving the *Chicago Daily Mail* for last.

A blast of sunlight, very intense and golden, came through the big window behind his desk and he blinked, blinded for an instant, the words blending together, so he had to reread Rebecca's food column to make sure he'd gotten it right.

THE CHICAGO DAILY MAIL
SUNDAY FOOD

SPINACH VICHYSSOISE

1 cup finely chopped white and pale green part of leek, washed well

2 tablespoons unsalted butter
1¼ pounds boiling potatoes
4 cups chicken broth
2 cups water
½ pound fresh spinach, stems discarded and the
   leaves rinsed, spun dry, and shredded coarse
   (about 8 cups)
½ cup heavy cream

In a large saucepan, cook the leek with salt and pepper to taste in butter over moderately low heat, stirring, until the vegetable is softened. Add the potatoes—peeled and cut into 1-inch pieces—the broth and the water, and simmer the mixture, covered, for 10 to 15 minutes, or until the potatoes are tender. Stir in the spinach and simmer the mixture for 1 minute. Puree the mixture in a blender in batches, transferring it as it is pureed to a bowl, and let it cool. Stir in the cream, the chives, and salt and pepper to taste. Chill the soup, covered, for at least 4 hours or overnight, and serve.

Makes about 8 cups, serving 6 to 8

A Note from Rebecca Covington

Darlings, you must promise me to be extremely careful when you make this divine recipe! Herbs have been known to be harmful to a husband's health.

I know Desperate Housewives *has shown us not only how to cheat on our wayward men, but also how to "off" them when necessary. But let us not forget the Chicago socialite who perfected the technique years ago.*

The dear, put-upon woman added sorrel mixed with the spinach in this sublime soup recipe. The two are so alike in look and taste it is nearly impossible to tell them apart. Except her miserable, cheating husband was violently allergic to sorrel! Of course it wasn't quite enough toxic matter to actually kill him, but just enough to make him wish he were dead.

He ended up in the hospital for four days, which gave her time to clean out the wall safe and hide financial assets.

Isn't that just so deliciously, cosmically correct? Happy cooking!

Xo Rebecca

David fell back in his chair and laughed with real amusement. It was something he rarely did, but when it happened he was lighter, as if the dull ache of sadness so much a part of him the last five years vanished for just that moment.

In his mind, David saw the picture of Rebecca Covington that used to head her former column as vividly as if he was looking at it now.

Her glamour had hit him first. Only then had he detected courage in her tilted chin, and a certain spirit in her eyes. Those perceptions, along with what he'd read about her, had warned him she might sue him for age discrimination. He'd expected it, alerted his legal team to the possibility.

But instead, she'd surprised and amused him.

━━━❦━━━

When the newspaper finally hit Rebecca's door on Sunday morning, she rushed to retrieve it. She held it like a baby, carrying it to her favorite chair by the window, where the light was so good she could read without her glasses.

My God, my hands are trembling!

Getting a grip on herself, she took a deep breath and turned to the Food section. Heart pounding like the hammer of fate, she read her column.

Laughing, she read her column again to make sure she hadn't missed anything. It was funny, but would David Alan Sumner be amused? Or would he order Tim to fire her *again*?

The chilling thought that she'd put not only her job but Kate's in danger cut through her like a steel blade. Stricken with sickening guilt for not thinking of the danger to Kate sooner, Rebecca rushed to the phone to call her.

She picked up the phone and realized she didn't know the number. Information was no help—it told her Kate's number was unlisted.

Desperate, she tried Pauline.

Pauline answered on the first ring with a laugh in her voice. "Rebecca, I loved your Sunday column. I'm dying to know who tried to kill her husband with soup."

Still consumed with guilt about Kate, Rebecca had a hard time keeping her voice light. "Sworn to secrecy. Even to you. Pauline, do you know Kate's home number?"

"Gosh, I'm sorry. I don't know it. She's real private. Is everything all right?"

"Of course, sweetheart." Rebecca tried to sound reassuring. "Everything is fabulous. See you in the morning."

Each time the phone rang she hoped it was Kate, but it was always one of her many sources who had fed her dozens of gossip items over the years. The phone had been deathly quiet since last week's bloodbath. This morning it rang off the hook, with people feeding her juicy tidbits of news. Obviously they all assumed she was back in business as usual.

Was she on the way back to the top? Or had she recklessly sealed her fate and Kate's?

Chapter 5

On Monday morning, Rebecca put on her darkest, biggest sunglasses, clasped Sunday's Food section to her chest like armor, and walked as fast as her four-inch heels would take her to the Daily Mail building. Everyone in Chicago always seemed to know her business before she did. She didn't want to hear any *new* bad news from a cabbie or passerby before she dealt with Tim.

She had written the gossipy note out of damn-the-consequences outrage. *She* was prepared to face the possible dire consequences of her choice. But she wouldn't allow Kate to suffer.

If Tim does David Alan Sumner's dirty work and fires anyone this Monday morning, he's in for a real fight.

Chest heaving, Rebecca started to push through the *Daily Mail*'s door.

"Rebecca!" George's shout stopped her. She twirled to find him racing across the street toward her.

Breathless, his cheeks flushed, and his thick dark hair slightly windblown, he bent to kiss her cheek. "Hi. I've got a meeting down the block in the Wrigley building. I hoped I'd catch you. I've been calling you for days."

Rebecca forced a slow smile. After all, her raw nerves weren't George's fault. "Sorry, darling. I promise we'll get together soon."

He bent closer, his warm breath tickling her ear. "I'll hold you to that. I'll call you tonight."

She waited until he safely dodged traffic across Michigan Avenue before she swung through the door into the lobby.

Pauline looked up with her usual sunny smile, and unshed tears of relief burned in Rebecca's eyes.

"Everyone's talking about your column. Joe Richards has a betting pool on about who the Soup Lady could be." Pauline clasped her hands to her chest. "I wish you could tell me. I'm in for five dollars."

"Would if I could, but I promised never to tell." Rebecca laughed, suddenly feeling lighter and younger than she had in years. Well, *better* than she'd felt since this time last Monday.

"Wasn't that George talking to you outside?" Pauline giggled. "He's so handsome. He sorta looks like George Clooney. You're not done with him already?"

"No. He's sweet. Just too busy for him at the moment." Rebecca waved. "See you later."

This fabulous sensation of being lighter and younger carried her up the steps, through the chaotic newsroom, where she blew a kiss to Rose before sweeping into the relative quiet of Kate's cubbyhole office.

Kate looked up, and as suddenly as relief had come over Rebecca, it fled in the face of what this column might still mean for both of them.

Rebecca didn't flinch away from Kate's long, piercing look. "I'm sorry to have put you in the middle of my messy situation with the new owner. Tim suggested I kick up the recipe column with my old Rebecca Covington touch, so I did. If it costs your job, I'll never forgive myself."

"No need to worry about Kate's job." Tim's cheery voice startled Rebecca. Prepared to do battle if necessary, she whirled to confront him.

He positively beamed. "Our new owner thinks very highly of Kate's work."

"You mean David Alan Sumner?" Rebecca said, keeping her voice casual and light.

Color drained from Tim's ruddy cheeks. "How did you find out? Damn, I hope the news isn't all over town! If the *Courier* gets hold of this first, there'll be hell to pay. David's people are planning a big splashy announcement on Friday."

"Remember when you *paid me* to know everything, Tim. Obviously the deal is done, since he's calling all the shots. Isn't he?"

Tim took a stab at looking stern. "Yes. Yes, he is. And brilliantly. Reader response was favorable to your Sunday recipe column. You will be happy to know he has authorized judicious use of your gossip notes."

Blood rushed to her head, making her feel giddy. *I can't let him see what this means to me.* As always, she tried to heed what her granny always said about people only knowing what she was feeling if she let them.

Rebecca shrugged as if this meant nothing instead of everything. "*Of course* he liked the column. We knew he would." She glanced at Kate, hoping she'd play along, and she returned the look with absolute serenity.

"Yes, I thought he would be pleased," Kate said briskly. "This morning, advertising informed me Rebecca's column is already generating new income for the Home and Food section. One of the paper's bigger clients, LuLu's at the Belle Kay, ordered all its ads to be enlarged and placed directly under Rebecca's recipe column on Wednesdays and Sundays. The revenue from that account has now doubled."

Tim winked. "I told you David Sumner's a brilliant businessman. But don't push it, Rebecca. Judicious use of those gossip notes," he warned again before strolling away.

"You were fabulous!" Rebecca gushed, in awe of how well Kate had played along. She should have known any woman who kept her bottle of Prozac next to her Pulitzer had to be unflappable.

Kate leaned forward across the desk and grinned up at her. For the first time Rebecca noticed a mischievous glint in her brown eyes. "You look shocked. No one here knows, but I'm a killer poker player. I plan to tell people we're revolutionizing the Home and Food section, as well."

Embarrassed, Rebecca groaned. "You know about the stories I was spinning all along Oak Street. But I was serious about taking you shopping."

The mischief faded from Kate's eyes. "I think not at my present weight. It's time to get back down to business. I do agree a conventional recipe for Wednesday would be best. Keep them wanting more."

A thousand delicious ideas were dancing through Rebecca's head. There was one *fabulous* gossipy note she was dying to use while the fire of rebellion against David Sumner was still blazing hot. For Kate's sake, she'd rein in some of her giddy enthusiasm.

"I promise. But to celebrate, I buy us lunch tomorrow and then we stop at LuLu's to thank Laurie for those huge ads. You'll love the store. The decor is wonderful. You should do a story on it for *our* revolutionized Home and Food section."

Her poker face on once again, Kate nodded. "All right, but no shopping."

Barely containing her glee, Rebecca slipped around the ridiculously shoddy partition of the cubicle and slid onto her incredibly uncomfortable swivel chair.

The wisp of sadness about weight had been impossible to miss in Kate's voice and in her eyes. Rebecca had read that mood-altering medication could cause weight gain. It was time for Rebecca to call a temporary cease-fire in her war with David Sumner and keep her vow to help Kate with fashion choices. She picked up the phone to tell Laurie they were coming for a makeover. Tomorrow there *would* be shopping for Kate. She deserved some fun.

The next day Kate followed Rebecca into LuLu's at the Belle Kay, advertised in the *Daily Mail* as Chicago's most extraordinary store of vintage clothing and accoutrements.

They fought their way through the door, past customers leaving, arms full of fabulous finds. Women stood three deep at the register to purchase one-of-a-kind vintage treasures.

Kate pushed her glasses high on her nose to study the enormous gilt-edged mirror and the oriental rugs partially covering the patina of the old wood floor. She ran her fingertips over an antique chest displaying vintage costume jewelry. "Very tasteful. You're right, Rebecca. There is an article here for the Home section."

Thrilled at Kate's reaction, Rebecca urged her farther into the store.

Finally free of other customers, Laurie glanced up and saw them. She swept around the desk. "Rebecca, how nice to see you. This must be your friend." She smiled toward Kate, giving her the once-over.

Without a doubt Laurie was already at work to make sure Kate would leave here with some treasure. Rebecca felt warm with gratitude. "Darling, we just *had* to thank you personally for your support."

Laurie's shrug was a grand gesture that flipped her straight black ponytail over her shoulder, making her gold hoop earrings swing provocatively and showing off her wrist full of gold bangles and the big oval ring set in pavé diamonds on her expressive hand. "You know me; I'm all about business. Why wouldn't I move to your new section? Everyone will be reading your recipe column to see what you do. Besides, you're a brilliant writer."

All at once Laurie swayed backward, studying Rebecca the way Kate had the decor. "Normally I don't do suits, but I've found the most extraordinary one with your name on it. You're going to die when you see it! Absolutely no one will have anything like it. It would be perfect for a date with that gorgeous guy I saw you with at Gibson's. Or better yet, for Dayson Cottington's Handbag and Halo luncheon on Friday."

Rebecca tried to surreptitiously signal Laurie to get on with Kate's makeover, but she ignored the frantic gesture. She turned toward one of the beautiful built-in closets without doors that lined the walls.

Trying to buy time, Rebecca looked at Kate, who had suspicion in her eyes. "The luncheon Friday is a fund-raiser Dayson does for the Howard Brown Health Center."

"I know. I read about it in your column," Kate said quietly.

Of course *this* year Shannon would be writing about it instead of Rebecca, so there was no professional reason for her to attend. But she *wanted* to go, as she'd done for years. Would it make Shannon uncomfortable if Rebecca showed up?

Rebecca jumped when Laurie twirled back to them, a black broadtail suit in one hand and a black crepe dress in the other.

"I have this beautiful dress from the forties for you to wear, Kate. Very simple. Very elegant," Laurie raved. "In those days the dresses were cut to make a woman's body look phenomenal. Classic and chic. You can slip this on, while Rebecca tries on the suit."

Kate appeared slightly dazed. With clothes and accessories, Laurie *was* a force of nature.

Kate shook her head and perched on the edge of the cream settee in the middle of the room. "No, thank you. I'll wait while Rebecca tries on the suit."

"No, Kate, I don't want to keep you waiting while I try on clothes." Rebecca looked pleadingly at Laurie for help.

"Go!" Laurie demanded. "I'll show Kate some accessories while she's waiting for you."

Behind the heavy rich brown velvet curtain, Rebecca slipped off her clothes and carefully put on the black broadtail suit. She peeped out to make sure Laurie was still at work.

She was holding up a beautiful vintage rhinestone brooch and earrings to the crepe dress. Kate's face lit up with interest.

Laurie's right again. If Kate feels too heavy to buy new clothes, she can always accessorize.

Unable to stall a moment longer, Rebecca stepped out to stand before the gilt mirror.

Laurie gasped. "Your body looks amazing in that!" She expertly pushed the collar up to frame Rebecca's face. "There! Wear your pearls. Black heels. Carry one of your fabulous Nancy Gonzales bags in some color that will pop the outfit."

She'd had absolutely no plans to shop today, but she had to admit the way the jacket nipped in at the waist and the skirt slid over her hips made her look sexy but still chic.

Good battle gear for Friday.

She met Kate's approving eyes in the mirror. "What are you buying?"

"The beautiful rhinestone brooch and earrings. They are signed Eisenberg Original pieces."

"Good. Then I'll take this suit."

"It will be fabulous for Friday's luncheon," Laurie declared.

In the mirror Rebecca saw a flash of concern sharpen Kate's features. "It is a beautiful suit for any occasion," Kate agreed and stood to pull a credit card out of her shapeless jacket pocket. "Now we need to pay and get back to work."

Rebecca changed as quickly as she could, still cavesdropping as Laurie urged Kate to reconsider the forties dress.

It *was* perfect for the Allen's opening in a few weeks. Rebecca fully intended to drag Kate to it, regardless of protests. Kate was entirely too serious. She needed to smile more.

Rebecca would tackle *that* problem after she confronted Kate's obvious concern about Dayson's party. She knew why Kate looked so worried, but she'd reassure her. Rebecca had no intention of interfering with Shannon doing her new job. Well, maybe just the tiniest bit, but she vowed not to embarrass either one of them.

Just as Rebecca stepped out of the dressing room, she saw Kate reverently stroking the black crepe dress Laurie still held out. "You're right. It is quality fabric and workmanship." Kate sighed. "Perhaps some other time."

Encouraged, Rebecca scribbled a note for Laurie to hold the dress before she paid her bill.

In the cab Rebecca was painfully aware of the prolonged silence between them and Kate's fixed stare straight ahead. Obviously Rebecca needed to level with her immediately.

"Kate, I know you're concerned about my attending the Handbag and Halo luncheon on Friday, but you don't need to be. I always receive a personal invitation plus the press invite." Did Rebecca hear a shadow of defiance in her own voice? She tried to soften it. "People would think it odd if I didn't attend, since I've supported the charity for years."

At last Kate turned, a searching expression on her face. "If you are attending Dayson Cottington's benefit because you believe in the charity and wish to personally support it, then I agree, you should go. But I can't help believing your real motive is to prove your worth to David Sumner so he will be forced to admit he made a mistake in choosing Shannon over you."

Rebecca shifted in her seat, wanting to avoid Kate's unflinching eyes, but her pride wouldn't let her. She knew clever, tough Kate had pierced her facade in a vulnerable spot.

David Sumner had rejected Rebecca because he thought she was too old and stale to do her job, and it hurt no matter how she spun it. She refused to accept *this* rejection without a damn good fight.

She respected Kate so much, she wanted to be completely honest. "I know my motives are flawed. I know I might not be playing this hand the way you believe I should. But you should know I'll do whatever it takes to get my identity back."

"Your identity isn't gone, Rebecca. Only your job as Chicago's most notorious gossip columnist. They are not the same," Kate warned.

Afraid, Rebecca did look away. Her facade was so thin Kate might see the truth.

You're wrong, Kate. For years, even before Peter discarded me, my job was my identity, the armor I put on every day. I need it back to feel safe.

Chapter 6

Strolling into the Empire Room of the Palmer House on Friday, Rebecca hoped she looked more confident than she felt. Even with the gorgeous suit, and her good pearls from her granny, and a red Nancy Gonzalez bag that was the most beautiful one she owned, Rebecca didn't have her usual feeling of well-being when she knew she looked good.

This was her first party in fifteen years as a guest instead of a source of publicity. Just Rebecca, with no perks. How *would* people treat her? Would they be dismissive, like Jessica at Très Treat? Or supportive, like Simone at Luca Luca?

She'd thought about nothing else but Kate's words for the last few days. *Of course* Rebecca wanted to attend this party for charity. Just as the invitation requested, she had brought a beautiful collectable Judith Leiber bag to donate to the Howard Brown resale shop. *But* there was another reason, one that kept her up at night. Certainly she recognized her behavior was reckless, but she needed to show David Sumner that she would not give up her identity and would do whatever it took to get it back, with as little bloodletting as possible.

Just inside the wide double doors of the ballroom, Dayson, as always splendidly dressed from head to toe in Ralph Lauren, waited to greet his guests. "Rebecca, hi. Love your suit!" Usual air kisses. "I'm so glad you could make it."

It was shocking how relieved she felt at his exuberant greeting.

Normal. No need to worry I've been forgotten already.

His cherub cheeks growing slightly rosier, he blinked rapidly. "I'm sorry. I'm not sure where you're seated this year."

Feeling like she had in high school when she'd been one of five friends *not* invited to the biggest and best graduation party, she forced a laugh. "Darling, put me anywhere."

"We would love to have Rebecca at our table," Lynda Silver offered in her strong, cultured voice.

Saved!

Rebecca turned to smile at Lynda, who looked impossibly chic from her platinum hair to her impeccable brown Chanel suit and matching slingbacks. No, wait. The shoes were actually Dolce & Gabbana and perfectly accented the suit, instead of being an exact match. *Très chic.*

Dayson's smile widened. "Lynda, hi. That's wonderful. Have fun, ladies!" He rushed off to greet three of his swans, Dolly, Mamie, and Hazel, who were waiting politely in the doorway.

"The Service Club of Chicago has put together a table, but if you'd rather sit with the press?" Lynda inquired politely.

"Thank you. I adore the Service Club ladies. Lead on." Rebecca followed her across the crowded room to a table for ten already half-full.

Before they reached it, Shannon loomed in front of them, with Chuck, the *Daily Mail* photographer, hovering behind her. Shannon's narrowed eyes and tight lips screamed that there was going to be a scene. Now that she knew how bitchy Shannon could be, the idea of verbal combat with her sent a little shiver along Rebecca's skin.

"What are you doing here, Rebecca?" If Shannon could have spoken and hissed in the same breath, Rebecca felt sure she would have. Instead it came out a sputtering croak of rage.

"I was invited as a contributor to this charity." Rebecca smiled, her vaunted self-control kicking in. She would behave well and channel Shannon's nastiness into some good. "I know you stopped us because you want a picture of the Service Club ladies. It *is* one of the oldest and finest charities in the city. And with no paid staff!" In truth, these ladies who lunch actually *did do* all the hard work themselves, and they deserved some publicity.

Chuck, obviously relieved to have something to do besides listen to his colleagues snipe at each other, immediately started posing the six women staring expectantly toward them.

Unblinking, Shannon continued to glare. Rebecca glared right back, but of course with more finesse, as she was older and wiser.

God forbid we start tearing out each other's hair at Dayson's party!

Thinking of Kate, Rebecca vowed to be especially conciliatory. "Relax, Shannon. I'm only here to support a worthy cause. Please don't wor—"

"Don't you dare write a word about this event!" Shannon interrupted her. "It's my job now, and don't you ever forget it."

A flurry of excitement in the doorway made Shannon turn. "Quick, Chuck!" she yelled. "Nadia's here. She's back from the Paris couture shows. I want her picture."

Shannon shoved past Rebecca, stomping on one of her new Manolos and sending a sharp pain through her foot.

Refusing to acknowledge the burning ache in her toes and trying not to limp, Rebecca seated herself at the Service Club table. All the women were watching Nadia strike several perfect model poses. Dark chocolate hair swirling around her shoulders and her exotic eyes smol dering, she played to Chuck's camera.

"She's wearing Yves Saint-Laurent straight from the runway," Lynda whispered. "I heard she bought the entire collection."

On Rebecca's right, Evie, a tiny former opera star, sighed. "Look at that waistline."

In unison all the women at the table pushed away their bread plates. Except Lynda. "I refuse to stop eating. I'll exercise tomorrow." She took one bite of roll and glanced over at Rebecca. "I prepared the soup recipe from your hilarious column for our alumni group. It was quite good."

Her toes and dignity ached from Shannon's footprint. She needed this compliment. "Thank you. I'm glad you liked it."

"You know, the Indiana University alumni group is still eager to honor you as a distinguished alumna." Lynda raised her perfectly arched brows. "Perhaps this is a good time to finally allow them to do so."

The implication that her bruised ego could use some

stroking was not lost on Rebecca. But the reason she had always declined this honor hadn't changed.

"I'm not sure this is the right time," she demurred, still fearful of that skeleton in her closet. But it *was* tempting to wallow in the memories of those halcyon years at IU.

In those carefree days she could eat *two* helpings of a decadent dessert like the chocolate soufflé she had planned for Sunday's column and not worry about carb bloat. In those days she had truly believed the world was hers for the taking. She could have it all.

That was before Peter proved her parents' desertion was not a fluke. She was easy to forget.

She wrapped her arms around her shoulders to protect herself from that particular life lesson. She *needed* to focus on the good years. Why not? She was very good at rationalization. It had been decades ago. Old news. Silly news, actually. Although at the time, her lie had been deadly serious. She'd needed to put a roof over her head and eat. Did IU even have computer files in those days? No one had ever bothered to look. Kate might have folded on this hand, but Rebecca felt reckless and she bluffed.

"On second thought, Lynda, I'd be delighted to accept the honor this year. Please call the paper on Monday and let me know the details."

Lynda smiled like she was sharing a secret. "Wise decision. You know, we're all in this together."

During the luncheon, Rebecca began to understand that Lynda's words were a call to arms for "women of a certain age." *They* approached Rebecca in droves, eager to offer their support, yet no one under forty came near her. In the old days, meaning two weeks ago, before evil Monday, Rebecca would have been surrounded by everyone eager to have their pictures and names in her column.

Of course, she'd always known much of her appeal was based on her power to put people in the limelight for good deeds or bad, as the case might be. Had any of them ever *really* liked her? Thought she was even *mildly* interesting in her own right?

Today those same beauties were fawning over Shannon. All except one.

Nadia glided toward her. "Hi, angel," she called in her lilting Eastern European accent. No air kisses from Nadia. A soft fragrant brush on Rebecca's left cheek, right cheek, and left again. "You're too beautiful to work, angel."

Nadia's way of acknowledging Rebecca's altered status was positively charming, but she felt compelled to be honest. "I liked what I did."

Laughing, Nadia shrugged her elegant shoulders. "Then everything will be wonderful when David arrives in town. You'll love him. I met him in Paris. He's one of the great guys, like my husband. And I've only met four such men in my life." Three more quick cheek kisses. "Must go, angel. I can't be late to pick up my bunny, Chloe, from junior high."

As Nadia floated away, Lynda turned to Rebecca. "Are you encouraged?"

"*Encouraged?* Far from it." Her image of David Sumner was becoming clearer, and, for the first time, pinpricks of fear shot down her spine at the thought of meeting him. "Of course he was charming to Nadia. She's beautiful. Sexy. And has yet to see forty."

"You have a point," Lynda murmured while they both

watched Nadia slip through the door with Shannon a few steps behind. "I would be careful of that Shannon, if I were you." Lynda offered her opinion with cool confidence. "She'll bury you if she can."

A great rush of affection for Lynda nearly undid her composure. "Thank you for your concern, darling. I'm so grateful not *everyone* believes I'm already dead and buried."

Chapter 7

As David drove out of the city toward the Pizza Palace near Ellen Sumner Park for the end-of-the-season party with the Little League team, his cell phone buzzed in his ear. He hated the damn earpiece he wore but had no choice since he refused to have a driver.

"I wanted to let you know some news." David heard the excitement in Tim's voice. "I got a call tonight from the Culinary Institute. They want Rebecca to be a guest chef at their big fund-raiser. We couldn't have paid for better exposure for the Food section, or a bigger PR opportunity for you as a new player in Chicago."

David smiled, thinking of Rebecca's last column. "I'll bet she's pleased to be showing off her cooking expertise."

"I'm telling her in the morning." Tim's hesitation was nearly imperceptible, but David caught it. "I think she'll be pleased, but honestly I didn't know she was such a good cook until she took this job."

Again, David felt that jolt of amused surprise at Rebecca's actions. But this time his instincts, like a burning itch, told him something wasn't ringing true. Great cooks usually liked to show off their talents.

"In all the years you've worked together, Rebecca has never had you over for dinner?" David asked incredulously.

"No. But she sometimes brings in cakes and cookies whenever anyone has a birthday. She brought in a delicious cake for Rose Murphy about a month ago. Until now I always thought she picked the stuff up at a bakery in Lincoln Park."

David's itch spread. "When is this fund-raiser?"

"In two weeks. I plan to do a promo on it in every edition."

David rapidly thought through his schedule. The party for the team to give out new uniforms was tonight. He hoped it would keep the kids looking forward to next season so they would all continue to play. Tomorrow he flew to California to be with his sons to celebrate Ellen's life, like they did every year on the anniversary of her death.

He tensed, gripping the wheel tighter. Like the last four years, he would put on a good act for the boys. No sorrow. He would continue to embrace life like Ellen wanted for all of them. But he knew deep inside he could never escape the pain. Even though the boys told him he was too rigid in his faithfulness to Ellen's memory. She'd thought him rigid sometimes, too, especially in business. He knew he had the tenacity of a terrier when it came to getting what he wanted. He brought his type-A game to improving the worth of the *Chicago Daily Mail.*

He made his decision and did his best to hide the interest in his voice. "Tim, I've decided to come into Chicago earlier than planned. Book me for the fund-raiser. It's time for me to meet Rebecca Covington in person."

～✖～

On Monday morning, Rebecca stepped inside the *Daily Mail* revolving doors and through the glass saw Kate, Tim, Pauline, and Shannon staring back at her.

What now?

Resisting a powerful urge to keep whirling right back onto the comparatively safe sidewalk, she stepped into the cool lobby.

"Here's our celebrity chef now," Tim called out.

"I beg your pardon?" Totally confused and hoping it didn't show, *especially* in front of Shannon, Rebecca looked pointedly at Pauline for help.

Pauline gave her a brilliant smile. "Rebecca, you've been invited to be a guest chef at the Chicago Culinary Institute of America's Black-Tie Benefit for Young Chefs. Celebrities prepare their favorite dish in front of everyone," Pauline blurted out. Reddening to her scarlet roots, she glanced at Tim. "Sorry, Mr. Porter."

He nodded, his face flushed. "I know. I know. I didn't think you could do it, Rebecca, but you rose to the challenge. Now I recognize I was a genius for moving you to the Food section. When David Sumner heard about this great exposure for the new Food section, he decided to fly in early to watch you do your magic."

Complete and utter disaster! She wasn't ready yet to meet her foe face-to-face.

Faking a show of excitement and totally ignoring Shannon's existence, Rebecca moved slowly forward. "Fabulous news! When did this all happen?"

Kate was watching her carefully, a furrow deep between her eyes. "They called Tim last night, and we agreed this morning to accept on your behalf. I hope you don't mind."

"Mind? I'm ecstatic." Rebecca lied, smiling so wide her cheeks felt numb. "Now I have a good excuse to shop for a new evening gown."

"Oh, Rebecca, you always have the best clothes of everyone on the paper." Pauline sounded as proud as she did bragging about her darling daughters. "Indiana University called this morning, too. About the local alumni group honoring you this year. They want to do a piece on you in the national alumni magazine." She glanced past Rebecca. "Oh, Shannon, you should write something in your column about it."

Hiding a smile, Kate coughed carefully into her palm.

Watching the happily calculating look on Tim's face, and the carefully controlled blankness on Shannon's, Rebecca felt mild hysteria tickle her throat.

"Excellent idea! After all, we're all on the same team. Take care of it, Shannon," Tim ordered like he'd thought of the plan himself.

"You know I will, Tim." Shannon nodded and managed a slight smile toward Pauline. "Would you please contact IU for me so I can get all the details for my column?" Her soft, wispy voice couldn't quite cover a sharp edge of annoyance. "And . . . um . . . congratulations, Rebecca."

The tickle of hysteria in her throat changed course to become a nauseating twinge of fear in her stomach.

The horror of cooking in public, Shannon exposing my silly secret by digging into records at IU, and David Sumner arriving early in town are the final straws. It can't get any worse.

Feeling *this* ill brought back memories of a particularly nasty "commode-hugging" episode she'd suffered through in her mildly misspent youth. As Walton Julius, the most fascinating older man in Chicago, had taught her, there was only one surefire cure for a queasy stomach after a rowdy night of fun or, in her present case, gut-curdling stress.

To hell with the calories. All day she downed can after can of sugar-rich, caffeine-infused, *real* Coke. She sat at her desk burping as discreetly and politely as possible until finally, midafternoon, her stomach stopped roiling and her blood sugar spiked. While experiencing this momentary burst of false optimism, she rationalized both looming horrors.

She had two weeks to plot with Harry before the potentially disastrous cooking event and the inevitable meeting with David Sumner. The only way to make it all less catastrophic was to have Harry at her side. She called the Culinary Institute to request that he be her celebrity chef assistant, and after she was given the pleased approval she called Harry to plead her case and beg for his help. He was in surgery, so she left the message on his voice mail.

Her other little problem drove her down the steps to find Pauline. They'd protected each other for years, but lately it seemed their personal crises had multiplied. Even though she *always* vehemently squashed any office gossip about Pauline deliberately getting the switchboard lines crossed—gossip that explained why she was so well informed—Rebecca *knew* Pauline would have the answer she needed.

"Did Shannon call IU?" Rebecca whispered.

A grimace of disgust crossed Pauline's pretty round

face. "I don't know! She used her cell. She's already gone for the day." Pauline leaned closer, her red curls falling into her eyes. "She'll have to write something nice about you, since Mr. Porter told her to. Right? Or should we be worried?"

"Not to worry. I'm just curious." Rebecca blew a kiss and hurried back to her desk, before Pauline saw her slight edge of panic. Pauline had enough to worry about, being a single mom with two energetic little girls.

Rebecca sat mulling over the silly lie that had started her journalistic career. Once or twice she'd thought about how embarrassing it might be if anyone found out she'd lied about her age, but she rationalized that no one cared enough about such things to dig into records.

If the truth had been revealed any other time in the last fifteen years she would have laughed it off and been charmingly contrite. But given her newly vulnerable state, it loomed like the cannon shot that would knock down her facade, completely exposing her to the world.

Maybe if she knew if Shannon cared enough to dig up that cannonball she could shore up her defenses. She called IU to thank the alumni director for the coming honor.

She was told someone from the *Chicago Daily Mail* had already spoken to the director before she left this afternoon on a two-week vacation.

Her intuition warned her this was not good news, but her common sense told her there was nothing more she could do about it until she accosted Shannon tomorrow.

The next morning Pauline brought both of them Giant Gulps from the deli.

"What else can I do to help you?" Pauline whispered.

"I haven't been able to find out anything about Shannon's column. Except that she's running a picture of someone in her bra and thong dancing on a bar."

"Charming." Rebecca shook her head and started gulping Coke. "Honestly, I'm just curious, that's all."

"Okay, if you say so." With a wave, Pauline drifted back to the switchboard.

After devouring twenty ounces of caffeine, Rebecca pushed herself up and walked past her old office. She peered in. Shannon wasn't there. The computer beckoned to her, so she stepped inside the door.

"Rebecca, are you looking for our Shannon?" Tim's nosy secretary, Maybella, shouted from the end of the hall.

Damn! Rebecca poked her head back out and smiled. "Yes. I'll just wait in here until she gets back."

"No. Come back later. You'll have a long wait. Shannon's in Mr. Porter's office on a conference call with Mr. Sumner." The little note of pleasure was unmistakable in Maybella's voice.

When I get this office back, no more chocolates for you. Rebecca shrugged. "I'll catch Shannon later." She strolled away, feeling Maybella's cold eyes boring into her back all the way down the hall.

Rebecca forced herself to work at her lonely, pathetic desk until she glanced at her watch and decided enough time had passed and she could stroll over to the executive offices again.

Waiting like a vulture, Maybella never took her eyes off Rebecca. "They're still in that important meeting," she drawled. "Can I take a message? Shannon's a real busy little lady."

"No, I'll be back." She stalked away, frustration burning a hole straight through her stomach. Back at her desk, she called Pauline. "Does Maybella *ever* leave?"

"Only for Starbucks venti double carmel frappaccino with extra whipped cream. Do we need her to go for one soon? I have a break in twenty minutes." Pauline giggled. "It's her turn to treat."

"Perfect. I owe you." Waiting, Rebecca read her recipe column over and over again until she could recite every ingredient and word by heart. Disgusted with herself, she marched into Kate's cubbyhole-size office and placed it on the desk. "I added a gossip note this week. I think you'll like it."

Looking up from the computer screen, Kate poked her wire-rim glasses higher on her nose. "Let's take a look." As she read the column, she burst out laughing. "This is hilarious. Did it really happen?"

"I was there," Rebecca admitted.

"Amazing! Wednesday's edition should be interesting. I'm almost finished with our section." Kate looked back down at the computer screen.

Not wanting to hamper Kate meeting her deadline, Rebecca backed out of the office.

Time to discover if Shannon is meeting her deadline.

As Pauline promised, Maybella had deserted her desk for a Starbucks run. Tim's office was dark. Rebecca sidled up to Shannon's door to find her typing madly.

I've never seen her look so happy. Dear heaven, what is she writing?

Rebecca's gaze darted around the office looking for something, *anything,* that would give her an excuse to barge in. Her gaze fell on the poster of the Chicago skyline she'd bought when she first moved to this office.

Perfect. She rapped on the doorframe. "Hello!"

Shannon glanced up and all but threw herself in front of the computer screen. "What do you want?"

Shannon's bark gave Rebecca pause, but the need to know what was coming drove her on. She gestured toward the print. "I just realized I left my print of the skyline in here when I moved out. I'll just take it back now." She stepped closer to the desk to take a look. Leaning forward, she squinted at the computer screen.

"Stay right there!" Shannon reached for the phone, shifting her body strategically to block the screen completely. "I need to check with housekeeping first to make sure it belongs to you."

"Don't be ridiculous, Shannon. Trust me, it's mine." Rebecca inched closer.

"Stay back!" Shannon repeated. "As I was saying, I will call to make sure the print belongs to you. If it was in the office originally, then it belongs to the office, which means it now belongs to me. It's despicable to take things that don't belong to you."

Shannon clenched her jaw, and loathing shot out of her limpid eyes.

If looks could kill I'd be drawn and quartered. "Are you all right?" Rebecca asked and stepped closer. True, she had hoped to catch a glimpse of what Shannon was writing, but this girl looked so flushed and agitated, Rebecca honestly feared for her health.

"Why don't you go away? Can't you see I'm busy?" Shannon's trembling lips twisted in such a nasty smile Rebecca fell back one step. "I have two and one-half pages to get out. You still remember what a real column is like, don't you?"

Rebecca thrust up her chin. "This is the second time you've told me to get lost. You know, the third time I might start getting offended."

"A threat, Rebecca?" Shannon mocked.

Odd, Rebecca's laugh sounded genuine to her own ears, although her insides quivered with rage. "No, *darling,* it's a promise." Her dignity shaken, she forced herself to stroll slowly out.

That night at home, Rebecca set the timer on her treadmill for ten miles and stuck in a DVD of *The Thomas Crown Affair.* The pounding soundtrack caused her to quicken her pace on the treadmill. The thrill of the first robbery brought images of stealing every copy of Wednesday's edition racing through her head. If she didn't steal *all* the papers, then she could take just the pages with Shannon's column, which might or might not expose Rebecca's embarrassing secret without her consent.

This is crazy. I need endorphins.

She ate ten pieces of Leonidas' fabulous chocolates, even the raspberry ones she didn't like, while she watched the hot love scenes between Pierce Brosnan and Rene Russo. She loved this movie because Pierce had an age-appropriate leading lady. And she looked damn good.

The goal of still looking fabulous in her forties usually kept her from late-night snacking. Lately, she had *no* willpower. She yanked open the refrigerator looking for her stash of bleu cheese and grapes to fill the gaping stress ache in her stomach.

She knew she shouldn't do yoga on a full stomach but pulled out old tapes anyway.

I'll think happy, positive thoughts.

The dead man's pose always put her right to sleep. But tonight her mind raced with horrible humiliating scenarios. Shannon and a faceless David Sumner were evil puppeteers, pulling her strings, making her dance around in a bra and thong.

It must have been something I ate.

She glanced at her watch for the hundredth time. Four a.m. Only an hour and a half until the first edition hot off the press landed in the lobby—and she would be there.

CHICAGO DAILY MAIL
WEDNESDAY FOOD

BAJA CHICKEN

8 boned chicken breasts
Salt and pepper to taste
1½ cloves garlic crushed
4 tablespoons olive oil
4 tablespoons tarragon vinegar
1 cup dry sherry

Sprinkle chicken with salt and pepper. Crush garlic into oil and vinegar in a skillet. Sauté chicken pieces until golden brown, turning frequently. Remove. Place in a baking dish. Pour sherry over pieces and place in 350-degree oven for 10 minutes.

A Note from Rebecca Covington

Darlings, please don't ever experiment with these skinless, boneless chicken breasts like a certain embarrassed divorcée chose to do. For a totally organic push-up bra, she shoved chicken breasts in her low-cut formal gown and went off to a black tie at one of our most posh hotels. After three drinks, she was dancing so gleefully one chicken breast popped out and tumbled onto the dance floor.

A woman slipped on it and fell, and her escort picked up the meat and screamed. He thought she'd lost a body part.

Enjoy!
Xo Rebecca

Chapter 8

On Wednesday at five twenty-nine a.m., Rebecca pushed through the *Daily Mail* doors. She stopped, stunned by dread. Pauline and Kate were at the reception desk, reading today's edition.

Pauline lifted her head, her face so pale her freckles stood out across her nose and cheeks. "Oh, Rebecca, I'm so sorry."

Kate squared her shoulders. "Yesterday Pauline told me you were concerned about Shannon's column. We agreed to meet here to get the earliest edition." She held out the paper.

Rebecca forced herself to take it. The bright lights in the lobby provided enough illumination so she didn't require glasses to peer down at Shannon's two-page spread plus pictures.

Right below Shannon's smiling picture and her byline, "Shannon Shares with Her Friends," Rebecca's name jumped off the page in bold letters.

Everyone in town (yours truly included) constantly raves about how fabulous **Rebecca Covington** *looks for 39. Well, get ready to heap on even more accolades!*

Our Rebecca actually turns 45 next month! We all agree she looks closer to 35, which is why she can still date all those 30-something hunks. I'm sure all those under-grads will make her the belle of the ball at the Indiana University alumni gathering where she will be honored. Remember, Rebecca, those hunks you chase after better be over eighteen or they're jailbait!

Rebecca couldn't move. Couldn't lift her eyes off the paper. Only her fierce pride kept her standing. It wasn't her true age being exposed that caused her entire body to cramp up in a ball. It was the ugly dig about younger men. It slashed at old scars from Peter dumping her for a nineteen-year-old. All the old weakness and vulnerability came rushing back. She'd never forgotten the horrible desperation that drove her to date young guys so she could say to Peter, "See, you bastard, twenty-year-olds want me, too!"

Now it made her feel so stupid and pathetic. Another crushing reminder of how easy she was to leave behind.

Only Pauline's deep, ragged sigh broke through Rebecca's haze of memories and forced her gaze away from the hateful words.

"It's my fault," Pauline whispered. "I gave Shannon the person to call at IU."

"It's not your fault, Pauline," Kate said briskly.

"No, it's *my* fault." Rebecca faced her friends. "There was always the risk my lie would come out. I'm not ashamed of shaving six years off when I was twenty-seven to get a plum job with a prominent teen magazine. They refused to hire anyone over twenty-one regardless of their credentials. I'd do it again!" She thrust up her chin. "And I'm not ashamed of dating younger men. Why not? Look at Demi Moore. I was ahead of the trend."

She'd never talked about the real hurt, not even to Pauline or Harry. All her pent-up fears about abandonment, all her issues about protecting herself, her decision to shun commitment to avoid possible pain—she kept these to herself. They were all too weighty to burden her friends.

Now, as always, she called on her survival skills. *Rage needed here.*

It roared to life, making her entire body burn. "Where is that *bitch*?"

Bitch echoed off the marble floor. Pauline sat up straighter. "Shannon took the day off. She's going to the Peninsula Spa to have the works."

"Rebecca, stay calm." Kate sounded stern, but Rebecca saw the concern clouding her eyes. "Therapy made me understand what motivates these young women coming up so fast on our heels. Society has given Shannon nothing to mark her transformation into equality and community with mature women in the workplace. That's why she behaves so badly. We need to have patience with her. She needs our guidance."

"*Guidance* is hardly what I have planned for her once I find her!"

"She'll be at the Allen's opening tonight. You can get her there. Are you still going?" Pauline asked hopefully. "I wish I wasn't busy with the girls, or I'd go to support you."

A plan to confront Shannon took root in Rebecca's fertile imagination. "Of course I'm still going, sweetheart. I wouldn't dream of giving Shannon the pleasure of my absence. Besides, I would never disappoint Harry and Kate."

"I told you earlier I wasn't sure about attending." Kate shook her head, the deep eyebrow furrow of worry back in place. "Are you sure you can control yourself when you see Shannon there?"

"Of course I can control myself! I *pride* myself on self-control. I plan to have a divine time at the party. So will you and Harry. I plan to *guide* Shannon through the rules of the female community. At the right time. *My way.* Certainly with more finesse than this cheap shot she took at me. Please come tonight," she pleaded softly.

Kate tugged at her shapeless black jacket. "I don't have anything to wear."

To hear the age-old lament of every woman standing in front of her closet coming from Kate made Rebecca laugh. It felt good to hide her pain and embarrassment in something fun for Kate. "Go buy that fabulous black dress at LuLu's."

A soft positively wistful expression flashed across Kate's face. "I'm sure it must be gone by now."

"It has your name on it." At Kate's shocked look, Rebecca tried to reassure her. "That's just a Laurie-ism for 'It's perfect for you.' Please come with me tonight. I'd really appreciate your support."

"All right." Again, Kate squared her shoulders, like a soldier going into battle. "I'll be there to remind you to keep hold of your self-control. I'm taking Chuck to LuLu's this afternoon to shoot photos for the article I'm doing on the decor. If the dress is still available, I'll buy it."

Once Kate was out of sight and hearing, Pauline leaned across her desk. Her eyes burned with bloodlust. "I want to help you get even with Shannon. What are we going to do to her?"

"Sweetheart, we're going to do what I planned from the very beginning. I'm going to take back my identity."

*   *   *

All day Rebecca repeated her granny's sage advice to "always behave like a lady, so when the smoke of battle clears you'll still be standing."

It took every ounce of willpower she possessed to laugh at the dozens of callers curious about Shannon's story. Some callers were snide. Others frankly pitying. *Those* were the worst.

By midafternoon she was exhausted from brazening it through. She pretended amusement at the friendly jabs about her age and dating habits from friends. But she became coolly unrepentant when confronted by the not-so-kind remarks from certain other colleagues.

By the end of the day she was nearly consumed by embarrassment and anger at herself for not being able to let go of the past. She cringed at the thought of walking through the newsroom to be the focus of more friendly, and not-so-friendly, ridicule.

She kept her eyes straight ahead and walked quickly down the narrow aisle. In front of Joe Richards' desk, the applause started. "You're a hottie at any age, Becca!" Joe bellowed at the top of his lungs.

His compliment drew approving hoots and hollers from the other male sportswriters.

Nearly overcome with gratitude after this day from hell, Rebecca waved and swept past them.

At the door, a determined-looking Rose waited for her. "Miss Covington, I want you to know I think you are an icon of nuanced, generationally appropriate glamour." She blushed and quickly sat back down at her desk.

Touched that someone as shy as Rose would speak up for her, Rebecca blew her a kiss. "Thank you, Rose. You've made my day."

* * *

That night, standing in front of her open closet, Rebecca remembered Rose's kind words. Like a general before an important battle, she checked her combat gear.

The Valentino asymmetrical-neckline ruched cocktail dress in black silk georgette, which she'd saved for months to buy, *always* made her feel incredibly glamorous.

The Christian Louboutin four-inch gold sandals showed off her legs and gave her the added height she needed.

Diamond drop earrings sparkled against her pale skin and light hair.

Illusion is everything. It works. I'm ready to face the world.

An hour later, strolling into Allen's restaurant, Rebecca lightly held Harry's right arm. An elegant Kate, wearing *the dress* and vintage rhinestones, clutched his left. Rebecca encouraged them both to pause with her in the doorway to make a more dramatic entrance. She needed to survey the packed Prairie-style restaurant for friends and foes. A quick glance told her Shannon had not yet arrived.

Cathy Post rushed up to greet her with a glass of champagne. "Be happy. Everyone's talking about you. Remember, there's no such thing as bad publicity unless you're a serial killer or a child molester."

"Of course, I'm thrilled, darling." Sipping the champagne, Rebecca glided into the room.

The society scene was her true element. For fifteen years she'd been working rooms like this. She moved among the tables with expertise. It was almost an out-of-body experience. She could *see* herself greeting players, kissing cheeks, stopping to engage in brief repartee.

She knew the stories of most of the people in this

room. The old money and the ones who married it. The couples who got wealthy together. The others, like her, who had worked hard and paid their dues to get here. The thing they all had in common, and the thing she really loved, was their choice to *do something* with their money. They could be lazing around their pools and boats, doing nothing, but they chose to give back.

I've never cared if they do it to get their pictures in the press.

Because they chose to play the society game, battered women had shelters, inner-city kids went to camp and decent schools, dozens of charities made Chicago a better place to live. Some might dismiss "Café Society," but she knew better. *This* was part of why Chicago was such a great city.

This made her happy. *This* made her feel whole. Most were charming and gracious, giving her news, both good and bad. Occasionally there was a bad apple. Leering and joking in a way that made her skin crawl. Tonight it was mostly gossip about *her.*

Finally they reached their reserved table. While Harry pulled out a chair for Kate, Rebecca turned to scan the room one last time.

Across the tiny dance floor she saw a man who bore such a striking resemblance to Pierce Brosnan she gasped.

Is he is town shooting a movie?

Their eyes locked.

My God, the item I dropped in my column about brain cells stirring a pleasure circuit when you lock eyes with someone you want is true.

She knew the man coolly staring back at her had a little too much muscle beneath his expertly tailored dark suit to be the former 007.

You're so yummy! Who are you?

Her pleasure circuit on overload, she cast him a smile calculated to beckon him to her side. He took a step toward her. Her pulse raced in anticipation.

Shannon appeared, grabbed his arm, and led him to a table for two. Rebecca felt like a bucket of icy-cold water had been dumped over her.

He turned his head back toward Rebecca and smiled, causing a slight dimple to dent his left cheek.

She was transfixed with longing and regret. "I can't believe it," she murmured to no one in particular.

"Believe what?" asked Harry. He was standing behind her chair, waiting for her to sit down.

"The best-looking man in the room is here with Shannon."

"Better-looking than me? Where?" Harry turned to look.

"Directly across the dance floor. Do you know him?"

Harry shook his head. Kate reached into her small bag for her glasses.

Her pulse still pounding from her reaction to the stranger, she couldn't stop staring at him. "*This* is the perfect ending to my miserable day. Older men date younger women and they're considered cool. An older woman dates a much younger man and she's considered a fool. Honestly, *this* injustice is too much for me."

She swept away from the table and across the dance floor as quickly as her four-inch sandals would allow. Harry tried to catch her hand. Kate called her name, but self-righteousness drove her on.

Rebecca reached his table and the stranger stood. He gave her the same look from cool blue eyes that made her want him even more. She hated that such a fabulous-looking man didn't have the good sense not to date a girl young enough to be his daughter.

Just like my ex.

"I just came by to say hello." Rebecca barely glanced at Shannon's shocked face. She curved her lips into her most insincere smile. "I know I shouldn't be interrupting this charming father-and-daughter outing, but, well, here I am." She held out her hand to him. "Hello. I'm Rebecca Covington."

He curled his fingers around hers and the earth shifted beneath her in a strange, silent shudder that started at her toes and rushed up to her brain. Every nerve in her body tingled.

The caress of his warm, dry skin against hers quickened her pulse.

His perfect masculine scent made her light-headed.

The brilliance of his blue eyes, crinkled at the corners with obvious delight, dazzled her.

His deep, rich, sensual voice throbbed through her. "Hello. I'm David Sumner."

Chapter 9

Around her the world spun faster and faster, growing darker and darker at the edges.

Oxygen. Breathe in. Breathe out. Or pass out.

Drawing in a deep breath, she flung back her head and laughed as loud as possible through her suffering lungs. "Of course, you're David Sumner. I knew that." At last she pulled her hand free. "Well, it's been lovely meeting you at last. *So* looking forward to working with you."

His mouth turned up at the corners. "I'll escort you back to your table. I want to introduce myself to Kate." He glanced down at Shannon, whose triumphant smile was nearly blinding. "Wait for me."

His hand felt warm on the small of Rebecca's back as he guided her through the crowded dance floor. Ignoring her galloping pulse, Rebecca tried to focus on not making more of a fool of herself. But the only thought front and center was the same one causing her to be light-headed.

David Sumner held my hand one second too long—and I let him. My God. I have the hots for my boss-from-hell.

Both Harry and Kate were on their feet waiting for her. Ready to collapse, Rebecca wanted to fall into the chair

Harry held out, but she forced herself to sit down slowly. She'd made enough of a fool of herself.

He extended his hand to Kate. "I'm David Sumner. I admired your work for *Wealth Weekly*. You richly deserved your Pulitzer, Kate."

"Thank you," Kate stated in her normal brisk tone, but she blushed ever so slightly. She cast a quick worried glance toward Rebecca. "I see the two of you have already met."

"Evidently." David's blue eyes were steely with silent amusement.

At my expense. But no more.

She gathered her control back from its lustful leanings and defied him by refusing to look away in embarrassment. He finally took his gaze off her to turn to shake Harry's hand.

Now breathe, for heaven's sake.

"Have a good evening." David nodded. With one hand in his trouser pocket, he walked away with almost a swagger.

Still standing, Harry watched David cross the room. "Good bones and muscle tone. He'll age well. I'm not sure he's my type, but he could be yours. It would be the perfect revenge on Shannon."

"Harry, please. Rebecca doesn't need any more encouragement to live dangerously," Kate scolded.

"Do you think David is dangerous?" Harry asked. A cocky grin spread across his face. "Sorry, sweet pea. If the man is dangerous, I want him for myself."

Delayed shock shuddered through Rebecca in waves.

David is dangerous. No, it was my brain being starved of oxygen that made me breathless. Of course I'm not attracted to him!

Kate frowned at her. "Rebecca, are you all right?"

His long fingers on her pulse, Harry lifted Rebecca's wrist. "Accelerated. However, she'll live to conquer another day."

"Very funny." Rebecca slid out of his gentle grip. "I was just thinking about how to answer Harry. David isn't right for either one of us, darling. Obviously he likes his victims young."

"So do you." Harry leaned down to kiss her cheek.

Rebecca glanced over his shoulder and met David's intent stare before he turned away to usher Shannon out the door.

Rebecca felt the same rush of pleasure when their eyes locked.

Not good. Not good at all.

The next morning, Shannon spun through the *Daily Mail* revolving doors only steps in front of Rebecca.

"Is there a message for me from David Sumner?" Shannon gaily called out to Pauline.

When Pauline shook her head, Shannon glanced over her shoulder at Rebecca to smirk. "I'll call him later."

Exhausted from a sleepless night reliving her humiliating meeting with David, Rebecca didn't have the energy to react except to thrust her chin into the air and silently repeat her newest mantra. *I won't give Shannon the satisfaction of thinking I give a damn about anything she does, including her cheap shot at me in her column.*

With a smug smile, Shannon strutted away.

Pauline, her eyes flashing with vengeance, leaned closer. "That b-i-t-c-h has his private number."

"Too bad I don't," Rebecca sighed. She glanced at the fistful of phone messages Pauline handed her. "George called again. We keep missing one another. He's sweet and sexy, but sometimes dull. I must talk to him about our dinner date at RL's. Harry called already? We're supposed to get together for lunch. I need to call to confirm that."

Pauline leaned even closer, her green eyes bright. "Kate told me David Sumner was at Allen's last night and you met him. She said he was very handsome. Is he really dreamy?"

"As my granny would have said, 'Dreamy is as dreamy does.' So far he's been a *nightmare* for me." Seeing Pauline's face pale in concern, like it did when she was worried, Rebecca smiled and shrugged. "He was . . . attractive. As Tim says, we're all on the same team, so I'm sure we'll all have a fabulous time working together once we get to know him better. Which I can't wait to do. I'll talk to you later."

Fifteen minutes later, Rebecca's phone rang.

"Oh, I hope I did the right thing. I know you're eager, so I put through the number you wanted," Pauline whispered.

Surprised, Rebecca laughed. "Sweetheart, that's fine. Thanks." She settled back in her awful chair to vent to Harry. "Hi, darling. What a night! After you dropped me off I didn't sleep a wink. *Why* did you let me drink so much champagne? Of course I needed it after my ordeal."

"Rebecca?"

David's deep voice shot through her like a hot spike. She gripped the edge of the desk to keep from falling off the ancient swivel chair. Instinct screamed to hang up. Common sense warned he had caller ID. No choice but to brazen it through *again*.

"I'm sorry, David. The office lines must have gotten crossed." She tried to sound as sincere as possible.

"Evidently this happens quite often."

If Shannon causes problems for Pauline, I really will hurt her.

"*Au contraire,*" Rebecca purred through clenched teeth. "Pauline is absolutely indispensable. *Everyone* who calls remarks how fabulous it is to talk to a *real* person. The *Daily Mail* switchboard is the lifeblood of the organization."

"I appreciate your passionate input." He sounded amused.

Good. End it with humor.

"Fabulous! Again, I'm sorry for the confusion. Good-bye—"

"Rebecca," he interrupted.

Her heart raced in dread.

Surely he won't have the bad taste to mention last night?

"Last night Shannon shared information with me about certain letters that have come to the newspaper concerning your recipe column."

"My goodness, has Shannon been getting *my* fan mail?" She glanced around, glad Kate couldn't see her childishly sticking her finger down her throat.

"Not exactly. I have no doubt there will be more letters about Wednesday's chicken breasts."

Is he laughing at me? Dear God, what is he plotting against me now?

✌

David tried to school his voice, but every time he thought about the chicken breast flipping around on a dance floor, he laughed.

"We need to discuss your current work in the Food section," he finished as smoothly as he could muster.

"David, I'd *love* to discuss my current work with you."

Insincerity dripped off her every syllable, and again David tried to keep the amusement out of his voice. "Where would be the best place to talk about food with you?"

She laughed lightly. "Over a delicious dinner, of course."

From what he'd now seen of Rebecca, he knew she was thinking the most outrageously expensive restaurant in town. Time to spring the trap.

"Thank you, Rebecca. I look forward to sampling your cuisine. When do you want me?"

"Want you?" She gasped.

"Us. Dinner. Your place."

He smiled, listening to her take a deep breath. "I know you're terribly busy. I understand if tomorrow *won't* work for you."

Satisfaction rushed through him. "Seven o'clock?"

"Perfect! I look forward to it. Good-bye."

David flipped closed his cell phone and lay down on the bed in his suite at the Peninsula hotel. Smiling, he stared at the ceiling, remembering the way Rebecca had tried to handle him by suggesting dinner and how he'd outmaneuvered her by getting her to cook for him. Now he only had to wait until tomorrow night to test his theory about Rebecca Covington, gourmet chef. Not that it really mattered if she was for real or not, since her column was a moneymaker for the newspaper. But what did matter was that he was so intrigued he'd invited himself to dinner at her place.

He stood and paced to the windows to look out at

Chicago spread below him. It was a beautiful city with the lake, like a blue sea, lapping at the beaches. More beautiful than he'd thought it would be.

Like Rebecca.

He'd wanted to meet her because she kept surprising and amusing him. He hadn't expected to feel such desire when he'd first seen her across the room last night. God knew there had been many women the last three years, but he couldn't recall one who had stirred such an instantaneous reaction; he couldn't take his eyes off her or stop wanting to touch her.

He rammed his hands into his pockets, a dead give-away he was confused by his reactions. Ellen used to tease and warn him about it before every important business meeting. And dinner tomorrow with Rebecca was business. That was his plan, and he would stick to it.

❧

As arranged, Rebecca arrived at Harry's at noon to plot strategy for the rapidly approaching celebrity cook-off. His kitchen had been restored to pristine perfection after her three-hour ordeal preparing Baja Chicken for Wednesday's column.

She pulled out the food-spotted, frayed-edged recipe card from her IU college days for "Not Low-Cal Triple Orgasmic Fudge Pie." It was the only thing she'd saved from her married life. The rest she'd burned or given to the Salvation Army.

"This can't be messed up," she promised. "Not even by me. But we need to practice. Do you get the Food Channel on your cable? We could watch and learn." Talking a mile a minute, she ransacked his neat cupboards, looking for a pie pan. "If we undercook the pie it has a yummy molten center. If we overcook it tastes like the chewiest delicious brownie you've ever consumed. The only possible place for error is with the shell."

At last she pulled out a pretty blue and white painted ceramic pie pan. "We can cheat and use an already prepared crust in this. If we're careful, no one will ever know we didn't make it ourselves."

The zealous glint in Harry's eyes worried her. "No, sweet pea. We won't cheat." He removed the pan from her viselike grip. "I'll prepare the pastry."

"But, Harry, you don't cook, either!"

"I've been experimenting since we started this madness. Trust me." His Roman-god face, with cheekbones women would kill for—or have Harry implant for them—grew rigid with concern. Gently, he clasped both her hands. "Now tell me what's truly bothering you."

"David Sumner is coming to dinner tomorrow night," she blurted out at last.

"My God, how did that happen? Why didn't you tell me immediately!" He led her to a chair and she plopped down on it, putting her elbows on the glass breakfast table and burying her head in her hands.

"I was too embarrassed to tell you. Maybe it was the dreaded hormone fluctuations that all women fear that made me so stupidly slow. Simple truth. He outmaneuvered me!"

"I'd say so. For this, you need food, sweet pea." Meticulously, he arranged Brie, stone-ground crackers, and organic red seedless grapes on a plate and put it on the table in front of her. "Champagne?" he asked, holding up a chilled bottle of her favorite.

She shuddered. "My head is still pounding from what

I drank last night. Besides, I need to keep my wits about me. *If* I have any wits left."

Harry sat down across the table from her and popped grapes into his mouth, watching while she fed her stress. She crammed cracker after cracker piled high with cheese into her mouth.

"What are you planning to do?"

"*Originally,* I planned to be stricken by a serious, non–life threatening but extremely contagious illness at noon tomorrow."

Harry lifted one dark eyebrow.

"I know. I know. Too obvious. Besides being cowardly. So I called Cathy Post, hoping to get more info on David that could help me."

"Perfect. Cathy knows her dirt. Anything interesting?"

"David mourned his late wife for two years and dedicated two parks in her honor for children in depressed city areas. He volunteers at both of them. At one he's the Little League coach."

Harry stopped eating. "Noble, don't you think?"

It was noble; in fact, she'd felt a strange powerful warmth in her chest when Cathy told her. "*Then* he started dating women the same age as his sons. So get that grin off your face, Harry. Tomorrow night is strictly business with little *old* me."

"Are you a tiny bit piqued if that is true?" he asked, lifting an eyebrow.

"I'm a *lot* worried about what is left of my career. Why did he maneuver dinner at my place? Does he somehow know I can't cook? Is this his way to finally get me off the paper? I can't figure him out, and if I can't figure him out, how am I ever going to convince him to give me back 'Rebecca Covington's World'?"

Harry rolled his long-lashed eyes. "The other day in this very room you declared David was like every other CEO you know. And that you would dazzle him with your brilliance. That he'd be dough in your lovely, delicate hands. Your insecurities are showing."

Wounded, she stared at him. "*Best friends* are supposed to make *best friends* feel *better* when they've been horribly wrong."

Smiling, he clasped her fingers before she could reach out for the last comforting bite of Brie. "You weren't wrong. You can dazzle him. By being your charming, wonderful self. I can read sexual vibes. You're what the man wants."

"The man *wants* dinner, Harry."

He leaned closer. "Then we'll give him dinner. He would be charmed if you served him one of the recipes you've whipped up for the new column. How about the quesadillas?"

She closed her eyes against the horrible memory. "Never! I'll never make those ghastly things again. Although . . ." She opened her eyes to find Harry smiling at her. "The idea of using recipes from the column appeals to me. I can do the spinach soup ahead. If we start early enough we can make Baja Chicken. Maybe serve it over rice?" At his nod, she became inspired. "I'll finish with a selection of fresh fruit and whipped cream. I'll impress him and use my granny's Staffordshire china and the family silver. Thank you, darling. I'm already feeling better."

"What are best friends for?" He pulled her to her feet. "Now we must go shopping. We have to cook the chicken here because of your unfortunate oven situation. The rest can be done on your stovetop."

Rebecca meekly followed along as Harry prowled slowly through Whole Foods, the way she did at Saks Fifth Avenue. She felt guilty that she hadn't confessed *everything. Why didn't I tell Harry about that five-second-too-long hand holding with David?*

Because there is nothing to tell, she sternly reminded herself. The *aha* moment, the sensual current drawing her across the room to David, the tingle along every nerve ending when they touched were all a figment of her stressed imagination. Brought on by oxygen and sleep deprivation. *But then what was that thrill on the telephone today?* She shook her head in denial and stuck to her story. Tomorrow night was strictly *unavoidable* business with David Alan Sumner. The first step in figuring out how to convince him to give her back her real job.

Chapter 10

Rebecca zipped up the third little black dress she'd tried on for this dinner with David and stared at herself in the full-length mirror on the inside of her closet door.

Why is it when I'm dreading an event it comes way too quickly, but when I'm eager, time creeps along? Tonight I can't figure out if I'm eager or anxious.

"All I know is I want this dinner to be over with!"

"Are you talking to me, sweet pea?" Harry called from the kitchen.

"I'm talking to myself," she shouted back.

"Bad habit." His laughter drifted to the bedroom, along with delicious aromas. "Hurry! It's almost seven o'clock."

"Don't I know it," she spoke again to her reflection. She slammed the closet door.

This is as good as it gets. I don't care if the dress is too tight or too low cut, because it's too late.

Disgusted, she slipped into her Brian Atwood sling-backs, clasped Granny's pearls around her neck, and fastened on the matching earrings.

When she walked into the kitchen, Harry picked up a

beautifully wrapped package from the counter. "You look perfect. Here is the finishing touch."

"Harry, you shouldn't have." She kissed his cheek and opened the present. "An apron." Casting him a rueful glance, she laughed. "*Exactly* what I've always wanted."

"Exactly what you need for tonight. Let me help you." He flicked the folded apron open so she could see the deep ruffle along the bottom.

Once he'd slipped the apron over her head and tied the wide sash in the back, she studied the pristine white cotton. "It looks new. Shouldn't it have a food spot or two on it?"

"Donna Reed's aprons were always clean. Or was it the *Brady Bunch* cook?" He shook his head. "One of those early domestic goddesses on Nick at Nite." He studied her with his surgeon's eye before pushing some short hair behind her left ear. "There. A little disheveled from preparing dinner for the media mogul. Now I must go. Wouldn't do to be caught in the kitchen. Remember, be yourself. He'll be enchanted."

The minute Harry and his optimism were gone, Rebecca started fretting again. She wandered around the condo making last-minute adjustments. Since it was one of those rare perfect fall nights in Chicago, she opened the doors to the narrow terrace.

We'll have drinks out here.

Harry had re-created the table setting from a picture in one of his late aunt Harriet's Carolyne Roehm home-living books. He'd used Granny's antique linen tablecloth, the large blue Venetian glasses, and the blue and white Staffordshire china. In the center he'd placed a white soup tureen full of dahlias in reds, ranging from Bordeaux to champagne. At the base of the large tureen, he'd mounded red grapes and plums. Rebecca backed away, not wanting to shift even a napkin, spoon, or flower for fear of messing up its perfection.

She wandered back into the kitchen.

There's something wrong with this picture. Too neat if David comes in here.

She lifted the lid on the soup, dipped in the ladle, and dribbled a few green drops along the burner.

Much better.

Still unsatisfied, she opened the refrigerator and took out the bowl of whipping cream for the fresh strawberries. Two smears on the countertop looked right.

The phone rang and, her heart pounding, she answered it. "Mr. Sumner to see you, Miss Covington," her doorman, Malcolm, announced.

"Please send him up. Thanks." She just had time to put the whipped cream back in the refrigerator and light the candles on the table before her doorbell rang.

It feels like my heart jumped into my throat. Stop. I'm not afraid of anything.

To prove it, she opened the door on David's first ring.

He didn't look quite as much like Pierce as he had at first glance across Allen's dance floor, but he possessed enough movie star looks to make any healthy woman's pulse flutter.

Even if he is the enemy.

"Hello, David." Feeling breathless again, she ushered him into the tiny mirror-lined foyer.

"Hello, Rebecca." His mouth curling in his slow, sexy smile, he handed her a large bouquet of pink roses in various stages of bloom and a bottle of chilled Cristal champagne.

The dimple dented his cheek as he removed the white

linen handkerchief from his breast pocket. "May I?" he asked and touched her cheek. "Dessert, I presume."

His touch sent hot shivers along her skin. She was surprised the chilled champagne bottle she clasped didn't start sizzling. Catching sight of her flushed face reflected again and again in the mirrors, she tried to regain control.

"Yes. Dessert." She twirled away. "Make yourself comfortable on the terrace. I'll bring you a drink."

Stop trembling! Put roses in water. Fix his scotch on the rocks. Open champagne. Pour into glass. Place drinks on tray. Like a robot, she went through the motions of a good hostess while wrapping her mind around the fact she'd definitely felt something *real* when David wiped whipped cream off her cheek.

Pulling herself up to her full height, she held the tray carefully in front of her and marched out of the kitchen. David had followed orders and retreated to the narrow terrace. When he saw her, he took the tray and placed it on the small iron-and-glass table next to the large pot of golden mums.

He handed her the champagne flute and held up his scotch. "I'm impressed. You know my drink."

Their eyes connected and Rebecca felt light-headed again.

Did I eat today?

"You'd be surprised what I know about you, David." She tried to sound mysterious while sending a silent thanks to Cathy Post. "If you stand right in this spot"— she shifted so they could change places—"you'll have a view of Lake Michigan."

"That flash of blue between the John Hancock and Water Tower Place? Nice."

God, he has a great smile.

For a second she lost her train of thought. It came searing back when they both moved at the same time and her breasts made contact with his arm. "Dinner is nearly ready. Make yourself at home."

She escaped back into the safety of the kitchen.

Get a grip.

She plopped down on a chair, closed her eyes, and practiced five deep yoga breaths. After the final *ohm,* she poured herself another glass of champagne and gulped half of it. *Better.* She flew around the kitchen, pulling out her granny's bowls and cream from the refrigerator, while drinking champagne.

Little flutters of euphoria and nearly letting the bottle slip through her fingers warned she was buzzed from gulping expensive champagne like it was Diet Coke.

She slurped two tablespoons of spinach soup to get something else in her stomach.

Not bad. Tastes yummy.

Plus it looked pretty in her granny's deep old bowls when Rebecca garnished the top with a minute droplet of cream, which for some reason reminded her of tiny white hearts.

Gripping the dishes like a vise, she moved them carefully out onto the table at the short end of the L-shaped dining room. David had deserted the terrace for the living area, where he was busy studying the photos scattered all over her bookcase.

There was such a sad look on his face she stopped to stare at him. *He looks lost.*

Studying the photo of three little girls, the tiny dark-haired one in the center reminding him of Miguellia, he was lost in thoughts of Ellen's park and the kids and what it all meant to him.

Warmth rippling along his spine warned he wasn't alone any longer. He glanced up to find Rebecca watching him. "The little girls in this picture must be related to Pauline Alper. That red hair is unique."

Slowly, Rebecca walked toward him. "Her daughters. Patty and Polly. Aren't they adorable?"

"Yes. Who's the little dark-haired girl in the middle?"

"Angelina, my ex-husband's daughter. She's a doll, too."

A hot jolt of shock hit him in the gut. "You're still close to your ex?" he asked, strangely interested in her answer.

"Heavens, no!" she laughed. "But Angelina and I are friends."

Intrigued, he gave her a long look. "Interesting. A child should never suffer because adults can't get along."

"I absolutely agree."

She hesitated, and he knew she'd made some kind of decision about him.

"I had a nasty divorce." She did a mock shudder, trying to make it sound light. But he could see in her eyes there had been nothing easy about it. An ache filled his chest the way it had watching Miguellia take a swing with everything she had at an impossible pitch. He'd sensed Rebecca had courage. Now he knew he'd been right.

"Then four years after the divorce my ex called and said he and his very young wife were taking some family relationship seminars. Their instructor insisted it was imperative that we all have closure so they could become better parents to Angelina. *We* were ancient history, but as you said, none of it was the child's fault." She shrugged. "Long story short. We met. Angelina walked in, plopped herself on my lap for the duration of the visit. Very strong like at first sight for both of us. Whenever I get extra tickets to Broadway shows coming to town, I send them to her. This picture was taken when Pauline and I took all three girls to see *The Lion King*."

Their eyes locked, and the strongest sensation of tenderness he'd felt in years flooded over him. He rammed his hands into his pockets and stepped back to put some space between them. "You surprise me, Rebecca."

Her blush made her brown eyes large and luminous in her beautiful face. "Well, then, I hope I keep surprising you. Starting with dinner. It's served."

~~≈~~

With the table between them it was easier for Rebecca to regain control. To try to forget the brain-chemical reaction or whatever it was between them that made her comfortable enough to tell him about Angelina. She needed to rekindle her dislike of him.

"Delicious soup," he complimented like a well-behaved guest. "This is from your first recipe column with a gossip note?"

Good. Let's get to the point of this evening. "Of course." Settling back in her chair, she sipped champagne instead of her soup. "You wanted to talk about my column?" she asked sweetly and took another gulp.

Mirroring her, he leaned back in his chair, sipping the

Duckhorn Sauvignon Blanc Harry had read would be the perfect accompaniment to spinach soup and fowl.

"I wanted to get to know you. Discuss the reasons I made changes at the *Daily Mail*. Particularly how they affect you."

Affect me? You pulled my world out from under me.

It was safer to feel angry at him than drawn to him. Widening her eyes, she tried to disguise her disgust with interest. "Do tell."

The cool, calculating gaze from his suddenly narrowed eyes charged the air with so much tension she could have sliced it with her granny's priceless sterling silver butter knife.

Damn it. Now he knows I'm angry.

He leaned forward. Instinctively, she pressed back into her hardwood chair.

"Let's lay our cards on the table, Rebecca. I chose Shannon over you because I'm taking the newspaper in a new direction. Reality journalism. I want Shannon out at parties all night. Climbing over people to get the pictures and interviews with local and national celebrities playing in Chicago. If someone famous is dancing topless on a bar, I want Shannon there to share the sexy excitement with the reader. It isn't a job I believe you can do."

Of course I don't want that job! Oddly unsure what to say or do next, she jumped to her feet. "I smell something burning in the kitchen. Excuse me." She grabbed their bowls and escaped.

There was no need to deliberately slop food around the kitchen to make it look real. She took out her frustration by slapping the Baja Chicken and rice onto dinner plates. She was furious at him for taking the paper in a direction she believed wrong, but she was even more angry at herself for being so confused about him. Tonight she'd glimpsed someone in him she might actually like.

When sauce splattered on her apron, she stopped to look down. In despair, she tried to wash off the huge red spot. When she failed, she took the apron off and hung it over a kitchen stool to dry.

Sorry, Harry. About everything. I am going to be myself, but David will not be enchanted. He may be handsome and he may have noble tendencies, and I might feel an odd kind of connection to him, but he turned my world upside down for all the wrong reasons and I'm going to tell him so.

David stood when she returned to the table to set the full plate in front of him. He glanced at the deep vee neckline of her Dolce & Gabbana dress, with the little smile that dimpled his cheek. "This must be the infamous Baja Chicken."

"The only chicken breasts are on our plates," she snapped.

A red flush, which started at his pale blue starched collar and worked its way up over his cheekbones, caused his sapphire eyes to flash and his smile to deepen. "I never doubted it."

She felt herself flush, too. "Sorry, I couldn't resist." She sat down across from him and crossed her arms over her chest, which had the unfortunate effect of swelling her cleavage. "I hope everything is to your taste."

"It is," he answered over a forkful of chicken breast. All the while, his cool eyes appraised her.

I'm so tense and a little drunk. If I eat one morsel of food I'll throw up. She clenched her hands in her lap. She needed to get the evening back on track. "David, since you've been so honest with me, I feel I should reciprocate." She tried to smile but couldn't. *This* was so important to her. "I violently disagree with you on your vision for the paper. What you call reality journalism is what I call yellow journalism."

"The world has changed since journalism school, Rebecca." He lifted the bottle of Duckhorn from the ice bucket to pour himself another glass. "Reality programming is the wave of the future."

"Then God help us all! The main impact reality TV has had on the world is that now everybody believes they can be famous. Once fame was earned by working hard to enhance a talent to act, sing, dance, paint, write, heal, invent. *Add* something to the world. Ten years from now, an entire generation of kids reared on reality programming are going to be visiting therapists daily because they didn't become famous for eating enough bugs. That's *my* personal *Fear Factor*."

Leaning back, calmly drinking his wine, David didn't appear moved by her passionate outburst. "Do you watch *Project Runway* or *Dancing with the Stars*?"

Again she felt a hot flush of embarrassment rush up from her chest to burn her cheeks. "Those young designers *create* something. The others *learn* a skill."

"Those programs are fresh and innovative examples of good reality programs. The type of product I plan to use to revive WBS-TV, which I picked up in this deal. The same way I'm reinventing the newspaper."

"With topless babes, instead of reporting on Chicago's philanthropists at play in black tie?"

He shrugged. "Outdated reporting. Inquiring minds want to know everything. The good. The bad. The ugly."

She was grateful his attitude was making her furious enough to ignore the excitement pulsing between them.

She glared across the table. "When did we start believing we have the right to know every dirty little secret about one another and enjoy watching while people make fools of themselves?"

His rich, deep laughter filled the room, whipping her into a deeper frenzy.

"*What?* What's so funny?"

"You." Still chuckling, he leaned so close they nearly touched. "Have you forgotten the blind item that started all this? The senator and the babe? You've done your share of exposing dirty little secrets."

Stung by the truth of his outrageous claim, she rose to tower over him on four inches of steel stiletto. "It's not the same. I *always* change the names to protect the dirty little secrets of the guilty. The innocent don't need protecting. I give them credit for their good deeds. Or I should say *I did* before you fired me."

He stood, his hands rammed into his trouser pockets. His eyes were mesmerizing in their intensity. "I'm glad you chose to stay. Otherwise I wouldn't have known who you really are. I like who I see."

A second ago she wanted to strangle him. Now she had a warm, glowing, nearly overpowering urge to sit back down and let nature take its course. She'd been handling men for years. Obviously this one had a slightly different effect on her.

I need to regroup.

"It's been such an . . . interesting . . . and *informative* evening. I'm sorry, but I'm suddenly exhausted." She marched to the condo door and held it open. At her pointed look he had no choice but to cross the L-shaped room to her side.

Ignoring her obvious desire to be rid of him, David

lingered in the open doorway. "May I ask you a personal question?"

Anything to get you out of here. "Yes, if you must."

"If rumor is true, you only date much younger men. Why?"

You hypocrite. "Why do you date much younger women?" she threw back at him, holding on to the part of her that still wanted to strangle him.

The mischievous grin that crossed his face sent a tidal wave of tiny shivers down her spine. "For the excitement and lack of commitment."

"At last. We have something in common," she purred before closing the door on him.

Breathing deeply, she fell back against the wall. David was hypnotically sexy even at his most insufferable. He wasn't her type, but she could *almost* understand why some women would want him.

She stared at her flushed face in the mirrored foyer. "Who are you kidding? You're the hypocrite. You wanted him the first moment you laid eyes on him and again tonight."

The stress of *this* confusion needed to be fed. She stalked back to the kitchen, yanked open the refrigerator, and pulled out the bowl of fresh strawberries and whipped cream. She ate standing up, plunging strawberries into whipped cream before slowly licking and eating them.

Finally she faced the awful truth. *Okay. All right. I want him even though he's the enemy. The one I must defeat, or charm, or reason into giving me back my job.*

Now what should she do about that, not to mention his horrible plans for the paper?

A deep sadness drove her to fall into a kitchen chair, carrying the strawberries and whipped cream with her.

Was she truly outdated? Was there no place for her in this *unbrave* new reality world?

She played the evening in her mind, like watching the scenes in *Groundhog Day* repeated over and over. How could she have changed it for a better outcome? The intangible connection she felt for David had deepened tonight. She knew he had depth and compassion from the way he conducted his life after his wife died and the glimpses of it she saw tonight. He was a man of strong character. If she appealed to that, perhaps she could change his mind about the direction he planned to take the paper.

Finally having a plan, she warmed to the idea, deciding it would strengthen David's moral fiber if he opened his mind to new possibilities instead of the current rage for shock journalism. Plus she'd be doing a good deed for all her writing colleagues who couldn't get work because no scripts were required for reality shows.

But what should be her first move? Every womanly instinct told her she challenged and intrigued him. There was power in that for her. Unfortunately, he intrigued her, which gave him power. Plus he was her boss. Unfair advantage in this battle of wills.

Smiling, she licked another strawberry while visions of sparring with David for his own good, and hers, danced through her head.

Chapter 11

Rebecca was so accustomed to her usual Monday morning disasters she felt mildly let down when she arrived at the *Daily Mail* and no one waited to sabotage her in the lobby. Where was David? Thoughts of how to put her plan in motion had kept her awake most of the night. If David was intrigued with her, then he would be more likely to actually *listen* to her about the future of the paper.

Today, Pauline, busy taking calls at the switchboard, merely waved at her. On the landing, Rebecca glanced down the short executive hall. Maybella was totally engrossed with work and didn't bother to throw Rebecca her usual morning scowl.

She arrived at her desk and sat down. *Where is everyone? I'm ready for action. It feels like being all dressed up with nowhere to go.*

She heard David's voice and then Kate's, growing louder. As they came around the corner from the newsroom, David's eyes locked with Rebecca's. The air around them crackled with sexual tension.

We're still intrigued.

She smiled in relief, then caught herself, making her face go blank.

"Good morning, Rebecca." Kate appeared flustered, running her fingers through her very short white hair, causing it to spike on top.

It's a great look for her. I must tell her.

There was a look of fondness in Kate's eyes as she gazed at her inadequate cubicle. "David is planning to update my work space."

Coolly assessing Kate's cramped alcove, David's gaze fell on Rebecca's desk. "How is your work area, Rebecca?"

She arched, rubbing her lower back. "My chiropractor was recently able to buy a second home."

His lips curled in amusement, just as she had hoped. "I'll see what I can do about that." He strolled away, his confident walk somewhere between a swagger and just plain sexy. Rebecca could hear him joking with Joe in Sports as he worked his way through the newsroom.

"David is taking me to dinner tonight at RL's to discuss business," Kate said quietly.

"*Our* business? Home and Food?" No need to fake being solemn now. Kate's flushed face was worrying her.

"Something else. I can't talk about it just yet. I must look a mess." Kate dropped her hand from worrying her hair.

"Actually, it's a great look for you. Cultivate it."

For the first time, Kate smiled. "You're good for me, Rebecca. I wish you could be there tonight."

"I will be . . . kind of. I agreed to have dinner with George at RL's tonight. But I don't want to make you and David uncomfortable. Maybe we should change restaurants."

"Please don't. If I need help, you'll be within shouting distance."

Really worried now, Rebecca decided to pry. "Do you have any idea what David wants to talk about?"

"I'm afraid I do." With that cryptic remark, Kate disappeared into her tiny cavelike office.

Really, really worried, Rebecca followed her to make sure the bottle of Prozac Kate always kept on her desk next to her Pulitzer was still there.

Her poker face back on, Kate peered up at her. "I'm fine. You don't need to mother me the way you do Pauline."

Relieved that everything appeared normal, Rebecca pretended to be indignant. "Mother Pauline? Have you seen what a disciplinarian she is with Patty and Polly? I wouldn't stand a chance."

Kate's slow smile took away any sting. "I appreciate that you care about all of us. If I need you, I'll let you know tonight."

That night, ready if she was needed, Rebecca sat tensely on the edge of one of the prized corner banquettes at RL's. She had a perfect view of the wide door leading from the wood-paneled bar into the dark green wainscoted dining room full of paintings and brass. *Totally Ralph Lauren lifestyle setting.*

"Looking for someone?" George asked, giving her his trademark squinty-eyed smile.

"I am. The new owner of the paper, David Sumner, and my editor, Kate Carmichael. They're having dinner here tonight."

"You're not going to ask them to join us, are you?" He asked with such a little boy pout she almost laughed.

"No. They're having a business dinner."

"Good." He reached across the table with his palms up.

Not wanting to be rude, Rebecca placed her hands on his. As she knew he would, he began to play with her fingers.

"It's been too long since I've had you to myself, Rebecca."

Tonight his playfulness was tickling her. Resisting the urge to wiggle away, she clasped his hands together to stop him. "George, you are tenacious."

"Always. When I want something," he uttered, staring intently into her eyes.

You are so good-looking and so young. "George, you *do* know I'm actually *more* than ten years older than you?"

"Yeah, I read the papers." He kissed the inside of her left wrist. "I think it's sexy."

Over his shoulder, she saw David standing in the doorway. Their eyes locked and shock sizzled along every nerve. Embarrassed to be caught holding hands with George, she pulled away. "Behave," she scolded. "My bosses just walked through the door."

❧

The instant David's gaze swept the room, he found Rebecca holding hands with some young guy. The tightness in his chest surprised him.

A feeling of tremendous urgency drove him to lead Kate across the room to Rebecca's table. David smiled, eager to make trouble. "I just came by to say hello. I know I shouldn't be interrupting this charming outing, but, well, here I am." He held out his hand. "Hello. I'm David Sumner." He said, almost word for word, what Rebecca had uttered the first night they met.

Blushing, Rebecca threw him a quick stunned glance. "George, this is Kate Carmichael, my editor, and David Sumner, the new owner of the paper." She sounded calm, even though her eyes were shooting bullets at him for his tit for tat. Just like she'd done last night at dinner when she'd ripped into him about the newspaper. He'd spent half the night pacing his suite, mulling over everything they'd said to each other and trying to figure out why the hell he couldn't think of anything else.

George stood to shake hands. "Nice to meet you both."

David found the guy's handshake weak. Although it was obvious George worked out, he needed ab work. He had a hint of a beer gut coming.

David felt Kate grip his arm.

"Our table is ready, David. We should go. Have a nice evening, Rebecca." Kate said in her brisk, matter-of-fact way.

David looked long and deep into Rebecca's angry eyes before he allowed Kate to lead him away. He knew it was time to go. Now that he finally admitted to himself the tightness in his chest was jealousy, he sure as hell needed to take a step back. He had always been rigid in his rule never to mix business and pleasure, and he was too set in his ways to change now.

~ᘇᘓ~

Rebecca's view of David's face was blocked by the waiter placing beef tenderloin and grilled asparagus in front of her. She tried to concentrate on her food but kept flashing back to David's cool appraisal. She didn't have an *exact* script to make David see the errors of his ways, but *this* development was spinning all her plans out of control.

During dinner, Rebecca tried really hard to listen to George's stories about mergers and acquisitions, and his plan to teach weight lifting at the local youth center. It was *too* rude to keep glancing over his shoulder to watch David and Kate, who seemed involved in intense conversation.

When Kate walked past and gave Rebecca a long, beseeching look, she jumped to her feet, nearly toppling her half-full champagne flute. "Please excuse me, George. I'll be right back."

She met Kate in the small wood-paneled back hall, in front of the elevator to the ladies' lounge below. Two other diners were also waiting, so Rebecca had no choice but to hold her tongue, even though Kate looked ashen, until they reached the lower hallway, where the others went into the restroom.

"What happened? Are you all right?" Rebecca whispered, shifting in front of Kate to shield her from any curious onlookers coming off the elevator.

"David wants to add a weekly feature on women and finance." Kate ran her fingers restlessly through her hair. "He wants me to write it."

Suddenly Kate appeared incredibly fragile. Worried, Rebecca thought hard about the best way to respond. "Kate, is the extra responsibility too much for you on top of everything you do for Home and Food?"

"David wants me to shift some of the workload onto you."

"*Me?*" Rebecca shrieked. A woman coming out of

the restroom gave her an odd look before stepping into the elevator.

Kate shook her head. "I know you have no plans to stay in the Home and Food section for any longer than necessary."

Seeing how scared Kate looked, Rebecca knew what she needed to do. "Of course, I'll do whatever helps you for as long as you need me."

"I told David I needed time to think about his offer." To Rebecca's shock, Kate gave her a quick, intense hug. "Thank you, Rebecca. I feel calmer after talking to you."

Unlike Pauline, who wore her emotions on her sleeve, Kate held hers close. This unexpected show of affection was a clear sign Kate needed help. Rebecca vowed to give her whatever she needed, no matter what happened.

When Rebecca got back to the table, George had a cappuccino in front of him and a hot tea waiting for her. Over their steaming cups, he smiled. "Should we go back to my place for a nightcap?"

She remembered the last time they'd gone back to his place and enjoyed a particularly energetic sexual romp. She suddenly realized it had happened weeks ago and was the last time she'd had sex.

Too long.

She glanced over at David smiling and felt a little catch in her lower abdomen. *Is sexual starvation why I have this unnatural attraction to David? If so, surely I wouldn't be turning down George.*

George's sexual expertise, and all his brawny good looks and little boy charm, just didn't turn her on any longer. But she liked him, so she wanted to be kind. "No, George. I think we should call it a night."

He leaned closer. "Tonight I'll take no for an answer. If you promise to say yes to another dinner soon."

Trying to concentrate on him instead of David, Rebecca demurred. "Maybe in a few weeks. I'll be busy until then with the celebrity cook-off."

"I know. My firm bought a table for Saturday night. Then it's a date for us to celebrate."

The next morning when Rebecca walked into the *Daily Mail* lobby, Pauline jumped up from the switchboard and clapped her hands. "Do we have something to celebrate!"

"They've called off the celebrity cook-off?" Rebecca asked with real hope in her voice.

"Oh, Rebecca. You're so funny! You'll be great. This is something so amazing I'm coming upstairs with you so I can see your face. And don't ask me to tell you, because I promised I wouldn't." Pauline pretended to button her lips. Her face rosy with excitement, she nearly pulled Rebecca up the stairs.

Everyone in the newsroom stood clustered around the entrance to Home and Food. Except Joe, who was snoring under his Cubs cap.

They parted for Rebecca.

She laughed. "If this was a movie the music would be building to a crescendo. What's going on? . . . My God!" Rebecca breathed, staring at the former Home and Food section. Overnight it had been transformed into a mini version of the executive hallway. Where Kate's cubicle had been there was now an actual office, complete with a real glass door. A smaller version had replaced Rebecca's lonely desk.

She walked through the open door and found a large

blue ribbon on the ergonomically correct chair behind a new desk. "My *old* chair!" Rebecca shrieked, throwing herself into it and swiveling around madly.

"It is?" Pauline asked. "How can you tell?"

Laughing, Rebecca pointed to the small chocolate-brown stain on the arm. "This is from a two-chocolates-in-each-hand deadline day. Besides, it fits me in all the right places." She wiggled deeper into the seat. "How did David get this done overnight?"

"I asked him the same question not five minutes ago." Kate walked in, looking slightly calmer this morning, although her hair was spiky on top. "David had a large construction crew in here all night. I've already thanked him profusely. Your turn."

Kate's crisp, direct order was so out of character, Rebecca blinked up at her, trying to understand.

"Rebecca, last night I may have been grossly self-absorbed, but I'm not blind to what is going on between you. David is using the large office across from Tim as a command post to organize both the paper and the television station. He's there now. Go thank him yourself."

Warmth seeped through every pore. *I thought I was so good at hiding my attraction to David.* "You warned me about being reckless, Kate."

"The only person who can determine your course of action is you, Rebecca. I'm merely suggesting you thank David yourself."

"Should I leave so the two of you can stop talking in code?" Pauline piped up, a hurt look in her usually twinkling eyes.

"Of course not, sweetheart! Come along. I'm going to follow Kate's advice and thank the boss."

On the landing, they met Shannon coming up the

stairs. "There you are, Pauline. Why aren't you on the switchboard?" she snapped. "My phone is going crazy."

Pauline glared back. "I'm on break."

"At nine a.m.? I must ask David if the rest of us can have your schedule." Tossing her flat black hair over her shoulder, Shannon pushed past to the executive hall.

"I'll see you later," Pauline mouthed to Rebecca and flew down the stairs.

Chalking up yet another reason she didn't like Shannon, Rebecca strolled past her, lounging at Maybella's desk. Before Maybella could stop her, Rebecca rapped on David's open door and walked into his office.

With the shock of wavy hair falling across his forehead, very Hugh Grant meets James Bond, his harassed look was *too* appealing. *I shouldn't have come.*

～✵～

David looked up at Rebecca and the same rush of desire he'd felt the first night and then again last night fueled his blood. He wished she hadn't come.

He looked away, shifting papers on his desk. "If you're here to thank me, you don't need to. Kate was appreciative enough for both of you."

"Even if you don't want to hear it, good manners force me to. Giving me back my old chair was a nice touch. The ribbon was especially festive."

Relaxing back in his chair, David shoved the stubborn wave of hair neatly back into place. He couldn't resist the feisty look on her face. "I thought so. Hopefully, you won't be visiting your chiropractor on a daily basis. Unless . . . your doctor is the young guy you were with last night at dinner?"

She laughed, perching on the arm of the couch. He watched the way she smoothed the skirt over her thighs.

"George is in mergers and acquisitions. His firm bought a table for Saturday's celebrity cook-off."

His competitive bent got the best of him. "The paper bought two. The TV station a third. We'll all be there to support you. Not nervous, are you, Rebecca?"

"Of course not." She lifted her chin, defying him. But he didn't believe her.

"Then you've got everything under control for the big night?" He hadn't wanted to see her, didn't want to feel the desire to go down this particular forbidden path, but now he wanted to prolong it. To keep watching the play of emotions crossing Rebecca's face while they verbally sparred with each other.

"Of course I'm in control." She stared him straight in the eyes. "Harry and I have practiced making orgasm pie so many times I could do it in my sleep."

This he believed. He leaned across the desk, wanting more from her.

"Sorry, I didn't realize you were busy, David," Shannon called to him.

He hadn't heard Shannon come into the room; his attention was focused solely on Rebecca.

Rebecca glanced up, looking as startled as he felt by Shannon's intrusion.

"Should I come back later?" Shannon asked, even though she kept on moving into the room. "I need to discuss our plans for Saturday night."

David sucked in his breath to tell her to come back later. He wasn't ready yet to have the spell or whatever it was that drew him to Rebecca broken.

A smile played around Rebecca's softly curving

mouth. "Your timing is impeccable as always, Shannon. I'm just leaving."

He knew he couldn't stop Rebecca from leaving the room, but he wasn't happy to let her go.

~~~***~~~

Rebecca was happy Shannon had barged into the room, breaking whatever spell David had cast. She should have been working him, trying to figure out the best route to convince him to retract his plans for her and the paper, but all she did was wallow in a pool of sexual pleasure just talking to him.

Slowly rising from her perch on the couch, Rebecca threw Shannon a scorchingly disdainful look to disguise the odd jealousy burning in her chest. "Since I'm a celebrity chef on Saturday, I have important plans to make myself." Just to annoy Shannon, Rebecca flicked David a come-hither look. "I *guarantee* Saturday night will be a treat."

His responsive smile made her tingle with pleasure as she swept out the door.

Rebecca refused to admit to herself that David had *anything* to do with her decision to rush off to LuLu's to purchase a divine black crepe vintage Pauline Trigère evening gown for the culinary event. She repeatedly told herself she bought it in the hope that her exposed cleavage above the strapless gown would divert everyone's attention from her rusty cooking skills.

Chapter 12

As the Culinary Institute had requested, Rebecca faxed them her recipe three days before the event. For the price of their ticket, the four hundred guests would dine on recipes from each celebrity cook prepared by the Four Seasons Hotel kitchen staff that day.

On Saturday, fortified by Harry's air of confidence and the few weeks of practice, Rebecca dutifully arrived an hour early at the Four Seasons as demanded by the chairwoman of the event, Milly Peabody.

Milly, looking rather like a stalk of celery in a light green gown that hung straight on her tall thin frame, met them at the top of the grand staircase to the eighth-floor lobby.

"Welcome, Rebecca. You look marvelous." Milly flashed Harry a huge smile. "Yes. The dashing Dr. Grant."

On any other man, Rebecca would have hated the black tux shirt open at the throat, but on Harry it looked debonair instead of sloppy. "He'll break hearts tonight." Rebecca gripped his arm in affection and an edge of panic.

"Hope springs eternal," Harry drawled, patting Rebecca's hand, which was wrinkling his jacket. "Shall we go in?"

"Yes." Milly led them inside. "I must show you the setup. This year it is different than usual." The pre-assembly room, which was usually set up for cocktails, tonight was filled with white draped round tables and chairs. "This area and the adjoining State Room will be used for dinner. Because . . ." Grinning from diamond-studded ear to diamond-studded ear, Milly flung open a door to the Grand Ballroom. "Ta-dah, this year the kitchens are in here."

Rebecca walked into a chrome maze of miniature kitchens with two bars set up at either end of the ballroom. "Fabulous." She forced a smile, even though she wanted to run screaming for cover. "Everyone will be in here enjoying cocktails while we're cooking?"

"Yes." Milly clasped her hands. "Which reminds me. Rebecca, you and Dr. Grant are the only two celebrity chefs who haven't committed to the live auction."

Harry threw Rebecca a quizzical look. She shook her head. "I don't remember anything about a live auction."

"No. One of our board members suggested it a few days ago, and we all thought it was a wonderful way to add money to our scholarship coffer. All the other celebrity chefs have willingly agreed. I'm sure it's simply a silly mistake that the two of you haven't signed up."

Harry's eyes widened in disbelief. "You plan to auction off every one of us?"

"No, Dr. Grant. Only one celebrity name will be drawn to prepare dinner for a party of no more than six." Milly's thin face rounded in a grin as she looked toward Rebecca. "Yes. You will participate?"

Rebecca knew Kate would think a one-in-forty chance a good bet. Besides, Harry would adore being an auction prize.

"Of course we'll take part." Rebecca turned around to survey the room. "Now tell us which one of these delightful play kitchens belongs to us."

"Marvelous," Milly sighed. "Now let me show you your special kitchen. Our board members wanted you to be front and center."

Great, we'll stick out like a sore thumb.

Indeed, Milly led them to a kitchen placed strategically in the middle, where they could observe the entire room and vice versa.

"This kitchen is fully equipped with all appliances and has all the ingredients for your recipe. Have fun." Milly scurried away, gathering up more celebrity chefs in her wake.

Suddenly petrified with fear, Rebecca looked up into Harry's solemn face. "We're doomed."

"Sweet pea, these board members are either your biggest fans or out to get you."

Circling inside the half kitchen, Rebecca could see they were the center, with all the other kitchens forming the spokes of a wheel around them. "Out to get me," she sighed.

"They shall fail." Harry hugged her tight to his side. "Together we are unbeatable!"

To reassure him and herself, she smiled and stepped away as a waiter approached with a tray of drinks. Stoically, Rebecca resisted the urge to drown her stress with a magnum of chilled champagne. Instead, she yanked up her slipping strapless gown and took out her recipe card. "We might as well get started."

Expectantly, Harry looked around. "Shouldn't we wait for an audience?"

"They've just arrived." A little of Rebecca's anxiety vanished in the joy of seeing Patty and Polly, red curls streaming behind them, race toward her.

"We're here, Aunt Becky!" they chorused in unison.

She blew them kisses. "Hello, darlings."

Pauline followed behind, wearing a new emerald green dress that exactly matched her eyes. "Slow down, girls. I told you we're only staying for the cooking, not dinner. What do you say, girls?"

"Thank you for the special tickets for tonight, Aunt Becky," Patty recited politely.

"Me, too," piped up Polly, younger by eleven months at nine. "Mom, can we walk around?" The girls were already heading toward a kitchen manned by Gozo, the beloved clown from WXY-TV.

The doors opened and other guests surged into the room, surrounding them. Amid the chatter and clinking of glasses, Harry deftly prepared the crust for their pie.

"Keep smiling and hand me the things I ask for, just as we practiced," Harry whispered. Obedient, Rebecca shoved him some flour and salt while keeping an eye on the door.

At last, the group from the *Daily Mail* came in, and her heart started pounding. Where was David? She saw Kate, the little frown line of concern between her eyes, as she scanned the room. When Kate finally saw Rebecca, she smiled and hurried over.

Harry looked up when Kate arrived at their mini kitchen. "Divine Kate. Your hair and that forties-style dress make you look ten years younger and ten pounds thinner. Please don't tell others your secret, or I'll lose all my patients."

Touching her slightly spiked hair, Kate smiled. "Stop joking, Harry, and concentrate on your cooking." She turned to study Rebecca. "How do you feel?"

"Like a winner!" Rebecca declared. She was a nervous wreck as more and more guests poured into the room, but she was determined not to worry an already burdened Kate. "Go check out our competition and report back to us."

"I'll be back later," Kate promised before joining Pauline and the girls in a group from the office.

Rebecca caught a glimpse of Tim talking to Charlie and Martha Bartholomew. It always amazed her how Tim could be so polite and complimentary to Charlie in public, when he had nothing good to say about him in private. Maybe it was because the rivalry between the papers made money for both of them.

George strolled up and leaned in to kiss Rebecca's cheek. "You look beautiful," he whispered, trying to nuzzle her ear and look down the front of her gown.

Embarrassed, she pulled away. "Behave, George."

Out of the corner of her eye, she caught David staring at them, with a serious, appraising look on his face as he sized up George again. Beside David stood Shannon, her face turning a sick shade of pale, pale lime green.

Why does she always look like she wants to murder me? I'm the injured party.

Determined to ignore her fluttering nerves and breathless anticipation of sparring with David, Rebecca concentrated on melting butter and chocolate in a saucepan over low heat. Very carefully, she transferred the mixture into a bowl without spilling a drop and slowly began to beat in sugar, eggs, syrup, salt, and vanilla.

Remembering Harry's instruction to smile, she looked

up at the large crowd surrounding them and directly into David's amused face.

The wooden mixing spoon slipped out of her fingers to disappear beneath a sea of chocolate.

The collective gasp got Harry's attention. "Never fear! I'm here!" he declared. From a clear plastic bag he took out what appeared to be oddly shaped stainless-steel scissors.

He held them up to the rapt audience. "These are DeBakey forceps, used in face-lifts."

Some women self-consciously stroked their cheeks and throats.

"As you can see, this forceps is longer than normal, with nice strong teeth at the end." He plunged it into the chocolate depths. "By using the correct touch, I will grab the wood without marring it . . ." He stared down into the chocolate and twisted his wrist ever so slightly. ". . . and then we will . . . have it!" His face triumphant, he held up the dripping spoon.

An avaricious look in his eyes, he scanned the crowd. "Would anyone like to lick it?"

Although everyone clapped and laughed, Rebecca saw quite a few looks from men and women that told her they'd like to take Harry up on *both* offers.

"Can I have the spoon to lick, Aunt Becky?" Polly yelled, pushing to the front of the low counter.

"Of course, darling." Rebecca placed the warm chocolate-coated spoon on a small plate. "But you must share with your sister. And don't get chocolate on your pretty dress, or your mother will kill me."

Watching Polly run off, Rebecca caught sight of David and Charlie looking at her. Charlie, who always reminded her of Santa Claus, even in a tux, waved to her.

I know they're talking about me. What? My cooking ability? Or lack of it?

Turning her back on them, she at last placed the pie in the oven to bake for forty minutes. Collapsing back against the low counter, she tried to get Harry's attention, but he was engrossed in entertaining his fans.

Charlie and Martha, who was the perfect Mrs. Claus, pleasingly plump and always smiling, strolled over to the kitchen.

"Rebecca, I knew you would be a great success tonight. Remember at that dinner last year when we discovered we're both Libras? Our horoscopes predicted good things. You look so beautiful and did such a good job tonight, didn't she, Charlie?" Martha looked adoringly up at him.

"Yes, indeed. Fine job tonight."

"Thank you. It was for a good cause. Is someone here cooking from the *Journal and Courier*?"

Charlie's deep belly laugh made Rebecca chuckle. "We aren't lucky enough to have a beautiful celebrity like you in our Food section." He wagged a pudgy finger at her. "I'm keepin' my eye on you. You're doin' interestin' work lately."

Martha nodded as they wandered off.

What was that all about? Rebecca watched them move through the crowd. They were always friendly to her, but there was something definitely different tonight.

At the far end of the room Rebecca saw the judges, two well-known chefs and a famous restaurateur, start tasting. Wonderful aromas were filling the room.

Including our pie, thanks to Harry.

By the time the judges arrived at their mini kitchen, Rebecca and Harry had the pie, topped with whipped cream, ready. With great ceremony, she sliced a small piece for each of them. Tightly clasping Harry's hand behind her back, she felt nauseated watching them eat. When each of them nodded and smiled in turn, Harry grabbed her in a bear hug.

"It's over, sweet pea. Now relax," he whispered into her ear. "I'm going to the bar. After this, I need a drink."

David walked toward her, carrying two flutes of champagne.

Anticipation poured through her like dark, warm honey.

❧

The shadow between Rebecca's breasts was the color of honey. David's gut tightened. He wanted to lick there to taste it. He'd seduced his share of women in the last few years, but never someone he knew was off limits. This was a game he'd play only so far. He placed a glass in her hand. "The lady deserves champagne."

"Yeah, the lady does," George drawled, strolling up, carrying two flutes of his own.

When George thrust one into Rebecca's other hand, she widened her eyes, looking back and forth between them. She laughed, shaking her head, and clicked each of their glasses simultaneously. "Thank goodness it's over," she toasted and took a gulp from each flute.

George tilted his glass of champagne down his throat, but David only tasted his, watching Rebecca. Her amused gaze told him she thought they were both acting idiotic. Yeah, he knew it, too, but he liked the rush of competition.

George squared his shoulders. "So, David, I understand with your business interests all over the world, you'll be leaving Chicago soon."

David shot him a short, cool look before focusing his eyes again on Rebecca. "Chicago's a great city. I'm considering making this my home base."

"Once you've experienced one of our winters you'll change your mind." George shrugged dismissively. "You strike me as a fair-weather kind of guy."

He slid George a bored look out of the corner of his eyes. No way was he letting this guy get the last word. "When I want to turn up the temperature, I'll hop in the jet with a friend and head to my place in the islands." He deliberately looked deep into Rebecca's eyes. Her lips parted ever so slowly.

Mesmerized by thoughts of how her luscious mouth might taste—had she licked the chocolate-coated spoon?—he was annoyed when a loud crackling came from the PA system. Like everyone else, he had no choice but to turn to Milly standing behind the podium.

"Your attention, please! Is this thing on?" Milly asked, tapping the microphone with her nails. Screeching reverberated through the room, like fingernails on a chalkboard, sending a shudder through most of the crowd. David steeled himself not to flinch. He felt mildly the winner when George did react.

"Yes. It is. Ladies and gentlemen, the judges have reached their decision." Milly paused and let everyone dutifully applaud.

"The winners will each receive their own frying pan with a copper bottom inscribed with their names. And the winners are . . . where did I put . . . yes, here it is." Milly's magnified sigh was greeted by a spattering of laughter. His gaze found Rebecca, and they both smiled.

"The winner, for his Pot Roast and Mashed Potato Casserole prepared to resemble circus animals, is Gozo the Clown and his assistant, fellow clown Winky Dinky!"

Amid the applause, Milly rapped again to quiet the crowd. "And in the dessert category . . ." she screamed into the microphone to get everyone's attention. "In the dessert category," Milly repeated in a modulated tone. "The winner, for her Not Low-Cal Triple Orgasmic Fudge Pie, is Rebecca Covington and her assistant, Dr. Harry Grant."

"I can't believe it," Rebecca breathed, her face flushed and her eyes wide and light.

David almost pulled her into his arms but stopped at the last second, thrusting one hand into his tux pocket and nearly snapping the flute stem with his other. "Congratulations, Rebecca."

"Yeah, beautiful, we have a lot to celebrate next week at dinner." George shot David a cocky grin.

David turned to shoot back, jealous at the idea of George having dinner with Rebecca.

Harry stepped between them.

"Sweet pea, we won!" Harry grabbed Rebecca in a hug that lifted her off the floor and swung her around. The way David had wanted to do. "Now we can really celebrate over dinner."

"You won, Aunt Becky, you won!" Patty and Polly shouted, pushing past David to reach her. He saw Pauline pale when she recognized whom the girls had nearly trampled in their eagerness. He laughed, and she blushed, before following the girls to Rebecca's side.

Polly stuck a finger in the whipped-cream topping and licked it off. "Mom says we have to go now."

"Can we take the rest of the pie home with us?" Patty asked.

"Of course you can take it home, darlings." Rebecca kissed them both on their smooth pink cheeks.

"Oh, thank you, Rebecca. One slice and they're going straight to bed," Pauline declared with a determined glint in her eyes.

"Here you are." Harry handed the pie pan to Pauline. "I wrapped it in foil for you."

David watched them until they disappeared out the door. A happy family. Like he'd once had. He turned back to Rebecca with the oddest wish that she would kiss him like she had the girls.

Heat scorched Rebecca's cheeks. She *knew* David wanted to kiss her. What scared her to the toes of her Manolos was that she wanted to kiss him, too. Not feelings she should have for the boss who had fired her.

Harry nudged her. "Time to go in to dinner, sweet pea."

"You're both at my table." David twined their fingers together to lead her out of the kitchen. The caress of his warm, dry skin against hers quickened her pulse like it had that first night at Allen's.

George grabbed her other hand, pressing a quick kiss on her palm. "I'll see you soon," he whispered, a husky note in his voice.

In a euphoric daze of happiness at winning, and total, absolute, delirious confusion at what she should do about these inappropriate feelings for David, she sat sandwiched between him and Harry, with Kate beside him. From the next table, Tim gave her a thumbs-up and beside him, Shannon, as usual, glared at her.

Again the PA system crackled as Milly stood at the podium, which had been moved into the dining room. She was holding up a fishbowl full of small pieces of white paper.

"It is now time to draw the celebrity chef. The fortunate bidder will have the services of the chef at a dinner for six. Shannon Forrester from the *Daily Mail* will pull the celebrity chef name."

Shannon stood to go to the podium and looked over her shoulder to flash a smug smile in Rebecca's direction.

All the breath went out of Rebecca's lungs. *She's going to pull my name!*

Rebecca clutched Harry's thigh under the table.

His eyes widened. "Sweet pea, the guy you want to do that to is sitting on the other side of you," he gasped under his breath.

"Shannon's going to pick me, Harry," she whispered.

He slid her a sideways glance. "Relax. The odds are in your favor she'll pick someone else."

Her heart banged painfully against her ribs, and she tightened her grip on Harry's thigh for courage as Shannon made a huge production out of stirring around the small white slips in the fishbowl. Very slowly, she pulled out one piece of paper.

"Rebecca Covington," Shannon called out and with a glittering smile crumpled the piece of paper in her fist.

Numb, Rebecca fell back in the chair. Instinctively, she smiled as everyone looked at her and applauded, but all the sounds in the room faded into the distance. An incredible calmness made the whole world seem to move in slow motion. She had been right on that first day. Shannon had been sabotaging her from the beginning.

Kate's face peering anxiously around David brought

her back to noise and reality. She'd been set up, and there was nothing she could do to fix it.

Milly tapped the microphone again. "Will someone start the bidding for Miss Covington at five hundred dollars?"

Harry held up his right hand while patting Rebecca's back with his left.

"We have five hundred. Do I hear six hundred?"

"Six hundred!" George called from across the room.

"One thousand!" David's deep voice sent goose bumps over her bare arms. She turned to him. Earlier he and George had acted like adolescents in testosterone overload, but *this* was ludicrous.

"Twelve hundred!" George answered.

"Fifteen hundred!" David countered.

At the podium, Milly looked dazed. A hush of anticipation fell over the crowd.

"Do I hear sixteen hundred?" Milly asked hopefully.

"Two thousand!" George called.

"Three thousand!" David didn't wait for Milly.

Neither did George. "Five thousand!"

David stared down at Rebecca with such a mischievous smile she couldn't take her eyes off him. "I'll give twenty thousand dollars for Miss Covington."

Everyone gasped, sucking all the oxygen out of the room.

"What are you doing, David?" Rebecca strained toward him, their faces only inches apart.

"It's good PR for me and the paper to support local charities. Look what happened to Macy's when they blundered the buyout of Field's. This is good business," he said coolly. But Rebecca saw the fire of competition in his eyes.

He's doing this so I won't cook dinner for George.

"Twenty thousand dollars once." Milly's voice quivered with excitement. "Twenty thousand dollars twice. Miss Covington is won by Mr. David Sumner for twenty thousand dollars!"

Amid wild applause, most of the *Daily Mail* staff came up to their table to heap on congratulations. Rebecca felt her simple plan to convince David to change his mind about her job and the paper's direction shatter around her.

How can I convince you to give me back my job, when all I can think about is having sex with you?

"Rebecca." She heard Kate's voice behind her. Felt Kate's hand on her shoulder. "Shall we go powder our noses?"

Dazed and emotionally bruised by confusion, Rebecca was eager to escape by following Kate. Before Rebecca reached the safety of the bathroom, Milly scooted up to stop her.

"Rebecca, may I speak privately to you for a moment?"

Resigned to doing her duty, after all, she'd agreed to the stupid auction, Rebecca motioned Kate to go ahead.

Clasping her hands, Milly looked ready to cry with happiness. "Yes. I must tell you how grateful we are to you. To think, I had doubts about your willingness to participate in the auction. And to think you were the last-minute celebrity chef added to our roster."

Rebecca's antenna went up. "Why was I last minute, Milly?" she asked slowly.

"I thought you knew. Yes. I was sure you did."

Rebecca shook her head and Milly looked startled, her eyes stretching wide. "Since you work with Shannon, I was sure she told you about the wonderful eleventh-hour e-mail she sent our board member Charlene Jones. It so elegantly described your marvelous cooking skills."

Rebecca clearly remembered Shannon hanging around the water cooler several months ago when people had been discussing leftovers and what to do with them. Rebecca had admitted she gave up on cooking when she gave up on her marriage, so now the only items in her refrigerator were Diet Coke and champagne. Shannon had laughed along with everyone else.

"Is Charlene Jones the same board member who suggested the live auction?" Rebecca asked quietly.

Milly perked up with pride. "Yes, she is."

"Did she also suggest that Shannon should draw the name?"

"Yes. The two of them are great friends."

Absolving this poor woman of any blame, Rebecca smiled gently. "I see. Thank you, Milly."

"Yes. Thank you again." Milly scurried off, none the wiser that she had sent Rebecca's thoughts careening in a new direction.

Rebecca stared back over the room at Shannon, who was gazing intently at someone at another table, who was hidden from view.

There is something more than blind ambition fueling your need to constantly hurt and humiliate me, and you have a willing helper. But why?

Rebecca's gaze instantly found David in the crowded room. He was relaxed and smiling as he stood talking to Harry. A ribbon of desire wrapped around her.

More importantly, what am I going to do about you?

CHICAGO DAILY MAIL
WEDNESDAY FOOD

NOT LOW-CAL TRIPLE ORGASMIC
FUDGE PIE

1 unbaked 9-inch pie shell
½ cup butter (1 stick)
3 squares (3 ounces) unsweetened chocolate
1½ cups sugar
4 eggs
3 tablespoons light corn syrup
1¼ teaspoons salt
1 teaspoon vanilla extract
1 quart vanilla ice cream (optional) or whipped
  cream

Melt butter and chocolate together in a saucepan over very low heat. Beat in sugar, eggs, syrup, salt, and vanilla with a rotary beater just until blended.

Pour into unbaked pie shell. Bake in a 350-degree oven for 40 to 45 minutes or until a knife inserted between center and edge comes out clean.

Do not overbake. Pie should shake a little. It will firm up in 15 minutes after being taken out of oven. Cool and serve with whipping cream (or ice cream) on top. Serves 8.

A Note from Rebecca Covington

Darlings, yes, it's true! I am the dessert queen and I have the copper-bottom frying pan to prove it.

Like all of you, I'm mad about chocolate and whipped cream. Such perfect foods on most anything are yummy.

Although I do have my limits, unlike a certain kinky businessman I know.

His favorite recipe for his favorite ladies is whipped cream, cherries, and chocolate sauce, and that's just for their toes!

In his banquet of love, the more serious body parts are smeared with pâté de foie gras, liver sausage, and caviar.

For this gourmand Don Juan, love is truly a bacchanalian orgy of rich foods. Unfortunately, if rumor be true, he's gained forty pounds in the last two months!

So, darlings, please be discriminating where you put YOUR whipped cream when serving my prize-winning pie!

Enjoy!

Xo Rebecca

Chapter 13

On Monday morning, Rebecca stomped into Shannon's office, ready to confront her about the false lead on the senator, her lie to the Culinary Institute, and the dastardly rigging of the celebrity auction. Any of these diabolically bitchy deeds would have pushed Shannon over Rebecca's line in the sand.

Sorry, Granny. No more acting like a lady. No more mantras. Little white gloves are off. Shannon must pay.

She found Maybella in the office tidying up the desk. "Where is she?" Rebecca demanded.

Maybella tossed her head, but her mahogany-streaked, shoulder length, flipped-up hair never budged. "You won't be finding Shannon in the office this week. She's taking a much-earned vacation."

On Tuesday Rebecca realized David was missing in action from the office. It wasn't long before she couldn't control the nagging jealousy rearing its ugly Medusa head. What if it wasn't coincidence that Shannon and David were both out of the office? After all, they obviously spent time together after work. Like that first night at Allen's restaurant. *What if David has hopped on his*

*jet with Shannon and they're frolicking on some island
paradise?*

That scene kept playing through her head like a bad
movie no matter how hard she fought to shut it off. It
should have been obvious to the most naive female that
David, handsome, single multimillionaire, could have
any woman he fancied in the slightest.

All the sexually charged moments they'd shared, the
looks, the intangible *something* between them hadn't
been real. It was what she wanted to believe, *her story.*
Like the one she'd told herself about her happy marriage.
Not reality. Simple, pure, wishful thinking.

*How could I have been so stupid to drop my guard and
let David into my heart! Worse, to believe he returned my
feelings. So much for the brain-chemical thing scientists
swear explains attraction!*

Finally, her self-flagellation became too depressing
to bear. To help her fully recover from her momentary
slip into stupidity and to get back to her normal self, she
needed a tad more cheering up. There was no better way
to get herself over the last hump than to take Pauline to
lunch at her favorite spot, RL's restaurant.

Indian summer lay in a haze over the city, like a balm
before the onset of another windy Chicago winter. The fall
sun felt softer but still warm on Rebecca's bare arms as
they sat next to the geranium-festooned half-trellised wall
that separated RL's outdoor dining from the sidewalk.

Pauline swiveled in her chair to scan the dozen or so
people seated around them. "Do you remember the time
we were having lunch here and Jennifer Aniston was sitting right over there?" She pointed two tables away. "Oh,
I just loved her and Vince in *The Breakup.* Maybe she's
in town again?"

Rebecca shook her head. "Sorry, sweetheart. Not that I've heard."

"Oh, well, maybe we'll see someone else famous." Pauline sat up straighter. "You always say RL's is the place in Chicago to see and be seen."

Half an hour later, even Pauline had to concede they were mostly seeing little girls with their moms or grandmas going into American Girl next door and inevitably coming out carrying multiple big red shopping bags.

"Look at that one coming now." Pauline pointed toward a happy little girl, clasping a redheaded doll while skipping along beside her mother. "She reminds me of my two girls." Pauline's eyes got misty. "They were just that thrilled when you bought them their American Girl dolls last Christmas."

Rebecca shivered at the memory. "Then it was worth my agony waiting in line outside to even get *into* the store. Did I mention it was snowing that day?"

"Rebecca, you should start shopping now. Christmas is just around the corner," Pauline said brightly.

Confused, Rebecca stopped dipping her grilled cheese sandwich into her tomato soup to look up at Pauline. "What are you talking about? You know I love last-minute Christmas shopping. It's only the middle of October."

"Oh, I know how much you love Christmas. You're always your happiest then. You should be thinking about Christmas, Rebecca. Remembering how much you love all the lights on Michigan Avenue, and going to all the fancy holiday parties, and shopping for your friends and just making people happy, like you did the girls."

Pauline did not have a poker face like Kate. Every emotion was written in bold, neon red letters across her pretty freckled features.

She thinks I'm depressed. Hoping to reassure her, Rebecca laughed. "Stop worrying. I'm fine."

Pauline's lips quivered as she pointed to the bowl of soup Rebecca was wiping clean with the crust of her sandwich. "Look what you're eating."

Rebecca had to defend her choice to feed her stress just a few more carbs. "My granny always said starve a cold, feed your stress. It's comfort food."

"Oh, I knew it!" Pauline leaned across the table, her curls falling around her stricken face. "I know you're trying to hide it, but I've never seen you so down. Not even when you got . . . fired." She dropped her voice on the last fateful word.

"I'm not *down,*" Rebecca insisted, feeling rotten for lying to one of her dearest friends. No way was she going to burden Pauline's gentle soul with this mess. "I'm frustrated." As always, when she had no choice but to fib, Rebecca kept it as close to the truth as possible. "I need to talk to Shannon about a work-related problem, but she's out of the office all week."

"Mr. Sumner's gone this week, too." Pauline went into deep-whisper mode. "That's just a coincidence, don't you think?"

Hoping the pain in her chest was heartburn instead of *heartache,* because she would have no more of *that* foolishness, Rebecca shrugged. "I guess it's possible they're together."

"But he paid twenty thousand dollars for you!" Pauline said, her voice loud with excitement.

The man at the next table looked up, a peculiarly interested gleam in his eyes.

"That was a business deal." Rebecca lowered her voice, hoping Pauline would do the same next time.

"Great publicity for him. It made him look good because I was up for bidding. It was nothing personal."

Obviously Rebecca hadn't kept her voice low enough. The man at the next table leered at her and actually scooted toward her in his chair. She stopped him with a scathing don't-you-dare glare.

He hastily paid his bill and fled.

Pauline had totally missed his crude behavior because she kept staring, like the Sphinx, toward Rush Street. "It should be just a few more minutes, and then I'll find out the truth about Mr. Sumner and Shannon. This is one of those moments that I need to be here for you," she declared, perching on the edge of her chair. "Look, Maybella!"

Wearing black cat-eye sunglasses, Maybella was slowly strolling along Chicago Avenue, sipping a venti Starbucks.

Waving, Pauline bounced to her feet. "Oh, Maybella, hi!"

Maybella stopped to stare in their direction.

Even from a distance Rebecca could see she didn't look happy to obey Pauline's eager gesture to join them.

Clutching her Starbucks in both hands, essence of caramel frappuccino clinging to her, Maybella hovered on the other side of the flower-festooned barricade. "Hi, y'all. It must be nice to get such a nice long lunch break."

Pauline nodded. "For you, too. We were just talking about how lonely it must be this week for you. With everyone gone in the executive hallway."

Visibly preening, Maybella flashed a toothy grin. "Mr. Porter's in and out so much this week, too. He left me in charge of everything. I'm so exhausted I had to have another frappuccino to make it through the afternoon."

"Poor you." Pauline looked wounded on Maybella's behalf. "When do you expect everyone back to relieve you?"

Rebecca watched Pauline in mounting disbelief, reminded of a special she'd seen on how a spider hypnotizes a fly into its web.

"Mr. Sumner comes back on Friday. Shannon not 'til Monday. Dear thing needs a break with all her new notoriety." Maybella smirked in Rebecca's direction.

She schooled her face for fear any sign from her might lead Pauline to inflict further torture on Maybella.

Pauline glanced down at her watch and her eyes widened in mock horror. "Oh, my gosh. It's almost two. If you're in charge, shouldn't you be back by now? What if Mr. Porter calls in? Or worse, Mr. Sumner. You might get fired!"

Maybella's lips, lined lightly with whipped cream, twisted into a frown. "I have five minutes left on my break. Don't you worry, I'll be back at my desk on the dot of two like always." With a last glare, she swung away.

Watching Maybella flutter frantically back toward the Daily Mail building to make that two o'clock deadline, Rebecca felt a twinge of sympathy for her. She turned to her always kind, sensitive, gentle friend. "Clearly I don't know you as well as I thought I did."

A fiercely protective look came over Pauline's face. "Oh, stop! Just because I'm not a mean-spirited person doesn't mean I'm not capable of defending my loved ones from those that *are* mean-spirited. Maybella deserves it for the way she sometimes treats you. I always tell the girls what goes around comes around. Besides, we got the truth. Trust me, if Mr. Sumner and Shannon were together, Maybella would give up a week of double caramel frappuccinos for the right to tell us. So see! You can be happy again!"

Rebecca wasn't so sure she knew the truth, and she was nearly positive she wouldn't be *truly* happy for quite some time, if ever, but who was she to burst Pauline's bubble?

She left Pauline content at the switchboard in the lobby. By the time Rebecca climbed the stairs to deliver Kate's promised treat of RL's Chopped Waldorf Chicken Salad, the nagging need to have the truth confirmed got the better of her. Before pride stopped her, Rebecca blurted it out. "Kate, do you know where David has been all week?"

Kate peered up over the top of her tortoiseshell half-glasses as she opened her lunch. "No. But I'm grateful his absence gives me a few more days to decide about the finance column."

"Shannon is gone this week, too."

Kate looked as startled as Pauline had earlier. "Surely you don't believe they're together?"

Rebecca shrugged. "They were together that first night at Allen's. And sort of together at the cook-off. So, yes, I think they might be together now." Unable to muster another fib, Rebecca flung herself into Kate's soft new black leather chair, which had replaced the hard, old, ugly one, and prepared to confess. "I *know* it's really none of my business if they're together. And I know it's my own stupid fault for thinking about it at all."

Kate was watching her with so much sadness and concern on her face, Rebecca had to look away. She intently studied her fingers twisting together on her lap, or she'd burst into hot, painful tears. "Pretty dumb, huh? For a woman of my age to so misunderstand his actions. To start believing my own publicity. *Never* a good idea."

She forced a smile before looking up, her eyes welling with tears despite her best efforts to hide her feelings.

"I'm sorry," Kate said quietly, her face etched with sorrow. "My instincts tell me you're wrong about David and Shannon being together. However, you're obviously in pain. How can I help you?"

"You can't, Kate." To Rebecca's horror, her own voice cracked a little. "As my granny taught me, ultimately, we all must save ourselves."

By Thursday night, nesting in her condo to lick her wounds, surrounded by scented candles and music, Rebecca called on all her years of practice in saving face. It wasn't quite as good as saving herself, because inevitably there was extra baggage that needed to be lugged around on a daily basis. Lately the baggage had become heavier than usual.

To get back to where she needed to be—confident, devil-may-care, able to lift her heavy baggage in a single hand, emotionally unattached, focused on getting her identity back—she went through her recipe for survival.

A pinch of self-pity. Granted, she'd allowed herself a smidgen more than she should have these past months since David fired her, and in the last days because of David himself, but she was still well under her recommended daily allowance.

A really healthy dose of anger. Yes, anger was good. When mixed with determination, focus, desire, and tenacity, it was incredibly delicious. She'd been feasting on it for years.

So why do I suddenly feel like I'm starving to death?

The phone's shrill ring startled her up off the plump pillows on the couch.

"Mr. Sumner to see you, Miss Covington," Malcolm, her doorman, announced.

Delight zinged through her body in a burst of bubbles, like too much champagne, making her giddy and reckless.

No, my survival needs anger now!

"It's late, Malcolm," she said coolly into the awkward silence that had fallen on the other end of the line during the time she was remembering who she was and what she needed to do to save herself.

"Miss Covington. Mr. Sumner to see you," Malcolm repeated, strain echoing in every syllable.

For a moment she'd forgotten the other half of the anger cup. *Don't dump it on those who don't deserve it.* She couldn't put Malcolm in the middle of her need to tell David to get lost to protect her heart. Pride demanded she do it herself.

"I'll see Mr. Sumner. Thank you." Once Malcolm hung up, she slammed down the phone and zipped the hoodie of her navy cashmere Juicy Couture sweat suit so tight around her neck she nearly choked.

Boss or not. Twenty-thousand-dollar date or not, David is not getting in here tonight.

She flung open the door to tell him so.

Directly across the hall, the elevator doors slid slowly open. There he stood, looking more casual than normal, wearing a black leather jacket and with a light scruffy shadow along his square jaw.

Their eyes met and his face became more alive, like some switch had been turned on. His blue eyes blazed and his long mouth curled in a deep dimpled smile. She was reminded of all the lights being turned on along the Magnificent Mile for the holidays, and she felt the same warm, joyous wonder.

Clearly I need another drink from the anger cup.

Crossing the hall in three strides, he held up the two frosty bottles of Cristal he was carrying. "Celebrate with me. I'm going to be a grandfather."

Determined to be strong, she fought her instant connection to his happiness. "Why little *old* me?" She put every ounce of sarcasm she could muster into her voice. "Your young girlfriend thinks being a grandpa makes you too old for her now?"

Watching the light go out of his face was like a kick straight to her heart. When he took a step back she had to bite her lip not to call out to him.

"I thought you'd understand. After the way I saw you with those little girls." His voice became firmer. "My mistake. I apologize for bothering you, Rebecca."

He turned away but not before she glimpsed his face. *I've hurt him.* "David, wait!"

He turned back, his face guarded, but he couldn't hide the emotion in his eyes. "No. You're right, Rebecca. This was a mistake. It's late. I'll see you at the office."

Determined to control whatever happened if she let him in tonight, she met him halfway in the hall. Without the advantage of her usual stilettos, she had to tilt her head back slightly to watch his expression.

"I'd like you to come in, David. I'm sorry. You caught me off guard. Besides, I can't bear the thought of wasting these fabulous bottles of champagne." As always, she tried to defuse the tension with humor.

Solemn, he stared down into her face. She knew these next few moments could change everything.

She put every ounce of her desire for him to stay into her eyes, willing him not to go. She backed to the door and pushed it wide open. "Please come in," she whispered.

Expressionless, his back stiff, he walked into her condo.

She closed her eyes for an instant in gratitude. Now she didn't have to hate herself or keep being eaten alive with remorse for her cruelty. She knew that was more baggage than she could handle.

She shut the door. "Please go on into the living room. There are champagne glasses on the library table next to the bookcase. I'll get the ice bucket and join you."

She needed the private time in the kitchen to try to understand why David had appeared at her door so late. She tried to tell herself the reason she let him in tonight was because since childhood she'd always taken in strays, feeling an affinity for their loneliness and need for love. My God, she'd even married one, and look how *that* turned out.

Here I am spinning another story. Truth needed here. David was no stray. He was powerful and sexy. Why did he want to celebrate one of the most important occasions of his life with her? Her need to understand shook her to her core.

The rose-scented candles she'd lit earlier had burned out on the glass coffee table, but their fragrance still hung in the air, and the CD of Patsy Cline's greatest hits was ending with her plaintive wail of walking after midnight.

David had thrown his leather jacket over the back of the hunter green tweed side chair and opened one bottle of champagne. He stood waiting for her, his blue shirt open at the throat and his dark hair wavy, like he'd run his fingers through it.

She placed the ice bucket on the table and he handed her a glass of champagne. His eyes were clear and vulnerable. "To a new beginning tonight?"

Afraid to face her feelings, she tried to make it light. "Deal." She curled up on the couch, burying her bare feet deep into the pillows, and patted the cushion beside her. "Now come here, Grandpa, and tell me all about it."

Joy flooded back into David's face, bringing her a rush of warm pleasure.

He threw himself down beside her in such a natural way, as if they'd shared this couch before and he knew exactly how close to sit. Knew how to snuggle into the plush softness and stuff a small green velvet pillow behind his head for comfort. Anticipation melted through her.

He turned his head to look at her, his eyes bright, yet lazy in a sexy, sleepy kind of way. It was the kind of look that reminded her she wasn't wearing any underwear.

Feeling sexy despite her best intentions, she snuggled down deeper beside him. The tail end of her self-preservation warned her *not* to focus on how it would feel for David to kiss her. She slammed the door on her common sense for the night. It was like the spell he cast that day in the office. She just wanted to wallow in this pool of sensual delight a little while longer.

"So tell me everything," she said, watching his face only inches away.

"The night of the cook-off I took the jet to the coast for meetings about WBS. I didn't get any time to see my son Ryan and his wife, Jasmine, in Pasadena until last night."

He smiled, and she *knew* he was remembering that moment of happiness.

"As soon as I arrived they told me she's going to have twins in the spring."

Rebecca sat up straighter. "My God, no wonder you're so excited. Twins! Double the pleasure."

"Often double the trouble with Ryan and Michael." He said it with such love in his voice she got goose bumps. "Your glass is empty, Rebecca. I'll get more champagne."

A sense of loss, for his warmth, for *him* next to her on the couch, made her watch him carefully. His almost-swagger. The way his strong hands grasped the ice bucket to carry the champagne back to the coffee table. His slow, confident smile. It all seemed so right for this moment.

Want became desire. *Desire.* Such an important ingredient of survival flavored life in so many delicious ways, she'd learned. Considering who he was, the kind of desire she felt for David needed to be portioned out carefully.

Surely one taste can't hurt me.

He settled back down and handed her another chilled glass of champagne. They were so close their thighs touched.

She raised her glass. "To the new twins."

"To the new twins and hoping their mother finds me a more satisfactory grandfather than she does father-in-law." He blinked as if startled. "I can't believe I admitted that to you. I haven't even discussed it with Ryan."

Rebecca refrained from asking why Jasmine didn't care for him. A few weeks ago she could have thought of several reasons, and she didn't even know the dear girl. Tonight she couldn't think of one.

"Don't worry about confessing. You'd be surprised what people have told me. Remember, it used to be my job to get people to tell me their deepest, darkest secrets."

He winced. "Ouch!"

"No. No. I didn't mean it *that* way." She didn't want to think about the *Daily Mail*. She didn't want to remember she'd once thought of him as the-evil-boss-from-hell. She didn't want to remember she'd once planned to do whatever it took to get back her job. Tonight she wanted it to be just Rebecca and David, with no expectations. No promises. Just the honesty of the desire beating between them.

She touched his thigh and their eyes met. She shifted closer, reacting to the invitation on his face. "Let's agree, David. Tonight nothing about the *Daily Mail* will taint the twins' celebration."

He laughed. "*Daily Mail*? Never heard of it." He poured them both another glass of champagne. "You didn't happen to give any advice to those other poor souls spilling their guts, did you?"

Sipping, she relaxed back onto the pillows. "As a matter of fact, I *love* giving advice. For your information, I wrote an advice column for my college newspaper. 'Ask Becky.' I was quite a hit, if I do say so myself."

He tried to look impressed but his dimple gave him away. "Why didn't Becky come to Chicago?"

"Becky *did* come to Chicago, eager to share her young wisdom with the world. But, alas, the world wasn't interested. In Chicago the only advice column that mattered belonged to Ann Landers. So I became Rebecca Covington."

Forbidden topic. She drained her champagne glass.

He immediately refilled it. "I'm interested. Can Ask Becky help me win over Jasmine?"

"Luckily for you, Becky still loves to practice giving advice as often as possible. Ask Becky needs to know how you reacted to the delightful twinner news."

"I took Jasmine's hand, like this." David picked up Rebecca's hand and held it firmly. "And I looked into her eyes, like this."

My God, his eyes really are the color of priceless sapphires.

"And I said, I'm very happy." His voice was deep, compelling, and so very sensual.

Why is it so hot in here?

Feeling incredibly flushed, like her skin was burning, she pulled her hand free to unzip her hoodie to the top of her breasts, where the cleavage started, and took another swallow of cold champagne. "Mistake, David. You should have kissed Jasmine's cheek. Then what happened?"

Really, she was trying to concentrate on his problem, but she found the way his hair fell across his forehead so utterly fascinating, she couldn't think of anything but running her fingers through it. It looked silky, and at the temples there was the slightest hint of beautiful silver.

"They're both veterinarians, so we discussed her absence from the clinic they run. And Ryan and I discussed the trust funds I'll set up for the children."

"Aha! Another problem. Of course the trust funds are a marvelous idea. But what are you doing for Jasmine? She's the one who's going to have morning sickness and swollen feet and gain twenty-five pounds. She needs a little TLC."

"What does Becky suggest I do?" He grinned and poured more champagne into her glass.

Ignoring the little buzz in her head, she took another sip. "Find out what flowers are Jasmine's favorite and have them delivered weekly. And a massage! Yes, definitely. A masseur to the house once a week to give her a ninety-minute massage. I believe such generous gestures will help her see you in a new light."

Like I do.

The idea of massaging David's shoulders and back held such appeal she had to tightly grip the stem of her flute to keep from touching him.

"Done. Thanks, Becky." He relaxed back beside her, leaned in, and kissed her. His mouth was warm and inviting, and it tasted of champagne. Her favorite.

Call me a glutton, I want more.

She touched her throbbing lower lip with the tip of her tongue and stared into his intent face. "I liked that. I'm going to kiss you back." The slow smile that broke over his face dangerously elevated her temperature even higher.

"It's my greatest hope." He removed the champagne glass from her hand and began to gently nuzzle the nape of her neck. "Do you like this, too?"

How did he know? She drew a short breath, shivers tickling every nerve ending. "*One* of my favorite erogenous zones."

"I plan to find every last one of them," he whispered, his voice husky. He slid his hands under her hoodie, his fingers making gentle circles on the aching sides of her breasts. "Like this."

Ribbons of desire pulled her insides so tight it frightened her, and she fought for freedom. "I'm highly competitive. I want to find your erogenous zones first."

She wrapped her arms around him and kissed him, fully, deeply, touching his tongue again and again.

She shuddered as he slid the cashmere hoodie down her arms. Her skin felt chilled and overheated in the same instant. "You're cheating."

"You're overdressed." He nipped at her throat. She

gasped when his mouth moved to the sides of her breasts, where they were so tender. Every brush of his lips tightened the desire wrapping them closer and closer.

"You're overdressed, too," she whispered. In spite of the heat rising in her abdomen, she forced herself to shift away from his wonderful, sensual mouth.

She slipped the top button of his shirt free to lick his warm, hard chest, and moved lower, opening button after button.

He stopped her at the fifth one, his taut stomach trembling beneath her lips. "You're getting ahead of me." His laugh was shaky.

"You're not the only one in control here." Slowly, loving his instant reaction, she rubbed her hot, tingling breasts against his lightly furred chest, making her way back to his mouth.

He groaned. "Becky, you're not playing fair."

"What do you plan to do about it?" she whispered before biting his earlobe.

"Where's the bedroom?" He stood, pulling her up and into his arms.

"David, we're not twenty anymore. I'm heavier than I look!" she warned, wrapping her arms around his neck.

He laughed and walked purposefully and without difficulty down the hallway to her open bedroom door.

She couldn't take her eyes off his face as he laid her on the down comforter and stood to shed his clothes. His body was lightly tanned except for a wide band of pale skin around his groin. His erection was taut and beautiful, and she wanted him.

"Safety?" she whispered.

"Always." He slipped on a condom before stretching out beside her.

"Do you like this?" He kissed her navel, and his mouth followed the trail of his hands stripping off her cashmere sweatpants.

Pleasure tremors racking her body, she gasped. "You're getting ahead of me."

"I know." He nipped playfully at the inside of her knee and then, slowly, his mouth warm and moist, he nuzzled along her inner thigh. Her muscles tightened in anticipation.

Desperate to let herself go, she tangled her fingers in his hair, urging him up over her body, loving his weight pressing down on her. "I'll relinquish control if you will," she whispered against his mouth.

"God, yes!" He kissed her so long and deeply her breathing changed, coming out in short gasps.

She closed her eyes, lost to everything except David finding and touching every delicious spot on her body, which throbbed to be stroked or caressed into pleasure by his hands and lips. The ache at her center expanded out in such hot waves she couldn't bear it another instant. Trembling, she arched up, demanding he cradle her hips with his palms and push himself deeper inside her.

"I want more." She bit her lip, frightened that she'd spoken her desire but unable to stop.

His eyes locked with hers as he moved deeper and deeper and faster until the spasms built.

Yes, this is what I wanted.

She held him tight, moving with him, their rhythm perfect, like this wasn't the first time. She *knew* what he wanted, just as he knew for her. Knew when to kiss, caress, thrust with her lips, tongue, and body until there was nothing but his taste in her mouth and him hot and throbbing inside her.

Shuddering waves of pleasure broke over her and she cried out, falling over the edge, lost to everything but swirling, scalding sensation beating between them.

They stayed tangled together, their breathing slowing to become more even, yet not quite normal.

"You're exquisite, Becky," he whispered into her damp throat. Kissing her shoulder, he shifted to gently pull her closer so she could rest comfortably beside him, her head on his chest.

It had been a very long time since she was like Becky. Free. Trusting enough to fearlessly go with her feelings.

Too long. By morning the spell would be broken. Time enough then to be Rebecca again.

Chapter 14

David opened his eyes, his senses filled with Rebecca. Her taste in his mouth, her breath warm on his throat, her soft body curled against him.

He stared into the darkness, blaming himself for letting things between them go this far.

Nothing had played out like he planned. Or had he planned this all along, since the first night he looked across the room and their eyes met? He rested his cheek against her hair. It smelled like almonds.

Contentment settled over him and he pulled her closer, being careful not to wake her. She sighed, shivering.

Afraid she was cold, he pulled the comforter up, tucking it around her bare shoulders.

Tired, he closed his eyes. He was falling asleep, and as he drifted off, he saw himself holding a woman's hand, looking into her eyes, twirling her around. They were both laughing, full of joy. It was the old dream from when his life had been whole with Ellen.

The dream fragmented into hundreds of pieces and slowly fit itself back together, jagged edge to jagged edge. He saw the woman's face again, but this time it was Rebecca's.

He tried to yell out that this was wrong, but his voice was blown away by the wind stirring the curls around Rebecca's small ears. Then she began to slowly fade into the light from the blazing sun in the blue sky above them. Only then did David let himself fall into a deep, dreamless sleep.

❧

Rebecca opened her eyes to the weak October dawn light speckling the wood floor through her half-closed cream drapes. David's even breaths felt warm on her cheek. Sometime during the night he must have drawn the comforter over them for warmth like a cocoon.

She slowly sat up, watching him sleep. With his wavy hair messed up and the shadowy scruffiness along his jaw, he looked vulnerable and adorable.

My God, what have I done? My first one-night stand. And with my boss. Insane, but worth it.

Remembering, her body tingled with pleasure. The spell wasn't broken yet.

Maybe I'll wake him up to do it again.

Seizing what was left of her self-control, she opened the door and welcomed back her common sense. *Get up and get dressed. This is not part of my plan.*

Determined to be smart, she slid to the side of the bed. She glanced back. He looked so sweet sleeping, she couldn't resist pressing one last farewell kiss on his warm, scratchy cheek.

Half an hour later, swaddled in a heavy terry cloth robe and a towel wrapped around her wet hair, she walked back into the bedroom. David was sitting up, stretching, the muscles in his back and chest rippling.

Yes, he obviously works out.

Since last night, the little spark of excitement he'd engendered on first sight had become a roaring blaze. She dampened it down with a healthy dose of cheerfulness, as if it was perfectly normal to find David naked in her bed.

God forbid there be an awkward moment. I'll make this light.

"Good morning, David. There are disposable toiletries in the guest bathroom down the hall, and it has the best shower. Help yourself."

His eyes were watchful as she moved around the bedroom, picking up their clothes, discarded in abandonment. "Natural beauty takes me about thirty minutes. Then I'll meet you in the kitchen. But you'll have to make your own coffee."

"Thank you, Becky," he finally responded in a husky I-just-woke-up-after-sex voice.

She fled into the bathroom, trying to focus on her goals. Her *immediate* objective was to get him out the door with as much grace and humor as possible. The other goals, to figure out exactly what last night meant to both of them, if anything, and her ultimate, gold standard goal, of changing his mind about the future of the *Daily Mail,* would have to wait.

The minute she walked into the kitchen and found David, showered and dressed, and brewing two cups of tea, she knew he wasn't going to make an awkward scene.

He looked very much at home. He used the strainer like a pro and handed her a steaming cup. "I noticed you like your tea weak."

She watched him pour himself a stronger brew. "*You* drink tea?"

"Sometimes. I developed a taste for it when I spent several months in London and Edinburgh putting together a deal." He leaned against the counter, watching her. She sensed he was waiting to take his cue from her.

Keep it light. Make him comfortable. We are two consenting adults. No drama needed here.

"About the Becky thing." She peered at him over her cup and tried to sound nonchalant. "I understand last night was part of the twinner celebration. *An enchanted evening.* Now time to get back to work. You know, the *real* world."

He stared at her for too long, like he'd held her hand. His face was guarded, like she tried to make her own. Their armor was firmly in place.

I wish I knew what he was feeling. Is he as confused as I am?

He placed his cup carefully on the counter. "I'll see myself out."

"No, don't be silly. I'll see you out." Holding her cup to her chest, she led him to the front door and opened it.

If she was still young and naive like Becky had been, she'd tell him the truth. *I've just had the best sex of my life with you, but I know it didn't mean anything, so let's be urbane and sophisticated about it. But if it did mean something, what should we do about it?*

But Rebecca had learned to hide her feelings. Watching him shrug into his leather jacket, she fought her confusion and desire to reach out to him.

David, his face strong, stern, and sad all in the same moment, stopped only inches away to gaze down at her.

"I want to tell you about my late wife, Ellen."

Rebecca's heart missed a beat. *Please don't say I remind you of her.*

"When she became ill and was dying, we were all devastated. It destroyed the foundation of our lives. I had to reinvent myself as a father and as a man. Ellen tried to make me understand that we all needed to move on and be happy, but I couldn't. I vowed to never love in that way again. Regardless of what we decide to do about what happened between us last night, I intend to honor that promise."

His eyes blazed with such sincerity she was speechless. That a man like David would make such a promise and, even more important, he'd tell her about it, loomed so large and compelling in her view of him, she needed to rewrite the script. This man deserved more than grace and humor. He deserved as much honesty as her self-preservation would allow.

"I understand what you're telling me, David. I have no expectations. I appreciate and respect your decision to tell me your feelings."

But if you don't leave, I'm going to embarrass us both by bursting into loud, messy tears from all the conflicting emotions bottled up inside me.

She willed him not to touch her. As it was, she barely contained her composure until she shut the door behind him. Then she collapsed in a heap, her heart pounding and her emotions flowing out of her eyes. For someone who prided herself on *always* remaining in control, she was suffering a serious malfunction.

Of course, she rationalized it. David *had* turned her life upside down, stolen her identity by firing her from a job that she believed defined her. So, naturally, he had a profound effect on her. How she'd chosen to respond to him last night didn't bear close scrutiny. And if she thought too much about the sadness she saw on David's face when he talked about losing his wife, Rebecca would never stop crying.

Rebecca finally arrived at the *Daily Mail* office an hour late due to the fact she had to *redo* her thirty minutes of natural beauty because of crying over David, or for David, or for herself. Her emotions were all over the map. How could this be perimenopause when she felt like an overripe, lustful teenager panting for the school's hottest hottie? At least here in her daily haunt she retained enough self-control to try to figure out how to get her life back on track.

Or so she thought, before she saw Pauline's chalk-white face, each freckle standing out in relief.

"Sweetheart, please don't tell me you're still worried about me!" She gave Pauline a quick, tight hug. "Look, I'm happy! No need to worry."

"Mr. Sumner came back early."

"Yes. I know." Rebecca smiled, still feeling incredibly warm and tingling all over.

Pauline's green eyes widened. "You've seen him already this morning? Is that why you're glowing?"

Rebecca tried to come up with a plausible, as-close-to-the-truth-as-possible explanation, like her skin looked dewy because she was wearing a new moisturizer.

Pauline gasped and sat down hard in her chair. "Oh, I can tell from your face that you and Mr. Sumner . . ." She pressed her lips together and shook her head. "Then I can't ask you to help me."

"*Of course* I'll help you. With anything." Totally confused now, Rebecca started fanning Pauline's flushed face with her purse. "But you *must* tell me what's wrong."

"Shannon came back early today, and she and Maybella had breakfast together at Starbucks. When they came in an hour ago . . ." Pauline stopped and shut her eyes. "They told me they'd been reliably informed Mr. Sumner is replacing me with an automated phone system." She opened her eyes and two tears squeezed out.

Heavy, painful dread took root in Rebecca's chest. "I don't believe it."

"If they can . . . fire you," she dropped her voice, like she always did when discussing Rebecca's predicament, "then they can sure do the same to me." Pauline's tears flowed in earnest now, and Rebecca let her cry it out, handing her pink Kleenex from the box on the desk. "I love this job. Plus the benefits are . . . great. I even have dental insurance for the girls. They're going . . . to need braces."

Patting her back, Rebecca made soothing noises. "Please don't worry. We'll get to the bottom of this."

"How? I can't go through my usual channels." Pauline glanced meaningfully at the switchboard. "It might add fuel to the fire. I thought you could find out for me . . . but . . . it might be too awkward now . . . if . . . you know."

The truth struck Rebecca like a bone-breaking blow to her already fractured emotions. She heard herself declaring she'd do anything to get her job back and cringed with remorse. It *would* be awkward now. Before last night she would have marched into David's office and demanded the truth. Now it would appear too calculated, like she expected more than he was willing to give.

Payment for services rendered.

Regardless of how Rebecca felt, Pauline's hopeful expression could not be denied. "Of course, I'll talk to him this very minute." Rebecca blew her a kiss and went directly to the executive hallway before she thought better of it.

As always, Maybella looked up when she heard Rebecca's heels striking the floor. Since she was practically running, she was noisier than usual.

"Can I help you?" Maybella asked with her usual smirk.

Today Rebecca didn't bother to smirk back. "I need to see David." Ignoring Maybella's indignant yelp, Rebecca walked past her toward David's office.

Early that morning David had wandered through the *Daily Mail* offices. Surrounded by the trappings of his growing media empire, he felt totally in command. Not like last night.

Christ, he needed to stop thinking about it. He hated weaklings who vacillated, refusing to chart a course. He'd been honest with Rebecca. Laid the truth on the line for her. Too much pain had gone into his decisions about the future to change anything now. It would go against the personal code he lived by.

Even if last night was the first time in five years he'd fallen asleep thinking about another woman.

Guilt ate into his gut. All right, so he wasn't quite back to normal. None of the casual affairs he'd enjoyed the last few years had fazed him. Yet one night with Rebecca and he was thinking she might be worth the risk of being hurt again.

He pulled himself up, tall and proud. He wouldn't give in to these feelings. He'd keep it light with Rebecca, like he had with the others in the past. Except this time he'd concede the rule of mixing business and pleasure.

In the sports department, he strolled toward Joe Richards' desk, and the three reporters who had been huddled there scurried away.

"What kind of betting pool do you have going this time?" David asked, smiling. "Can I get in?"

Grinning, Joe turned his Cubs cap around backward. "Hell, no, David. Conflict of interest. The bet is on how long it takes Becca to get back her gossip column from you. She always gets what she wants."

It honest to Christ felt as if his heart shifted against his ribs, causing a dull ache to pulse through him. Looking down at Joe, he narrowed his eyes. "What are the odds?"

"Five to one in favor of Becca." Joe laughed. "But hell, when she finds out about it she'll lay us all out in lavender. Sweet gal until you make her mad. Then look out."

Remembering last night, he smiled, the pain in his chest receding. "Thanks for the warning."

Forcing his mind to run through the possibility that she'd slept with him to get her job back, he headed to his office.

The sun came out from behind a bank of clouds and streamed into the room. The searing light seemed to pierce his brain, helping him to decide that he had known women the last few years who had had agendas where he was concerned, but he didn't believe Rebecca was one of them.

He heard her voice and looked up, to watch her walk into the room. Her eyes blazed with determination and her chin was tilted up in defiance. Maybella followed quickly behind.

He remembered how soft Rebecca's skin had felt along her heart-shaped face. Desire rose through every cell in his body.

Now that he knew exactly what he wanted to do he felt warm, eager, and ready to take action. He moved toward her. "Thank you for being so prompt for our meeting, Rebecca. Please close the door on your way out, Maybella."

~~~⚜~~~

Stunned by how David's face had changed when she walked in, Rebecca glanced around to see a disgusted glaze in Maybella's eyes. The way she shut the door with a little slam sealed the fact she hadn't missed a thing.

David reached for her and she met him halfway. He kissed her with all the lustful warmth she thought she'd never allow herself to have again. Relinquishing control yet *again*, she tangled her fingers in his thick, wonderful hair and kissed him back with just as much gusto.

They both came up for air, and he pressed a kiss on the top of her head. "I've been thinking about what you said this morning."

"Said? This morning?" She forced herself to step back from him, hoping it would clear her mind so she could control where this was going. But he still held her hands and gazed down at her with his combination of playful sexiness, which she found dangerously irresistible.

"About last night only being about the twins' celebration. Not the real world. I've decided the twins deserve to be celebrated in the real world for as long as you and I are both enjoying it. I want to continue to see you."

Her feelings careening between joy, excitement, disbelief, and, most powerful, fear of being hurt, she fell back on her Midwest common sense. "Considering you're my boss the new owner who ripped my power base out from under me, I'm not sure we have any foundation for a sustainable enjoyable relationship."

His grip tightened on her hands. "Replacing you with Shannon was a business decision. Not a personal one. We didn't have any difficulties last night or just now."

His slow, sensual smile had been her undoing from the beginning. "No, but—"

"Rebecca," he interrupted in a firmer voice. "We are two mature, intelligent adults who find each other invigorating and challenging. We can be discreet."

Although she was rapidly turning to the dark side, wanting things not good for her, she took one last stab at reason. "I'm a firm believer in discretion. But believe me, people *will* find out and they *will* talk. I'm sure Maybella thinks we're doing the dirty deed on your desk."

He glanced over his shoulder at the broad, heavy mahogany surface and back to her with such a hot gleam in his eyes, Rebecca wondered if the door had a lock.

"I'm game if you are," he said with a laugh.

"David!" More excited than shocked, she thought it best for both their reputations to pull her hands free and clasp them demurely in front of her. "Seriously, we should give this a lot of thought before we . . ." *My God, what are we doing?* ". . . continue," she finished lamely.

"I have given it a great deal of thought, Rebecca."

She felt compelled to set him straight. "David, a great deal of thought is not the two and one-half hours since you left my condo."

"I dreamed about it last night, and I haven't been able to think about anything else for the last . . ." He glanced at his gold Rolex. "Two hours and forty-five minutes. We need to settle this. I have an empire to run." He said it in jest, but his eyes demanded a response.

She knew women who slept with their bosses to move up the success ladder, but she didn't plan to become one of them. She fully intended to convince David to give back her job because of her talent as a columnist, her expert people skills, her knowledge of what made good copy in Chicago. Not her eager, dare she admit, *creative* lovemaking. Yet a part of her so very much wanted to follow where David was leading. If she continued to sleep with him, she couldn't try to get back her job. End of story. She couldn't have her cake and eat it, too. *Which do I want more?*

The answer seared itself into her heart and mind, but she cooled it with fear and icy self-preservation. "Let's see what happens," she demurred, needing more time to figure it out.

"Good. That's settled." He sighed as if he'd been as tense as she still felt. "I'll be back and forth between the paper and the TV station for the next week. I'll stay in touch. Discreetly."

Completely off balance, she stepped back. "Wait, David, I . . ."

"I'm sorry." He shook his head. "You came in here to talk to me about something else."

I can't now. I really can't. Pauline's scared face flashed in front of her eyes. "Are you replacing Pauline with an automated phone system?" Rebecca blurted out and then, for her self-respect, tried to soften it. "I'm not here to try to convince you one way or another. But I need to know the truth." She braced herself for his steely, narrowed-eyed look, but mercifully it didn't appear.

He looked slightly perplexed. "When I did my initial blueprint for the restructuring of the paper, I investigated making such a change. But I vetoed it at least a month ago."

Relief made her feel giddy. Before she threw herself at him, smothering him in grateful kisses that might lead to heaven knew *what* form of delightful debauchery, she backed to the door. When she could lean against the strong wood, she felt slightly more in control. "Well, that's great. I guess I'll be . . . seeing you soon."

"A great deal of me, I hope."

His grin was the last thing she saw before she shut the door behind her.

Tingling from her toes crammed into her Manolos to the top of her head, which was still warm from David's kiss, Rebecca turned to meet Maybella's judgmental glare and tried to appear businesslike. She resisted the urge to tell Maybella what she thought of the cruel lie she'd foisted on Pauline. Instead, she strolled down the hall as normally as possible.

But she couldn't let Shannon off the hook so easily.

She paused in the open door to her old office. Maybe Maybella had sent out the alert that Rebecca was on the way, because Shannon was waiting, sitting casually in her new chair.

Leaning against the doorframe, Rebecca crossed her arms over her chest and stared straight into Shannon's wide, pale blue eyes.

"I'm not one to backstab, so I'm telling you straight out, Shannon. Beat me up as much as you want. But don't *ever* make my friends pay for whatever this vendetta against me is all about."

Shannon tossed her hair over her shoulder. "I'm sure I don't know what you mean."

"Think about it, Shannon. Long and hard. Don't make the mistake of believing I'm weak because I've tried to behave well, even after your nasty trick."

For some reason Shannon looked very young and even the tiniest bit vulnerable, stroking the sides of the small aquarium where five little goldfish swam happily. Maybe there was something here to salvage, after all. Rebecca sighed. "Why don't you just tell me what your personal problem with me is all about so we can work through it? I know there's more to this vendetta than just ambition on your part."

Shannon's thin lips curled. "How typical of the legendary Rebecca Covington to think it's all about her. You might find this hard to believe, but most of us have more important items on our agenda than what happens to you."

So much for helping Shannon into the community of women like Kate suggested.

From Shannon's set face, Rebecca conceded it was a waste of time trying to get the truth out of her.

"Here you are, Rebecca." Tim's cheerful voice broke the heated silence. Shannon's face shifted into a welcoming smile, and Rebecca glanced up at Tim with little interest.

"I've been looking for you with great news. Kate is thrilled, and I know you will be, too." He paused for dramatic effect. "Since I moved you to the Home and Food section, their ad revenues have increased forty percent." He winked. "I wouldn't be surprised if David gives you a bonus."

I think I already got it. She blushed at her own racy thoughts.

"We did it, Rebecca. We revolutionized Home and Food." Tim seemed to have completely forgotten the real reason for the change.

She hadn't. "You're a genius, Tim."

Nodding, he walked into his office.

Before she turned away, Rebecca glanced back at Shannon, who returned the look with pure loathing.

There was no getting around it. While trying to stop her life from spiraling out of control because of David, she also needed to uncover why Shannon hated her before she struck again.

Kate was waiting in the small brown leather chair in Rebecca's office. "Did Tim find you to tell you the good news?"

"Yes. I told him he's a genius." Rebecca didn't like what she saw on Kate's face. Lack of sleep showed in new lines around Kate's eyes and in the slump of her usually square shoulders. "Forget Tim. What's wrong with you? You look terrible."

"I'm tired." Kate raked her fingers through her hair, but it appeared too weak to spike up. "I'm going home to work for the rest of the day."

"Don't work. *Sleep.* What can I do to help you?"

"I can't sleep, and there's nothing you can do. The deadline to give David my answer about the finance column is Monday."

"I wouldn't dream of telling you what to do," Rebecca said carefully, wishing she knew if Kate's fatigue had anything to do with depression. "But if the *thought* of writing the finance column is making you sick, maybe you should decline David's offer."

Kate sighed so deep she shuddered. "David isn't the problem. The problem is I want to write the finance column even though I know the pressure might not be good for me."

Having just had a similar conversation with herself about wanting what wasn't good for her, Rebecca empathized with Kate. "Darling, I know *exactly* how you feel. Do you want to go shopping this weekend? I do my best thinking when I'm helping the retail economy. Or dinner? You know *feed* stress is my motto."

"Thank you for the offer, but I'm fine," Kate replied in her matter-of-fact way.

Rebecca didn't quite believe her. "Honestly? Or are you bluffing?"

Kate raised her eyebrows. "Have you become a poker player, Rebecca?"

"No, but you can teach me. Take all my quarters, or dimes or chips or whatever you play with. Wouldn't that cheer you up?"

At last, a ghost of a smile curved Kate's firm mouth. "I'll call you if I feel up to some fun. Honestly."

As soon as Kate walked out the door, Rebecca picked up the phone to reassure Pauline.

"Sweetheart, all is well. David has absolutely no plans to replace you. In fact, he thinks you're wonderful," she ad-libbed a little to make Pauline feel even safer. "I think Maybella was getting back at you for the other day at RL's. Don't give it another thought."

"Oh, that Maybella and awful Shannon." Pauline gasped, a little catch of emotion in her voice. "Thank you so much. Wait until they want me to make a Starbucks run for them. Oh, Rebecca, you have a call coming in."

Rebecca heard a click, then answered. "Rebecca Covington."

"Rebecca, it's Charlie Bartholomew."

"Charlie, what a pleasant surprise!" She glanced around to make sure no one was listening to her conversation with the competition. "What can I do for you?"

His deep belly laugh made her smile. "How'd you know I need a favor? Any chance you're free to join Martha and me Saturday night? It's a little birthday party for her. Don't tell your boss, but Martha reads the *Daily Mail*'s Home and Food because of you. In fact, she's asked the chef at the Carlton Club to prepare some of your recipes for the birthday party." The belly laugh again. "Remember, the two of you are Libras. Thank goodness she reads the horoscope in our paper. She says things are goin' to be good this month for the two of you."

Laying it on a little thick, Charlie. This good old boy is up to something.

She didn't believe for one second this call was about dinner, even though she liked Martha very much. Curiosity demanded she find out what was going on with the competition.

"Rebecca, are you still there?" Charlie said.

"Sorry." She laughed. "I was looking at my schedule. Yes. I am free."

"Wonderful news. Martha will be thrilled to pieces. We're sure lookin' forward to seein' you on Saturday at seven."

After she hung up, Rebecca stared at the phone, debating whether or not she'd done the right thing. If something was going on at the *Journal and Courier,* she needed to know so she could give a heads-up to Kate.

The nasty memory of being blindsided by Tim, *and* David, she quickly reminded herself, played through her head. David, the enigma. Was he the commando mogul, taking no prisoners, or was he the kind, lost man who touched her heart in so many ways she needed to steel herself against the emotions?

She needed to think of David, the business mogul. After all, he had declared her demotion a business decision, not a personal one. Amazing how men could differentiate so cleanly, truly believing one thing had nothing to do with the other.

Women just didn't think in the same way. Of course the two were inseparable to her, even if she wished it wasn't true.

Her need to seize back some control in her life demanded she find out what Charlie Bartholomew had up his sleeve, before he pulled whatever it was out and hit them all over the head with it.

Chapter 15

The twelfth-floor lobby of the Ritz-Carlton hotel was busy on Saturday night with nearly every lawyer in town and their wives, dressed in tuxes and evening gowns, going to the Chicago Bar Association's annual dinner in the ballroom. A few of the women shot Rebecca curious looks but didn't speak. For years, she'd attended the cocktail portion with a photographer in tow to cover it for the paper. And though she felt a little ache of loss, it wasn't as wrenching as she'd expected. Perhaps it was because tonight she was on a different kind of mission.

Across from the huge, glorious bronze fountain of two phoenixes, the private members-only Carlton Club was a serene, elegant oasis off the lobby. She stood for a few seconds just inside the heavy, etched-glass double doors. A few steps down in the cozy bar area, a man leaned against the baby grand piano, making a request to the musician playing it.

The maître d' approached her in the same moment the pianist began playing "Send in the Clowns." It seemed somehow appropriate.

Smiling, Rebecca followed the maître d' through the

cranberry and taupe dining room, with the coved ceiling that kept the noise to a minimum. There were few diners, and the tables were placed far apart so privacy was ensured.

Martha and Charlie were sitting at a table by the large windows overlooking Lake Michigan. By seven p.m. in mid-October, the lake had disappeared into blackness, with the city lights strung out like jewels around its invisible shoreline.

Rebecca kissed Martha's blushed, round cheek and placed the small blue bag from Tiffany's on the table in front of her. "Happy birthday."

"Rebecca, you shouldn't have brought me anything." Martha smiled, her small eyes bright as new pennies. "Should I open it now?"

"Of course." Rebecca sat across from her and watched with interest as Martha tore into the small blue box with the sterling silver heart shaped bookmark. Her mind was racing with the possible reason why this birthday party was set for only three.

"Thank you. This is lovely," Martha exclaimed. With her rosy cheeks and beaming smile, she looked exactly like Rebecca's childhood vision of Mrs. Santa Claus.

"I'm an avid reader, you know. For years I've told Charlie I wished you'd do a compilation of your old 'Rebecca Covington's World' columns for a book. Haven't I said that, dear?" She gazed at Charlie with adoration.

"Yes, you have, Martha. Yes, indeed." His belly laugh was truly infectious.

Despite the legendary rivalry, Rebecca had always liked Charlie and admired his business prowess. Often more than she liked Tim.

Martha and Charlie's five grown-up children were the

topic of conversation before the Lobster and Mushroom Quesadillas arrived. Remembering how they had tasted dipped in chocolate, Rebecca contained her shudder of revulsion. Martha and Charlie dug into the dish with obvious enthusiasm. To be polite, she had to follow suit.

Pictures of the fifteen grandchildren came out with the soup course. They kept up a running dialogue about the joys of being grandparents until their entrées arrived. Listening to them, she couldn't get the image of David's face out of her head. She wondered if he'd carry baby pictures in his wallet, too. The idea made her feel toasty inside.

By the time Rebecca was picking through the Baja Chicken, her insides were so stuffed the waistband on her black silk Ralph Lauren cocktail suit was digging into her stomach, and her curiosity was stretched to the snapping point.

Daintily pressing a cranberry-colored napkin to her rosebud mouth, Martha sighed. "That was delicious. Rebecca, would you mind keeping Charlie company while I go powder my nose?" Not waiting for an answer, Martha stood, gave Charlie a pat on his shoulder, and disappeared.

Here it comes. Rebecca widened her eyes and smiled across the table at Charlie.

"This has been like havin' family to dinner. You know, the *Journal and Courier* is a big happy family." Charlie gave her his benevolent Santa Claus smile. "Remember, I told you I was goin' to be keepin' my eye on you."

Needing to be a little more proactive to get answers, Rebecca leaned toward him. "Charlie, you have a gossip columnist in the *Journal and Courier* family."

"We're announcin' her retirement next week." He held up his pudgy hands as if to ward off any accusations. "Her idea. Her choice. Fine woman, but her likability quotient never rose as high as your own." His eyes twinkled above his snowy beard. "Rebecca, you have talent. You're a real fine people person. And you know what the readers of Chicago want."

His words so closely matched her own thoughts yesterday about how she wanted to convince David to give her job back, she got the eerie feeling Charlie might be reading her mind.

"Thank you. Those are very kind words coming from a newspaperman of your caliber."

"I don't mind tellin' you, I'm damn impressed with how you've taken the changes at the *Daily Mail* in stride. Hell, you took that lemon of a recipe column and turned it into such tart lemonade the city can't get enough of it. That's the kind of grit we value at the *Journal and Courier*."

He put his elbows on the table and leaned closer. "The baby boomers are a market segment to be reckoned with. They want their own tellin' them how it is. Not a snip of a girl, half their age. Did I mention we're startin' a daily half-hour segment before the news on our station, WXY, devoted to the sort of thing you do best?"

If it wouldn't give her feelings away, Rebecca would have pinched herself to make sure she wasn't dreaming. Even if she'd still had "Rebecca Covington's World," this was such an attractive offer she would have had to give it careful consideration. Coming from her present status, this was like rubbing a genie lamp and having her dreams come true. She'd be back doing what she loved, with the added bonus, both financially and professionally, of having television exposure.

"Is this an offer, Charlie?" she asked, controlling her voice not to sound too eager.

"If you're interested, it's an offer." Again, laughter

rumbled up through his barrel chest. "If you're not interested, it's two old friends shootin' the breeze over a nice dinner. I'll wager you'll be lettin' me know which it is by Monday."

His final salvo gave her forty-eight hours to decide whether or not to change her life forever.

Maybe this was the answer. Separating business, meaning the *Chicago Journal and Courier,* from pleasure, David and the *Daily Mail.* Then she could have her cake and eat it, too.

On Sunday, sitting on a stool in Harry's kitchen, helping him prepare Wednesday's recipe of Sausage Surprise, Rebecca tried to convince herself and him that she should make a change. "Accepting Charlie Bartholomew's offer is a wise business decision, don't you think? Right, Harry? I'll have a real column again. 'Rebecca Covington's World,' *the sequel.* More money. Television exposure. I'd be a fool to pass up such a fabulous opportunity at my age. At any age!"

He turned away from the stove to level his physician-as-superior-being look at her. It didn't happen often.

"I know. I know," she sighed. "You told me it was a choice I have to make for myself."

"To be exact, I've told you ten times tonight. In answer to the ten times you've asked me the same question." He sipped at his red wine and stirred the bleu cheese sauce. "I'm not the one you need to convince, sweet pea. I will add I believe extreme change is not always bad. In fact, it's often a wise choice."

His voice sounded wistful. She tried to see more of his face, turned half away from her. "Harry, is there something you want to tell me?"

"Absolutely not!" He glanced over his shoulder to smile at her. "Only one midlife crisis allowed at a time. How long do you have to talk yourself into this life-altering decision?"

"Twenty-four more hours." If she left the *Daily Mail*, she could explore her feelings for David without her current baggage. No strings. No wanting anything from him. They were two consenting adults who would enjoy each other's company for as long as it lasted. It was enough for her.

On top of that, this was a career opportunity she couldn't pass up. Decision made, she slid off the stool and went to the stove to check on the progress of dinner.

"Are you sure about this recipe?" He lifted one eyebrow and gazed down at the ingredients of one large sausage and two organic figs. "Have you given any thought to how it might taste?"

"I've been reliably informed this dish was served at an aphrodisiac-themed dinner I'm going to write about for Wednesday's column. It does look a little gross, doesn't it?"

She placed the sausage on the serving plate and positioned the figs on either side of it.

"Good God, Rebecca, it looks like a penis and testicles!"

"That's the idea, Harry." They both eyed the bleu cheese simmering on the stove. "And that sauce is supposed to be dribbled over the whole thing, like . . . you know."

Looking pained, Harry took a gulp of his excellent Cab. "I feel ill."

"So do I. And so did most of the people at the

aphrodisiac dinner. It might be a fitting column to end my days at the *Daily Mail*."

Today is the first day of the best of my life. Rebecca kept repeating the refrain as she dressed for work, as she walked to work, and as she pushed through the revolving door at work. Strange how, *again,* her life was altering forever on another Monday morning.

Pauline didn't see Rebecca immediately, because Rose Murphy was getting her messages and a few sports writers were standing, talking around the reception desk.

I'll miss you, sweetheart. A rush of nostalgia for all their good times at work washed over Rebecca. She blinked back tears. Just because she wouldn't be working here didn't mean she couldn't see Pauline and the girls nearly as often. Or so she'd convinced herself over her long, soul-searching weekend.

When Pauline finally saw Rebecca, she jumped up from behind the desk and ran halfway across the lobby. "Thank you . . . thank you . . . thank you!" She gave Rebecca three strong hugs. Her face as red as her hair, Pauline did a little dance around the lobby. Breathless, she stopped. "I'm so excited I can't stand it."

Rebecca laughed, although her heart ached a little knowing how Pauline's mood would change once she heard the news.

"You're the best friend I've ever had, Rebecca. The best. If you hadn't been here on Friday, I don't know what I would have done; I was so frantic with worry. But you were here and you made everything better."

"No, Pauline. All I did was ask David a question and get the truth," Rebecca said gently.

"Oh, and I suppose you didn't have anything to do

with Mr. Sumner personally calling to assure me of my importance to the paper? Or Human Resources contacting me about evaluating my position for a possible raise?"

No, David did it on his own. He's so wonderful.

Her chest swelled with feelings so rich she knew they couldn't be good for her. She shook her head. "It was all David's idea. I'm happy for you, Pauline."

"Are you all right, Rebecca? You look a little pale." Pauline shook her head, her eyes widening. "Not that you don't look gorgeous. You do. I always love you in winter white. It's so perfect with your blond hair and brown eyes."

More people were spinning through the revolving door. The lobby wasn't the time or place to break the news. "I'm perfectly fine. Really. I'll talk to you later."

Rebecca had barely made it to her office and flung herself into her beloved ergonomically correct chair before Kate appeared in the open doorway.

"I did it, Rebecca." Kate squared her shoulders. "I accepted David's offer to write the finance column. I couldn't have done it without your support. Not only your agreement to take over some of my responsibilities for Home and Food, but you being here for me in all ways." Kate smiled. "You make it fun. I'd missed that before you came."

Speechless with remorse, Rebecca watched Kate visibly pulling herself together with a sigh and a tug on her black suit jacket.

"Rebecca, can we meet in my office after lunch to discuss the projects you will now be overseeing?"

This is the moment to tell Kate I'm leaving.

The moment passed.

Feeling an odd rush of mingled relief and regret,

Rebecca looked up into Kate's suddenly suspicious eyes. "I'm sorry, I zoned out for a second. Of course I'll meet after lunch. You look happy, Kate."

"I am." Kate's face changed as if she'd surprised herself. "I honestly do feel happy, Rebecca. Thank you."

After Kate left, Rebecca sat, trying to understand why she'd just canceled out every decision she'd agonized over all weekend. *I can't separate business and personal decisions like men do. People are depending on me. I can't leave right now. Even if it means I can't be with David in the way I want.*

She had the strangest feeling that the universe was trying to tell her something profound. But what? That she was torn about what she really wanted and now she had time to ponder what was really important to her?

Her phone rang, and she stared at it with the strangest sensation of expectation. *Another cosmic message, perhaps?*

Slowly, she answered. "Rebecca Covington."

"Hello, it's David." The sound of his voice sent warm little flutters through her. Not cosmic, but close. *This* message she got loud and clear.

"I'm at WBS, and I may have to fly to New York on business tomorrow. But I'll be back at the *Daily Mail* on Wednesday. Can I see you?"

"I'll be right here." She smiled, cradling the phone against her cheek. "Let's see what happens."

If Kate didn't need her, Rebecca would have already moved to the *Journal and Courier* before David returned on Wednesday. Would he have understood her leaving was purely a business decision and nothing personal? Yet, in a way it was so very personal. It was the door to the future, where she could have her identity back as

Chicago's most notorious gossip columnist and be with David.

An offer as attractive as Charlie's might never come her way again. The same could be said of a man like David.

Deep inside, behind her facade, fear flickered to life. Her relationship with David, whatever it might be, had played into her decision. Once, Kate had called her reckless, and now Rebecca realized she was taking the gamble of a lifetime.

Knowing she needed more time, hoping he wouldn't throw in his hand, Rebecca made the call to Charlie.

"I've been expectin' to hear from you, Rebecca." She could hear assurance in his voice.

"Charlie, I want to thank you and Martha for a lovely dinner Saturday night." She'd carefully planned her words. "I *so* appreciated shooting the breeze with such dear, generous friends. I'd like to do it again. But I need a little more time to fulfill my obligations here."

His silence was mercifully brief and ended with his rumbling laughter. "It was an interestin' night. We'd like to do it again real soon. I believe we still have a great deal to discuss. You give me a call when you're ready and willin' for another go at it."

Relief warmed her skin. Charlie was leaving the offer on the table, just as she'd hoped. "Thank you, Charlie. I'll be in touch." She hung up the phone and stared into space. If only she could see into the future and know where her choices, reckless and not, were leading her.

DAILY MAIL
WEDNESDAY FOOD

SAUSAGE SURPRISE

3 tablespoons oil
¾ pound fully cooked pork, chicken, or turkey
    sausages, thickly sliced into rounds
1 pound fresh wild mushrooms (such as crimini or
    stemmed shiitake), thickly sliced
4 garlic cloves, minced
½ teaspoon dried crushed red pepper
1 10-ounce package ready-to-use spinach leaves
1½ cups canned low-salt chicken broth
¾ pound penne pasta, freshly cooked
2 cups (about 8 ounces) grated Romano cheese

Heat oil in heavy large pot over medium-high heat. Add sausages, mushrooms, garlic, and crushed red pepper. Sauté until mushrooms begin to brown, about 10 minutes. Add spinach and broth; toss until spinach wilts, about 2 minutes. Add pasta and cheese; toss until cheese melts and sauce coats pasta, about 3 minutes. Season with salt and pepper. Serves 4.

A Note from Rebecca Covington

We all know about the megarich group of bachelors who invite wealthy, attractive, foxy, sexy single and married women to their Annual Mingle Party given in the most chic locales on Earth, including Chicago. Of course our fair city is chic—the rest of the world just hasn't accepted the fact yet!

One of the fascinating bachelors' claim to fame is that he once danced with Princess Di. Don't you love it? We adore this group of handsome hunks.

Alas, there is another subset of randy bachelors who are not so divine. They have their own party, called "Nooky Nourishment for Passionate Cannibals." I know, darlings, the title alone should have warned off the lovelies who chose to attend.

Absolutely every dish was a phallic symbol. A sausage with whole figs as testicles and bleu cheese sauce as . . . (shudder) . . . elicited a few nervous chuckles.

The next course, a pancake shaped like a woman's womb, with lobster thermidor spilling out, drove most of the ladies from the room, never to return.

The lesson for these clueless men—if they want to set the proper scene for seduction—is quite simple. Most women have not seen the "food as a sex toy" film 9½ Weeks, while all have watched and sighed over the elegant, sublimely sexy Breakfast at Tiffany's.

Yes, gentlemen, class counts.

Because I care so much, I changed Sausage Surprise from an X rating to a P. Perfectly Palatable.

Enjoy!

Xo Rebecca

Chapter 16

Wednesday morning, still wearing her bathrobe, Rebecca waited for Harry in her doorway. It reminded her of waiting for David, except her emotions had been charged in a completely different way. She loved Harry like the brother she'd never had. David, on the other hand . . . a little pleasure shiver ran along her skin.

How should I label what I feel for David?

"Happy birthday, sweet pea!" Harry called from the open elevator.

He was dressed in an impeccably tailored, subtle, pinstriped suit, his hair slicked back very Rupert-like. He couldn't have looked more debonair gently swinging the open picnic basket holding champagne, strawberries, and croissants. His annual early morning offering to Rebecca on her birthday.

"Harry, you're an angel, but I told you not to fuss this year." She tried to scold him, but her stomach growled at the aroma of warm, buttery croissants, overriding her feeble protests.

Bending, kissing her cheek, he smiled when he heard

the rumbling. "Thou protest too much. Let us partake of this feast before we must face the real world."

Over her mimosa and Harry's straight orange juice, Rebecca picked up the thread of a nagging thought from yesterday. Had she made the right choice by staying for Kate's sake? "Harry, do you think I smother people with my need to fix things for them?"

He blinked his ridiculously long lashes. "You're pensive this morning. Is it about your age? Haven't you heard, our forties are the new twenties?"

"Harry, I'm serious."

"I can see that." He reached across the small table to hold her hand. "You're the best friend anyone could have, and we love you for it. Pauline and the girls have baked a cake for tonight. Kate and I are bringing the champagne and chocolate. Today you will be celebrated in the way you deserve." His smile was so warm and kind, she actually could feel his love in the air around her. "You want the world to always be just to everyone in the same way. You particularly want it to be fair to those of us you love. When you perceive the world as being unjust, you shore it up until it equals out again. My only concern is that you are not always fair to yourself."

"So if I wasn't . . . say . . . here. Or at the Daily Mail office, you all would carry on quite well without me."

His grip tightened on her hand and his eyes bore into her. "Is there something wrong? A health issue I need to know about?"

She laughed to reassure him. "Heavens, no. I'm wonderfully healthy. Maybe it is my age. I just need a reality check to make sure I don't think I'm so important the world can't spin properly without my hand on the rim."

She could see the relief in his eyes. He kissed her hand. "Yes, sweet pea. We could carry on without you, but it wouldn't be nearly as much fun. Speaking of fun. I have two rhinoplasty surgeries to perform this morning. The real world beckons."

For a very long time, Rebecca's world had been the *Daily Mail.* She'd hidden behind the Rebecca Covington persona for so long it had become the biggest part of her. That's why she'd been so desperate to get it back. Now her view of the world had shifted because of David, and she'd gotten a part of herself back she had believed long gone.

Slightly dizzy from one and a half mimosas so early in the morning, coupled with serious soul-searching, Rebecca was already feeling a little surreal when she walked through the doors into the *Daily Mail.*

She gasped at the lobby transformed into a garden by dozens of red roses in vases placed on every flat surface, except Pauline's desk, where there was a perfect white rose in a crystal bud vase.

"There are forty-five long-stem roses," Pauline whispered, as if everyone in town didn't already know Rebecca's age thanks to Shannon's spiteful exposé.

Rebecca's fingers trembled slightly as she tore open the card.

They must be from David.

She recognized George's bold, black writing immediately and tried to disguise her disappointment. "The flowers are from George, reminding me that weeks ago I promised to have dinner with him Saturday night."

Pauline's mouth curled into a big "oh" of surprise. "You're dating . . . both of them?"

"No, I'm not dating either one. Well, not exactly," Rebecca amended. "Keep a vase of flowers and take another for the girls."

Kate walked into the lobby, and Rebecca handed her a dozen roses. "For your office."

Kate shook her head. "What are you doing? It's your birthday we're celebrating today."

Swinging a brown alligator briefcase, David strolled down from the executive hallway. His gaze stopped on Rebecca and then moved to the bouquets of roses. "What are we celebrating?" he asked in a friendly way.

"Today is Rebecca's birthday," Pauline exclaimed with her usual enthusiasm.

Again David's eyes met Rebecca's. "From an admirer?"

His voice held not a note of intimacy, but his gaze brought a flush to her cheeks. They might have been the only people in the room. *Or maybe it's the effects of champagne before nine in the morning.*

Believing discretion was the better part of valor, particularly in front of a rapt audience of her friends, Rebecca did her best to ignore the heat between them.

"Yes, they are from an admirer. But I'm sharing. Would *you* like some flowers for your office?"

His lips twitched in apparent amusement. "No, thank you, Rebecca. I'll be at the television station for the rest of the week. Have a good day, ladies."

The lobby seemed strangely empty after he was gone. And strangely silent.

She glanced around at Kate and Pauline. Questions burned from their eyes. Especially from Pauline, who was pressing her lips together to keep from speaking.

"I have to know," she burst out in a gasp. "Why do you think he didn't even wish you a happy birthday?"

Rebecca shrugged like it was meaningless, when in reality he'd disappointed her way out of proportion to what she should be feeling. Obviously he'd taken a step back from the relationship. Hardly a relationship, she reminded herself, a hot, heavy feeling in her chest. Whatever it was between them, she knew it was dangerous to her peace of mind.

She mustered a bit of relief that David had wisely decreed a cool-off, and laughed. "Hey, the man has an empire to run." She swept up another vase of flowers. "I'm taking these to Rose Murphy. I'll come down later to get the rest. See you."

Throughout the day, when she wasn't fielding birthday greetings from colleagues or taking calls from contacts feeding her juicy gossip, Rebecca was obsessing about David. She was relieved that she could dampen down the little flicker of fear in her heart, but the dull, constant ache of regret wouldn't go away.

One minute he's so hot. The next so cool. Of course, why shouldn't he be? She'd done the same thing for years. Obviously, they were both commitment-phobic.

❦

The boardroom at WBS-TV was long, narrow, and stuffy. David loosened his tie and leaned back in the heavy, uncomfortable chair at the head of the table.

He looked at Tim sitting at his left, talking about his perceptions of business as the liaison between the paper and the station.

David hadn't heard a word. He tried to focus on business, usually as natural as breathing to him, and immediately thought of the *Daily Mail* lobby filled with roses for Rebecca's birthday.

No doubt from George, the slack-gutted young guy who rubbed him the wrong way.

Tim looked at him again and, on instinct, David nodded. Satisfied, Tim continued to speak while David slid back into thoughts of Rebecca.

He knew it was a waste of time to feel such a tug of regret because he hadn't known it was her birthday. A savvy man would take action. They could still celebrate tonight

Tim turned to him again, and David had had enough. He stood, casting a long look down the table at the expectant faces of his board of directors. "Thank you, Tim. You've given us a great deal to think about. That's it for the day. Good afternoon, gentlemen."

David stalked out, fully aware he'd left a room of stunned men. He'd handle the fallout tomorrow. Today he needed to make something happen for Rebecca.

Restless, he left the studio and walked through Lincoln Park and onto the small streets of the Gold Coast, which reminded him of New York City. Racking his brain for something special for Rebecca, he came up with zero.

God, he hadn't bought a woman a gift since Ellen's last birthday.

The thought didn't bring the usual catch of pain.

He stood, rooted to the sidewalk, letting the feelings settle over him. First guilt stirred, then it receded a bit. But it was still there, only slightly duller than usual. It was all right, he told himself. He had stayed loyal to Ellen's memory.

He turned down a street heading back east toward the lake. At the end of the block David saw two guys putting a padlock on a chain-link fence around what looked like a vacant lot. He glanced in and then at their T-shirts emblazoned with "The Farmer's Market Nursery."

"Do you have roses in there?" he asked, disappointed in himself for not coming up with something more original.

"Nay." The taller guy shook his head. "Waste of money. Die in a week. We got perennials and annuals."

"Forget your wife's birthday, did ya?" the shorter one laughed.

"Not exactly." David relaxed, not minding being the butt of their jokes if they could help him out. "But I need a gift."

"We're closed, but hey, what's another five minutes." The short guy shrugged.

"How about a mum plant? Nice this time of year," the tall one offered.

David didn't know a flower from a weed, but a plant didn't do it for him. "Something bigger."

"How's about a tree?" the shorter guy said with a laugh, obviously the comedian to the other's straight guy.

"Where's she live? Trees need room to grow." The tall one looked solemn.

Remembering Rebecca's balcony, David became inspired. "How about a rosebush?"

"Just got a shipment in. Healthy batch. Last a lifetime. Full of blooms, too. Man, you look like a guy in deep trouble." The short guy smirked. "Better buy two."

David smiled back. "Deal. Do you deliver?"

Both men gave him the once-over. The shorter one smiled. "Sometimes. Depends."

David gladly took out his wallet.

❧

Rebecca waited in the office until after six so she could arrive home at the exact time Pauline had told her everything would be ready for her "surprise."

"Happy birthday, Aunt Becky!" Patty and Polly screamed the instant the condo door clicked shut behind her.

Like they'd done since they were toddlers, the girls grabbed Rebecca's hands to pull her into the living room. A slightly lopsided two-layer cake, surrounded by colorful happy-birthday napkins and plates, sat squarely in the center of the library table.

"What a beautiful cake. Did the two of you make it?" she asked as she did each year.

Both girls nodded and smiled so big their eyes squeezed into slits.

This is such a happy rut. I'm a fool to think I need more. "Thank you. I love it!" She gathered them both in a hug. "What flavor is it?" she asked, knowing full well it was chocolate.

"Chocolate!" they said in unison with the ringing phone.

Harry answered it. "Thanks, Malcolm. Send them up. Delivery!" he called out to the room.

"It's more presents!" Polly turned to dash to the door.

"No, you don't, young lady." Pauline caught her, twirling her around. "Let Aunt Becky get her present herself."

"Yes, girls. I need help putting the chocolates on a plate." Kate led them into the kitchen.

On cue, the bell rang and Rebecca went to open the door.

David stood flanked by two enormous rosebushes. Behind him the elevator doors were closing on two burly guys wearing "The Farmer's Market Nursery" T-shirts.

David stepped into the foyer, pulled her into his arms, tilted her chin up, and gazed down into her eyes. "These rosebushes will last a lifetime. Happy birthday, Rebecca." His voice husky, he bent, lips parted slightly, to kiss her.

"Wait," she squealed, painfully aware others might be watching her melt into a puddle of happiness.

He stopped and glanced over her head into the mirrors. "You have company. So much for discretion."

She twisted in his arms to find everyone grouped together just inside the living room, staring at them. If it were anyone but her most beloved friends, *her family,* this would be a disaster.

"I know you. You're Mommy and Aunt Becky's boss." Polly looked up at her embarrassed mom. "He's the new boss, right?"

David straightened and smiled. "Yes, I am the new boss." He slid Rebecca an apologetic glance out of the corner of his eye before walking into the living room.

Overcome by David's incredibly romantic gift, Rebecca waited to control her breathing before she followed him.

He shook Harry's hand and greeted Kate and Pauline. "I'm sorry to have crashed your party," he said to the girls, who continued to stare up at him.

"We made the cake ourselves. Would you like a piece?" Patty offered politely.

Rebecca pulled herself together. "Of course, you must join us, David." His intent expression told her a party of seven was not what he'd planned for this evening. Thoughts of what might have been made her insides tighten in anticipation.

"It's chocolate cake," Patty informed him.

"That settles it." He smiled down into her freckled face. "Chocolate is my favorite."

"Aunt Becky's, too. She loves it." Polly couldn't be outdone by her older sister. "Mom says she doesn't know how Aunt Becky keeps that figure with all the chocolate she eats."

"I do not say that!" Pauline went scarlet, looking at her youngest in a less than besotted way.

David's laughter, along with Harry's, and Kate's amused smile, broke apart the tension in Rebecca's chest. "Sweetheart, you're absolutely right. There are days I'd rather eat chocolate than real food. Like tonight."

"Then I believe it's time to sing 'Happy Birthday,'" Kate said, shepherding everyone into the living room.

Rebecca sat on the couch, dutifully waiting as she did every year for the candles to be lit and the cake carried over to her.

David settled down beside her, changing the whole dynamic of the party. Just as he'd changed everything else in her life. Before, she was always lazily relaxed, but tonight every muscle in her body quivered in anticipation.

Polly turned around, a frown curving her tiny mouth. "Aunt Becky, there are too many candles to put them all on your cake. So we gotta do only part of them. Isn't that what you said, Mom?"

This time Pauline just rolled her eyes.

"Champagne?" Harry offered glasses on a silver tray.

When David took one, he slid her a sleepy, sexy look. "This brings back fond memories, Becky," he murmured under his breath, barely loud enough for her to hear.

Not wanting him to get ahead of her, she batted her eyelashes at him. "Becky had fun, too."

"Excellent. Then Becky won't mind giving me more advice." He shifted closer so their thighs touched.

"Becky says, remember we're being discreet." She shifted away, leaving a little space between them. "Look at this cake," she said louder, clapping her hands.

"Make a wish and blow out your candles!" the girls demanded.

Rebecca glanced around at all these people whom she had made her family. *Please let everyone in this room find lasting happiness.*

She blew out the candles, knowing why the wish had not been to get her job back at the *Daily Mail*. Since David had come into her life, all her other wishes seemed vague and less important.

Sitting, listening to everyone sing "Happy Birthday," she realized how much her life had changed in so short a time. Last year Kate hadn't been here, or David. The way their lives were becoming intertwined meant more changes. Where would her feelings for David lead her? What should she ultimately do about Charlie's offer? If she was still Becky she'd embrace the growth, see where it might take root. Instead, she felt out of control. Especially where David was concerned. She could feel the foundation of her facade eroding, and it scared her.

Today in the *Daily Mail* lobby, when she'd thought he'd taken a step back, she'd realized he'd become too important to her. She was acutely aware of every nuance of David's voice, and her stomach tightened every time their bodies inadvertently touched.

She breathed a little easier when he and Harry got up to carry the rosebushes out onto her terrace. Directed by all the females, the men moved the pots around until everyone agreed they should be placed on the south end, where the light was best. The scent of roses filled the air.

One by one, everyone drifted back into the living room, leaving Rebecca alone with David.

He leaned against the railing, watching her. "Do you like your rosebushes?"

Pretense seemed a waste of time. "It's the most romantic gift I've ever received. Although I'm a little confused." She moved closer, hoping to catch the truth in his eyes so she'd know where this was heading to protect herself. "About the rosebushes lasting a lifetime. Sounds serious. What happened to for as long as we're both enjoying it?"

"Don't be alarmed. 'Last a lifetime' was a figure of speech." The darkness hid his expression. "Are you still enjoying it, Becky?"

She hoped the darkness hid her expression, as well. Part of her had hoped for a different answer. She was burning with disappointment, a rush of emotion so strong she struggled to find her voice. "Yes, yes, I am."

She was glad when the sliding glass door to the terrace opened behind her.

"I'm sorry to interrupt you." Kate sounded mortified. "However, Pauline is desperate for you to look at your watch. I'm assuming it is some plot to convince the girls to leave without incident."

"It is. Excuse me." Needing time to shore up her defenses, she was glad to have a reason to move away from David.

Standing in the middle of the living room, Rebecca looked at her thin gold watch. "Heavens! It's nine o'clock. Past my bedtime." Stretching, she yawned. "Party's over. You know Aunt Becky needs her beauty sleep."

"Let's go, girls. Bedtime for all of us." Pauline started gathering up their coats and book bags. Looking tired, the girls helped her.

Harry stood. "I'll clean up."

Kate came back into the living room. "I'll help."

"I'm happy to lend a hand." David walked up beside Rebecca.

Rebecca looked into his eyes. "It's a *very* small kitchen."

"I know." His smile spoke volumes.

Harry turned to her with a what-was-I-thinking look on his face. "Perhaps it would be better if David stayed to help you clean up. I'll drive Kate home."

"Harry, it's out of your way. I'm on the river and you're on the Gold Coast. I'll take a cab." Kate was already on her way to the hall closet to retrieve her coat.

Rebecca followed her, not sure what she should do. Ask David to stay? *Too indiscreet and dangerous.* Let him go? *Too lonely.*

While Kate lingered, putting on her coat, Rebecca kissed the girls and Pauline good-bye.

David walked into the foyer. "Let me drive you, Kate. I'm at the Peninsula hotel. It's only a few blocks to your place."

Kate gave Rebecca a long, level look, which reminded her she needed to protect herself.

"That's a great idea, David." Rebecca hugged Kate. "Thank you for the chocolates. I'll see you in the morning."

When Kate stepped out into the hallway, David moved closer. Smiling, he loomed over her. "My turn at last."

Wrong decision. I want you to stay. "Thank you for the rosebushes. They're absolutely beautiful. Good night."

She tried to kiss him on the cheek, like she had the others, but he turned his head just enough so their lips brushed too briefly in a kiss.

Her mouth still tingled long after he and Kate disappeared into the elevator. She turned to find Harry watching her.

"I'm sorry, sweet pea. I wasn't thinking clearly when I offered to clean up. You wanted David to stay."

"No . . . yes . . . maybe." She shook her head, roaming aimlessly around the living room, trying to figure out what was happening to her. She didn't want even Harry to see how scared and confused David made her feel. Yet she couldn't resist him. Didn't want to give up the way he made her feel when they were together.

She cast Harry a stern look. "I don't need to tell you mum's the word, right?"

Harry struck a pose of injured innocence. "I know nothing. Except this is the first time since your unpleasant divorce you haven't filled me in on your romantic interludes. Does that mean you're at last putting your fears and insecurities about your ex behind you?" He looked so hopeful Rebecca hated to disappoint him.

She plastered on her pat smile and hoped he believed it. "Darling, I'm honestly not sure of anything anymore. Maybe I'm in a midlife crisis, wanting change in my life. Then the next second I want everything to be back the way it was before David came into my life and fired me. Don't you have a pill for this?"

"If I had the cure for love I'd be as wealthy as Oprah." Harry's gentle, knowing smile caused tears to gather at the back of her throat. "Sweet pea, what you should do about David is one question you must answer for yourself."

Chapter 17

On Saturday when George called to tell her he'd picked her favorite Asian restaurant for dinner, the Shanghai Terrace at the Peninsula hotel, Rebecca's thoughts flew to David. *He's staying there. Maybe I'll see him tonight.*

Of course, her thoughts didn't have far to go, since he seemed permanently fixed in her brain. She, the notorious brown thumb, hovered over the rosebushes he'd given her, watering and feeding, like they were newborn babies.

Fall was still going out in a warm blaze of Indian summer, but she knew the weather in Chicago could change in five minutes. She worried the temperature might drop during the night and the roses would get frostbite. She thought about sending them to a nursery for the winter, the way so many Chicagoans fled to Florida to escape the cold. The roses remaining gloriously beautiful were tied up in her feelings for David and how she wanted this relationship to flourish for as long as they were both enjoying it. She didn't want it to wither on the vine like all the others since her divorce. They had all been killed off by her lack of interest or her fears about the emotional danger of commitment. A part of her accepted that there could be no lasting commitment with David. He had made that very clear. Yet the Becky part of her, the part David had brought back to life, yearned for more, regardless of the cost to her heart.

Thoughts of David and roses, and what she should do about both, consumed her to the point she had to think for a second where she was when George helped her out of the cab in front of the Peninsula hotel.

Why did I agree to come here with George? Feeling like an ungrateful wretch after he'd sent her so many beautiful roses, Rebecca pulled herself together. She *would* be an attentive and entertaining dinner companion tonight.

As they rode up alone in the elevator to the lobby, she smiled at him. "The Shanghai Terrace was a lovely choice, George. Thank you."

He slid his arm around her shoulders. "Remember when we had dinner here the last time?"

She didn't, but she kept smiling.

As she'd hoped, he took it as a yes and nodded. "I couldn't stop looking at you. You were wearing this same dress. It matches your eyes."

She looked down at her brown and gold beaded tulle Ralph Lauren dress and gasped in mock horror. "Please tell me I wasn't wearing these same suede boots and cashmere scarf, too?"

"All I can remember is the dress and wanting to rip it off you," he murmured very close to her ear.

Her heart sank into her stomach. She didn't want it to be that kind of evening.

The elevator doors opened, and in the hustle of stepping off while people got on, Rebecca was able to extricate herself from George's grasp. She didn't want to encourage him or hurt him.

Like most Saturday nights in Chicago, all the great hotels were alive with partygoers. People spilled out of the lobby bar, and at the bottom of the grand staircase there was a private party going on in the ballroom. Sounds of "Celebration" were leaking through the closed door.

In contrast, tiny, intimate Shanghai Terrace was Zen-like in its peaceful, quiet atmosphere. The two sets of French doors were open onto the terrace, lit by thousands of tiny Italian lights.

While waiting for their table to be ready, Rebecca wandered out to look at the city spread twelve stories below.

George joined her with champagne. "Happy birthday, Rebecca."

His truly handsome face, etched in moonlight, left her cold. She kept seeing David's face and wishing she was with him.

George deserves to be here with someone who would swoon at this romantic moment.

She felt so guilty, she blew him a kiss before taking the glass of champagne. "Thank you. I hope you got my note about the roses. They were beautiful."

"So are you." It was his coming-in-for-the-deep-probing-kiss voice. Low. Deep. Suggestive.

Taking evasive action to discourage him, she looked around and realized they were the only people left on the terrace. "I think the lovely hostess just motioned to us. Our table must be ready."

Trying not to appear too eager to escape, she stepped out of the shadowy intimacy of the terrace and into the softly lit ambiance of the romantic restaurant.

Directly in front of her, David and Shannon were being seated at a table.

Raw red jealousy roared through her like a Chicago L-train out of control. She drew a quick, harsh breath.

David looked up like he'd heard it.

Emotions played across his face, but she couldn't tell if she saw embarrassment or delight in his eyes as he stood.

Following his gaze, Shannon saw Rebecca and immediately her cheeks drained of color. Horror was written all over her face.

George's warmth and expensive aftershave curled around Rebecca's head. "Damn, it's your boss again," he murmured, his breath brushing the short blond hair around her ear.

The intimate nature of the narrow restaurant left her no choice but to acknowledge them.

Plastering on her most urbane smile, Rebecca strolled forward. "What a lovely surprise." Furious with David, but more angry at herself for this painful surge of emotion, Rebecca clung to George's shoulder and placed a possessive hand on his chest. "You know my . . ." Batting her eyelashes, she gazed up at him. "Friend. George Crosby."

"We've met." David's voice couldn't have been any frostier, but he went through the polite formality of shaking George's hand.

"Hello, George." Shannon dropped her eyes coyly, but not before Rebecca caught the hunger she couldn't quite disguise when she drank in George's tall, broad-chested, narrow-hipped body. "Long time no see," Shannon breathed in her softest voice.

"I've been busy. Nice to see you again, Shannon."

In that instant, Rebecca saw her life since evil Monday flash before her eyes. *This horrible vendetta is all about George!*

Rebecca mutely observed the play taking place between Shannon and George while ignoring the penetrating gaze of the man in her own drama.

"I'll tell Christopher and Kara I ran into you." Shannon looked up with the thinnest facade masking her vulnerability that Rebecca had ever seen. "They miss you. We all do."

"Yeah. I'll call them soon." George snaked his arm around Rebecca's shoulders in a possessive hug. "Our table is ready. We're celebrating Rebecca's birthday tonight."

Her eyes locked with David's. *We should be here together.* She felt his gaze burning into her in the few steps to the table.

She sat and stared at George. The thought that she had broken her iron-clad rule never to poach another woman's man made her feel ill.

"You never told me you had dated Shannon." Her voice was colder than a twenty-below-zero winter night in Chicago. If George had shivered, it wouldn't have surprised her.

"Dated her?" George reared back in his chair, his face a study in confusion. "I hardly know her. Her best friend, Kara, is married to my old college roommate, Chris Baxter. A bunch of us hung around together until Kara started playing matchmaker with her girlfriends. She did one fix-up and the couple got married. So Kara thought she had the perfect formula, like eharmony.com."

Smiling again, he leaned forward, making his usual

move by placing his hands, palms up, on the table. "I'm very particular about who I see."

"Behave, George. Remember, my boss is watching." Even though David was seated at a table behind her, she could still feel his eyes boring into her. The stress was giving her a headache.

"Yeah, I know. Both of them are staring over here. What's with that?" He drained his martini glass and motioned the waitress for another round of drinks, even though Rebecca had barely touched her champagne.

The idea of drinking made her faintly nauseous. She needed time to think. "Excuse me, George. I'm off to the powder room. I'll be right back."

"Should I order your favorite appetizer?" he asked, a hopeful gleam in his eyes. "Oysters, right?"

In her present state, food was the last thing she wanted, but she was being such a horrid dinner companion the least she could do was let George have his oysters. She tried to appear pleased. "That would be lovely. Thank you."

The short walk from the Shanghai Terrace to the ladies' lounge tucked beneath the grand staircase took only a few minutes. Not enough time to come to grips with the oldest cliché Rebecca knew to be absolutely true from experience.

Hell has no fury like a woman scorned.

❧

David watched Rebecca walk out of the room, barely able to stop himself from following her. What the hell was she doing here with George? He didn't like it. Christ, he'd wanted to grab her away from the guy on the spot.

Jealousy had roared through him like a train. He'd actually heard roaring in his ears when he looked up and saw Rebecca with the guy hanging all over her.

But the expression on her face made him ache for her. She looked hurt and angry, even though she tried to hide it. He could see through her now. She didn't like that he was here with Shannon. They should have been here together. As soon as he could decently send Shannon home, he'd make it up to Rebecca. He smiled, counting the ways.

"Are you having anything, David?"

He glanced at Shannon studying the menu. "No, just a cup of coffee." He needed to get the hell out of here as quickly as possible and find his way to Rebecca.

"Then I'll only have the green tea ice cream." Shannon looked up from the menu, stared intently over at the table where George sat alone eating oysters and back down at the menu. "On second thought, I'd like the chocolate lava cake, too."

"Have whatever you want." Too restless to wait another second, David stood. "Excuse me, I'll be back."

He stalked out to find the powder room, where he figured Rebecca was heading. He saw the sign tucked under the stairs. He propped himself against the wall to wait where he also had a view of the door to the Shanghai Terrace. She couldn't escape him. And if she didn't come out of the powder room soon, he'd barge in and retrieve her himself.

Rebecca threw herself down on the small leather love seat in the ladies' lounge and shut her eyes. Away from David's overpowering presence, she felt her headache dissipate. Now she could focus in on the crystal-clear answer to why Shannon had set out to destroy her.

Shannon was in love with George. Though she had never actually *had* a relationship with George, she *still had* a fantasy about a future relationship with George.

Rebecca remembered how purely magical such a fantasy could be. She'd done the same kind of imagining when she was younger. Every romantic dream came true because in her fantasy, her dream man didn't have any faults.

Shannon's fantasy George was right there whenever he needed to be conjured up in her imagination. Ready and willing to worship at her feet. Shannon had probably decided what North Shore suburb they'd raise their three children in. No doubt right next door to best friends Chris and Kara.

For the first time, she truly sympathized with Shannon. Rebecca had been here and worse. She'd ignored Peter's questionable traits to live in the fantasy world she thought she wanted in her marriage. The story she wanted it to be. Until he'd shattered it with the true reality of their relationship in such a cruel way she was forced to face the truth. She'd walked away without a fight, because she didn't care enough.

But Shannon was willing to rip out Rebecca's heart. All for momentarily captivating the man who had never been Shannon's in the first place.

Certainly Freud must have something to say about women dealing with women, dealing with sexual relationships. Certainly Rebecca would have something to say to Shannon on Monday.

I'll rip out your heart if you don't stay away from David, who is not mine, either. Of course, Rebecca would never expose herself so completely to Shannon. She knew exactly what would happen from this moment on, because she'd make damn sure it did.

By Monday, she would successfully and, with as little damage as possible to his ego, end this flirtation with George. Then she'd put a bandage on the beating her heart had taken tonight with David and sail forth to try to put a Band-Aid on her professional relationship with Shannon before they both bled to death.

Her resolve firmly in place, she opened the door to leave the safety of the luxurious lounge.

Propped against the wall beside a stunning painting of dogs sitting by a fire, his long legs casually crossed at the ankles, David waited for her. He straightened immediately when he saw her.

Her heart banged against her ribs, and she thrust up her chin in defiance. "I'm sorry, David. If you're waiting for Shannon, she's not in the lounge."

"You know damn well I'm not waiting for Shannon. I'm not here with her."

Rebecca forced her eyes to widen in shock. "Shannon has an identical twin who knows George, too!"

"Very funny." David ran his fingers through his hair, and instead of making it look messy, it became sexy. "If you'll let me, I can explain."

Anger was such a great acting coach. It helped her put just the right amount of amusement in her laugh and the perfect dismissive shrug in her shoulders. "You don't need to explain to *me*. My motto is, and always shall be, all's fair in the dating game until there's an engagement ring." She wiggled her ringless fingers. "Have a nice evening."

He caught her hand, all six foot one of him looming over her. She thrust her chin even higher and glared at him. "Yes? What's the problem?"

"You. Before you rudely interrupt me again, I want to

tell you I had a drink with Shannon to discuss the paper. Like I had dinner with Kate to discuss the paper. Shannon devoured every bowl of pretzels the waiter put on our cocktail table, saying she was starving and wanted dessert. Being a gentleman, I offered to feed her."

The overwhelming relief bubbling through her veins terrified her. *Why do I always believe what this man tells me?*

"In a few minutes I'm putting Shannon in a cab to go home alone. I'd like to do the same with George. I have a burning need to check on my rosebushes. It has been much too long." David gave her a tantalizing smile, promising delights.

Remembering their one night together, her body tingled all over. Anger was fading in a rush of blissful anticipation. "The rosebushes were looking a little peaked tonight," she lied, because she *needed* to remember her anger. It was part of the survival kit.

"I have just the TLC they need. I'll be at your place in an hour."

"Maybe I'll be there. Maybe I won't," she murmured, untangling their fingers. "We'll see what happens," she called back over her shoulder as she walked away.

She knew she was being a little cruel, but she didn't want him to think she was too easy to win over. They could make up taking care of the rosebushes.

By the time Rebecca returned to the table, George had eaten half the oysters. He stood and pulled out the chair for her. "Shannon and your boss are leaving. Now you can relax and we can order dinner."

She wanted him to believe he was the one to walk away, so she must be as outrageously demanding as possible. Like Kate Hudson in that movie *How to Lose a*

Guy in Ten Days. "Actually, I have a dreadful headache." Gently, she rubbed her temples with her fingertips.

He frowned and leaned closer. "It's stress. I've got some great massage oil my trainer gave me. We'll leave and go back to my place. I'll massage your neck and back until you feel better. Then we can get into the Jacuzzi," he added with a hopeful gleam in his eyes.

"That sounds lovely, George," Rebecca sighed. "That's the perfect spot to have our serious discussion. We have a lot of plans to make."

He winked. "I've got some plans of my own for us tonight."

She stared deeply into his eyes. "I'm serious, George. It's time for us to go to the next level. I need commitment from you. My biological clock is ticking. I want to hear the pitter-pat of tiny feet."

George's eyes widened, and a thin film of perspiration glistened on his skin. He sat up straighter, putting distance between them. "I'm not ready for that. I'm only thirty-four."

"Yes, I know. But I'm much older. My clock is tocking its last." She smiled gently. "If not the pitter-pat of tiny feet, then large ones. I've always wanted a Newfoundland dog. I've read they're wonderfully loyal to their family."

"A . . . Newfoundland dog . . . but aren't they . . . huge? My co-op doesn't allow pets over forty pounds." Stammering was new coming from George.

"My place has those same silly rules. That's why I'm thinking about us moving to the suburbs."

"The suburbs!" He said it with the horror of someone contemplating exile to the most desolate wasteland on the planet. He fell back in his chair, getting as far away from her as possible. "Rebecca, are you putting me on?" There was a thread of hope in his voice.

She smiled. "A little bit."

His eyes lost their glaze, and he swayed slightly closer. "Then let's discuss this again in the morning."

"Of course. While we're having our herbal tea I'll get on your computer and pull up the places my real estate agent has shown me for us to consider." She chuckled, giving him a coy glance. "You knew I was only kidding about the Newfie. I really want a pug."

George appeared to waver on the edge, his breath sucked in to utter something. He was definitely looking at her differently now. "How's that headache?"

She dropped her lashes over her eyes for an instant while rubbing again at her temples. "Still dreadful."

"Then that settles it. We'll skip dinner. I'm taking you home to get a good night's sleep. I'll get the bill."

Watching George walk to the front desk to pay the waitress, Rebecca sighed. One obstacle hurdled without any harm done. Within an hour George would be in a trendy bar, giving a pretty girl his signature smile and congratulating himself on his lucky escape from being trapped in the suburbs.

While she couldn't wait to get home to torment David over their rosebushes, she hoped George would be very happy. She certainly planned to be blissful tonight.

Rebecca walked into the quiet, wood-paneled lobby of her condo building expecting to find David. All she found was Malcolm napping behind the security desk.

A faint sensation of doom draped itself around her shoulders, really giving her a headache.

The click of her high boots on the marble floor woke

Malcolm. Blinking, he sat up and stretched. "Sorry, Miss Covington. Must have dozed off for a sec."

"I won't tell." She gazed around like David could be hiding under the tapestry bench or behind one of the Chinese red planters holding ficus trees. "Has anyone been here to see me?"

"Sure. Mr. Sumner." Malcolm nodded. "I put the groceries he delivered for you in your refrigerator and cupboard."

Interesting. Champagne and what else?

"Where did you put Mr. Sumner?" she asked, hoping to be funny.

Malcolm's deep, former-heavy-smoker raspy laughter shook his thin chest. "Good one, Miss Covington. He said he'd be right back. Ran out 'cause he forgot the plant food. I think that's what he said." Malcolm's veiny cheeks flushed redder.

He probably thinks David forgot the condoms. She smiled gently at the confused look on his face. "Mr. Sumner is an avid gardener. Please send him up as soon as he gets back. Thanks."

The elevator couldn't move fast enough for her. She had important things to do before David returned.

She raced around her condo, picking up saucers and half-full cups of cold tea littering most flat surfaces. She plumped up the pillows on the bed and switched off the overhead light, leaving just the two on her bedside tables.

She opened the closet door and started to unzip her dress. She caught a glimpse of herself in the mirror.

George was right. The dress exactly matched her eyes, which is why she'd bought it after seeing it in *Elle* magazine. The ad had read "*price upon request,*" which she knew meant exorbitant. But once the dress came into the Ralph Lauren store and she saw how it brought out her eyes and how the sweetheart neckline exposed just enough creamy décolletage to be tastefully provocative, she'd thrown down her credit card without a fight.

Deciding the suede boots might be a bit much for gardening, she pulled them off. The barefoot look brought back tantalizing memories of the last time she'd tormented David. This time, instead of being naked under her clothes, she was wearing a nude, silky La Perla strapless bra and thong. Shamelessly, she hoped they had the same effect.

Waiting, she paced around the condo in ever-tighter stomach-knotting anticipation. *Where is he?*

Finally the doorbell rang. She flung the door open and pulled David inside.

They were in each other's arms, kissing deeply, desperately.

"I love kissing you," he murmured against her lips, and he swept her up in his arms.

She wrapped her arms around his neck, rubbing her breasts against his chest, and returned the compliment by caressing *his* sensual mouth with her tongue.

As they moved through the living room and into the bedroom, their kisses grew deeper and hotter. Reaching the bed, he lowered her bare feet to the floor. His long fingers stroked her neck and made light circles across her breasts just above the sweetheart neckline of her dress.

"I love you in this. Take it off," he commanded.

In her head she was Becky again, free to go wherever he wanted. Being with David reminded her that once Rebecca had been spontaneous and a little wild.

"You first," she demanded back.

His eyes never left her face as he did a slow striptease, unbuttoning his shirt, shrugging it off, and tossing it toward a chair.

She ached to stroke his taut stomach. To press slow, wet kisses on his warm skin.

"Now it's your turn, Becky."

"No fair. I only have one piece of clothing."

"No underwear again?" The dimple deepened in his cheek.

"You'll see," she teased. Slowly she pulled down the zipper, and with one shrug of her shoulders, the exorbitantly expensive designer dress slid down her body to pool like a lagoon around her ankles.

His eyes roamed over her might-as-well-be-naked designer underwear. "Nice. I approve." Grinning, he held her hand to steady her as she stepped free of the dress and flung it across the end of the bed.

It had been too long since she'd had this much fun. Too long since she'd wanted to be with someone so completely. Had she *ever* felt this way before? "You again, David."

Quickly he undid his black alligator belt and pulled his trousers down. Kicking off his loafers, he was now barefoot, too.

Looking at his white briefs, barely containing his taut erection, she realized how lucky women were to be able to hide the fire burning between their thighs.

He lifted one eyebrow. "Next?"

She snapped open her bra and peeled it off her warm body.

He reached for her, but she gently pushed his hands away. She wanted those fingers stroking her aching breasts, but she was already giddy with anticipation. She wanted it to build higher. "No cheating. Keep going."

He groaned. "Becky, there is only so much a man can take. Especially at my age."

She smiled lazily at him. "You run empires. You're not so old you can't tough this out. You're almost there."

He slid off his briefs and kicked them under the bed.

His body was as beautiful as she'd remembered. Like before, he couldn't hide how much he wanted her.

She needed to show him how much she wanted him. Without words, she slid the last wisp of silk off her body and knelt in front of him.

David sucked in a sharp breath. "Becky?"

"I want to show you what I'm feeling." Her mouth closed over him, her tongue tasting and tracing every contour again and again and again.

He spread his fingers through her short blond hair, and his hoarse voice rang in her ears. "God . . . Becky . . . stop before . . ."

He hauled her up to slam their bodies together, and the sensation of his hard, hot skin rubbing against her drove her wild.

With shaking hands, she slipped on the condom and pulled him down onto the bed with her.

He caught her wildness, caressing her breasts, her stomach, and down her thighs, with more and more urgency. She tried to pull him on top so she could wrap her legs around his hips, to bring him where she needed him. He resisted, his mouth warm and wet on her stomach.

"David?" she groaned.

With a husky laugh, he dragged his lips toward her thighs. He nibbled and kissed and caressed her body until she was dying to have him inside her.

Gently, insistently, he stroked a finger inside her. The next instant she felt the searing rasp of his tongue.

Her need swelled. *Yes, more!*

She arched her hips, the climax growing unbearable beneath his mouth.

She cried out. "Make love to me. Now!"

He thrust inside her with deep, long strokes. Again and again and again, the rhythm growing more powerful, harder. They were both wilder, and more desperate to touch and taste each other, than anything she'd ever known.

"Christ," David groaned, thrusting deep and high, filling her.

She sobbed once, the blissful explosion shuddering through her. They clung together, gasping for air, before collapsing in an exhausted tangle.

She closed her eyes, savoring the sensual afterglow. She felt David's warmth and pulled him to her. She cradled his head to her breasts and caressed his silky hair.

She was so shaken by her strong feelings for David it frightened her. She fell back on old safe habits.

Keep it light. "That was fun," she sighed.

"Fun?" He shifted higher so their faces were millimeters apart on the pillow. "That was a religious experience."

Her heart actually felt bigger in her chest. "Are you a spiritual man?"

"I'm a convert. To the worship of Becky." His smile took her breath away.

Deep instincts for self-preservation made her close her eyes so he couldn't see her overflow with joy. "You know

Rebecca Covington had a thing or two to do with tonight, too." She opened her eyes to see his reaction.

The naked admiration on his face made her whole body burn. "You and your alter ego are nearly more than a mere mortal man can handle."

She couldn't resist him. She *didn't want* to resist him. She pressed a slow kiss on his wonderful mouth. "I don't know about hard to handle. But I know the two of us are starving. I didn't have any dinner."

"I brought you dinner. It's in the kitchen."

She'd forgotten. Now her stomach growled. They both laughed and got out of bed at the same time. Rebecca to wrap herself in her voluminous terry-cloth robe. David to pull on underwear, pants, and his unbuttoned shirt.

She found it appealing just to pad off to the kitchen with David. Tonight everything about David seemed perfect. She put it down to the lingering sensual afterglow, which hadn't diminished one iota.

She opened the refrigerator, bare except for what he'd brought: a bottle of Cristal, organic strawberries, and her favorite St. Andres cheese from Whole Foods.

"There's a box with two croissants and a smaller box of chocolates with soft caramel centers here." He pulled them out of the cupboard.

Surprised, she turned to him. "How did you know all my favorites?"

"Pauline communicates more information in the shortest possible time than anyone I've ever met. She should be in sales. Will you share? Like you did the roses?" He glanced toward the terrace. "I need to check on our rosebushes."

"After we eat. Come on."

He sat down at the dining table where they'd shared

their first disastrous meal. It was so different now. She laid out white linen napkins, dishes, and crystal champagne glasses. The intimacy of their lovers' laughter and the natural playful way she and David ate off each other's plates delighted her. It was almost like they were old marrieds, so comfortable and so much in love.

Wait a minute! Am I opening up too soon? Too fast? I'm setting myself up for more pain.

Now terrified at her thoughts of domestic bliss with this man, she stomped the fantasy to the ground and tried to concentrate on what he was saying.

"Jasmine has called three times to say how much she appreciates the massage and fresh flowers. I have you to thank for that thaw." The warmth in his voice was contagious. She could feel it seeping into every cold, empty hollow in her body.

"The boys and Jasmine are coming to Chicago for Thanksgiving. It's been a few years since we've had a real holiday together. I want you to meet them."

Still in sensual overload, she laughed. "I'd love to meet them. Why don't I cook Thanksgiving dinner here for everyone?" The instant the words left her lips, she knew she'd become deeply deranged by great sex.

David's luminous face made her descent into madness worth it. "That would be great. The kids would like a home-cooked Thanksgiving dinner. Especially from a great cook like you. I'll be traveling in New York for the next few weeks. By the time I get back, I'll know their itinerary." He glanced at his Rolex. "The jet is scheduled to take off at six-thirty tomorrow morning. Let's take a look at those peaked-looking rosebushes before I leave."

The terrace lights revealed several new blooms and dozens of buds.

"They've made a remarkable recovery tonight," she declared innocently.

He pressed a kiss on her forehead and a hot flash of sensation made her weak. "I feel the same way," he said with a laugh.

All the way to the front door he kept his arm casually around the area where her waist was located beneath her bulky robe. In the foyer he bent to pick up the plant food, which must have fallen to the floor in their mad rush to embrace.

He handed it to her with great ceremony. "Remember, TLC. I want those rosebushes to live to a hundred and ten."

I must remember it is just a figure of speech.

She wasn't a thirty-year-old like Shannon, weaving fantasies about her dream man. David was flesh and blood, and she was old and wise enough to luxuriate in these feelings for as long as they were both enjoying the relationship. No more. No less.

"I hate to leave. I'll call you soon." He lifted her chin with his thumb and tilted her head back. Her lips parted for his kiss.

In that moment, she fearfully acknowledged she was enjoying this way too much for her own good.

"You offered to cook Thanksgiving dinner for David's family?" Harry's wonderfully chiseled jaw dropped open, and he leaned back against his kitchen counter like he was too weak from shock to stand without support.

"Don't look at me like I've lost my mind." Rebecca continued to putter around the kitchen like she did every Sunday afternoon, assisting Harry, the *real* cook, with the recipe for Wednesday's Food section.

"Come here, sweet pea." He straightened, placed his hands on her shoulders, and, his face very serious, studied her. "A glitter in the eyes. Peachy flushed skin. Lips slightly swollen. Yes, you're definitely giving off a vibe of sexual satisfaction." He burst into a smile. "All symptoms of having had fabulous sex. Lucky you. David is a sly one, using sex to talk you into cooking Thanksgiving for a cast of thousands."

She smiled back, her body tingling with that satisfaction. "Including you and Kate and Pauline and the girls, it's only ten people."

"Your oven hasn't worked in months. How can we cook a turkey dinner for ten in your kitchen?"

The *we* was not lost on her. She flung herself against his chest for a quick hug. "Thank you, darling. I knew I could count on you."

"Always. Now let's plan the perfect menu." He pulled cookbook after cookbook out of his library. Thumbed through them and made copious notes in his food journal.

While he happily debated the merits of different sweet potato recipes, she called to have her oven fixed.

Two hours later, Harry was still totally engrossed in recipes. Rebecca laughed. "Harry, I haven't seen you this happy since you went to Paris last year for your medical convention."

"I'm thinking about going back to Paris, sweet pea." He looked up and smiled gently. "There's a cooking program I want to attend. The information arrived yesterday. It's there on the desk. Take a look at it."

While she read through the booklet on the Cordon Bleu in Paris, she felt a hard catch of old fear about being abandoned. She'd be lost without Harry.

"What are you planning to study?" she asked, trying to adopt a mature attitude.

"Haute cuisine, nouvelle." He glanced up and saw her face. He placed the cookbook on the counter and carefully marked the page. He walked to her and removed the booklet from her hands. "I'm not deserting you. It won't be forever. I can't be away from my practice for more than four months."

"I'm sorry, darling." She hoped her wobbly fake smile hid the dull, heavy pain in her stomach. "If it's something you want to do, you absolutely *should* pursue it. I read that we baby boomers reinvent ourselves every three to five years."

He looked down at the booklet and twisted it in his hands. "These days I'm happier cooking than with medicine." He shrugged. "I still get great satisfaction when I can help someone who has had a catastrophic event to their face. But much of plastic surgery has become about injectable products. Botox. Collagen. Restylane. Radiance."

He reached out and took her hand. "If I go, it doesn't mean everything will be different. We won't be different." A wicked grin curled his mouth. "Except I'll be better. Change will recharge the old brain. I'll be more fascinating than ever."

"I know, darling." She squeezed his fingers and held on. "I know. It's just old me. Being afraid of losing the people I love."

Chapter 18

On Monday morning, exhausted from a fitful, unrestful night of thinking about Harry leaving and already missing David, Rebecca walked into the *Daily Mail* lobby to find a blissful Pauline.

"Oh, what do you think?" Pauline twirled around so Rebecca could see the sleek, shiny, brilliant red hair that now only brushed Pauline's shoulders, instead of hanging down her back. Not a curl in sight except for the ends turned under perfectly.

"It took me an hour to blow it dry. My new stylist showed me how. She's the one who cut it. I decided to do something for myself with the extra money from my raise." A frown twisted her plump, glossed lips. "Don't you think that's okay, to do something for myself?"

"Absolutely! You look stunning. Love it! Turn around again."

Laughing, Pauline twirled, looking dazzling.

"Have you lost weight, too?" Rebecca asked, her mouth curling into a conspiratory smile. "Looks like you've decided not all men are bastards like our ex-husbands and you're on the hunt."

Pauline blushed. "Maybe. Oh, Rebecca, you found Mr. Sumner. He's wonderful. It's given me new hope that there's someone for me to love. Like the way you guys feel about each other."

Warmth filled every pore of her body just thinking about David, but she tried to be discreet. "Well, that's not *exactly* the way it is."

"Oh, sure. Stop!" Pauline rolled her eyes. "What about the rosebushes? If that wasn't the most romantic thing I've ever seen, I don't know what is. And the way he looks at you!"

"Yes, we have become closer friends lately," Rebecca tried to sound nonchalant, but even she could hear the thrill in her voice.

"See. I'll bet you're not worried this time that he's gone and so is Shannon."

"Again?" She'd accomplished her goal with George, and her own heart repair had taken quite a different delightful path, but she still had to confront Shannon. "Didn't she just take a vacation?"

"Sick days." Pauline leaned closer, and her new sleek hair fell charmingly across her cheek. "Maybella told me Shannon is suffering from a severe migraine. She'll probably be out the rest of the week. Something traumatic happened to her over the weekend to bring it on."

Rebecca knew from personal experience that reality was a nasty dose to swallow. There was no other choice but to wait until Shannon returned for her woman-to-woman talk. Rebecca didn't have the heart to accost someone prostrate in their bed with a headache and a heartache.

Rebecca arrived in her office to find a short stack of mail on her desk. On top was a blue envelope addressed in large, flourishing handwriting.

It was a thank-you note from Martha Bartholomew, raving about the birthday gift and gushing that every time she used the silver bookmark she thought fondly of Rebecca. It ended with hopes from both Martha and Charlie that they would see one another soon.

She tapped the note against her desk, debating her choices.

"Rebecca," Kate said from the doorway. "I'm sorry to interrupt. You appear deep in thought." She walked into the office.

Feeling guilty for fraternizing with the enemy on *Daily Mail* time, Rebecca slipped the note under her pile of mail.

"I need to hand over a few assignments to you this week." There was a new freshness to Kate's walk.

Rebecca thought she knew why. "Did you get the voice mail I left you early this morning? Your finance column in this morning's paper was brilliant!"

Kate's eyes looked brighter, more rested. "Thank you. I did get it. Several other people called or sent e-mails, too."

"I'm not surprised. I called my banker this morning and changed two of my accounts because of your column."

Kate's laugh sounded fuller and deeper than Rebecca had ever heard it. "That's funny. Two of my other callers told me the same thing."

"You're the baby boomers' new financial guru. Since we've vowed to stay young forever, we need the money to do it. You should write a book," Rebecca declared, warming to the idea.

The light went out of Kate's eyes. "Actually, I had a book contract before my breakdown. The project is outlined, researched, ready to be written."

"Then you should write it, Kate."

"The contract was canceled. My stay at the hospital was longer than expected. There was also the fact I no longer had my power base at *Wealth Weekly* behind me." Kate shrugged as if wanting to shake off those memories. "Yesterday's news. Now, for Friday, I need an article on the ultimate hostess gifts. And for Saturday, the best ways to store your summer clothes for the winter."

"Of course, I'll take care of the pieces. Don't give them another thought."

It gave Rebecca comfort to give in to her natural inclination to take care of others. It felt *right* to help Kate for as long as she needed her.

Harry didn't need to worry about Rebecca not taking care of her own needs. Like her quintessential heroine, Scarlett O'Hara, she'd think about what was good for herself tomorrow.

On Saturday afternoon Rebecca had to give serious thought to taking care of her own well-being. She caught the first wave of flu sweeping through the newspaper office.

Feverish, head pounding, her chest feeling like an elephant was sitting on it with the trunk wrapped around her throat, Rebecca lay spread-eagled, miserable on her bed.

The phone rang, and with a groan she rolled over to answer it. "Hello," she croaked, her voice nearly gone.

"Rebecca? You sound awful." David sounded very far away.

"I have the flu. Where are you?" She tried not to cough into his ear.

"On my jet. I'll be in Chicago for five hours tomorrow before I leave for the West Coast. I'll come see you."

"No!" The thought of him seeing her lank, oily hair, red, blotchy skin, and weepy eyes and nose made her feel sicker. "I'm contagious."

"Who's taking care of you?" He sounded alarmed, like he *truly* cared.

She curled up in a fetal position, feeling incredibly happy for someone with a hundred-and-two temperature. "I am. Pauline and Kate both have the flu, too, and Harry's got several surgeries scheduled this week. Can't take germs into the operating room. I'm fine."

"Stop talking. I can hear how much it's hurting you. I'll be in touch."

The phone rang early Sunday morning and woke Rebecca up. She didn't mind, because she thought it might be David.

She cleared her throat, hoping her voice would sound stronger. *"Hello."* She still sounded like a sick frog.

"Miss Covington? This is Malcolm. There's a Miss Gilda Parlinski from the Loving Hands Nursing Agency down here who says she's supposed to take care of you."

"What?" she croaked and sat up. She felt so light-headed. If she hadn't been in bed, she would have fallen down. "I didn't call any nursing agency. I only have the flu."

"She says to tell you Mr. Sumner hired her. She has a message from him for you."

Is this how it feels to be swept off my feet? If she could see herself, would her eyes be sparkling with this beautiful, joyous feeling of being cherished? Or was it just the fever making her hallucinate? "Send her up. Thanks, Malcolm."

Rebecca stood up gingerly, and the room tilted a little

to the left. Moving at the proverbial snail's pace, she managed to struggle into her robe. It felt too heavy on her weakened muscles. With great effort, she shrugged it off.

She decided she'd have to greet Gilda Parlinski wearing just her "If All the World's a Stage, I Want Better Lighting!" sleep shirt.

She made it to the living room and collapsed on the couch, resting until the doorbell rang.

When it did, the sound pierced her throbbing head like someone was sticking it with big, thick needles.

By the time she unbolted the door and pulled it open, she could hardly stand. "I surrender. *Please* come in."

Miss Gilda Parlinski had an ageless face and fair-colored hair and was dressed from head to foot in white. In Rebecca's weakened state she looked like an angel.

"Hello, Miss Covington. I'm Gilda. Mr. Sumner called in a message for you. I wrote it down."

Leaning against the mirrored wall, Rebecca read it: "Don't argue. For a change let someone take care of you. I'll be in touch. David."

She clutched the note to her bosom like it was a love letter instead of orders. *He cares.* There was simply no way she could talk herself out of the truth.

"Time to go back to your bed, Miss Covington. Rest is what you need. I'm unhooking the phone in your bedroom."

Meekly, Rebecca followed Gilda's orders, too.

She slept until three p.m., when Gilda brought in homemade chicken soup from groceries she'd ordered from Whole Foods and Malcolm had picked up.

After consuming half the soup, Rebecca fell back on the pillows and closed her eyes. The next time she opened them, the clock said two a.m. There was a fresh box of Kleenex on her bedside table beside a pitcher of ice water and a glass.

When she woke at five a.m., she felt well enough to stagger to the tub for a quick bath. It made her feel cleaner but weak as a noodle. Wrapped in a dry bath towel, she fell back into bed.

When she heard the door open, she lifted her heavy eyelids and quickly let them drift shut. "I shouldn't have taken that hot bath. I'm so weak I'm hallucinating. You look just like David."

"I've been called many things, but never a hallucination." David's voice was unmistakable.

She groaned and covered her head with a pillow. "I told you not to come."

"I would have been here last night, but the airport was socked in. We couldn't land the jet until two this morning."

She felt the mattress give as he sat on the side of the bed.

"Take that pillow off your face before you suffocate. I've seen you without makeup. You're adorable."

Too weak to resist, she pushed it aside and stared up at him. "Aren't you afraid of getting sick?" Rebecca asked in a small voice because her throat hurt again. This time it wasn't the flu but happy tears pooling there.

"If I get sick, you take care of me. Deal?"

Afraid to open her mouth for fear she'd start crying, she nodded.

"Glad that's settled." His eyes swept across her feverish face as he gently pushed her limp hair off her forehead. "Now eat the breakfast I made you."

Only then did Rebecca pay attention to the tray on the table. "Did you cook this yourself?" she croaked.

"I did." He moved the tray to the bed and handed her the juice. "Don't talk. You need to eat to keep up your strength."

She tried to remember if anyone had ever taken such tender care of her. Feelings she was too terrified to name swelled in her chest, making it hard to swallow the tiny bits of food David fed her.

Afraid she couldn't hold back her feelings another second, she shook her head. "I can't eat any more. I'm too tired," she whispered.

"Sleep." He kissed her forehead. "I'll be in the other room until I have to leave at midnight."

Blinking back tears, she watched him close the door. Only then did she shut her eyes and cry herself to sleep, because deep inside she knew happiness like this couldn't last forever.

❦

Every fifteen minutes David walked carefully into Rebecca's bedroom to check on her. She looked comfortable to him, her lips slightly parted, her eyes closed.

He brushed her hair off her forehead, pleased she felt cooler. He pulled the comforter higher, tucking it around her shoulders, before backing out of the room.

Shortly before midnight, he rose from the couch where he'd been working and headed toward her bedroom again. Gilda Parlinski's chuckle stopped him.

"Don't worry so, Mr. Sumner. Miss Covington only has the flu. Nothing life-threatening."

Memories stirred and his heart ached. At first the doctors thought Ellen's leukemia was a lingering flu.

He nodded at the nurse but still opened the door and entered Rebecca's bedroom.

He sank onto the side of the bed, and his eyes roamed over her, lingering on her mouth. He smiled, thinking of how she curled her lips when she was happy and how she thrust up her chin when defying him. Rebecca was clever and beautiful and special, and he cared about her too much.

Here with her, it was easy to forget the world outside and the promises he'd made himself.

He ruthlessly tried to push aside his feelings. He was too raw, too vulnerable to the pain of loss. He hadn't forgotten how it felt to lose the person he loved most in the world.

What if something happened to Rebecca? Fear seared through him. He'd come so far, he wasn't sure if he could back away from her.

He stood, watching her sleep, the even rise and fall of her breasts under the covers. He had to leave her now, for a short while. It would be good to put some space between them. Give him time to think.

He pressed one more kiss on her warm cheek and backed out of the room.

❧

She slept until the next morning, when Gilda came in carrying another breakfast tray and her phone. The instant it was turned on, it rang.

Gilda left when Rebecca answered it. "Hello." Today she sounded only slightly husky.

"Excellent. You sound much better," David said softly.

"David." Rebecca swallowed the aching lump in her throat. "I'm sorry I slept through your visit. You shouldn't have come and done so much."

"I did what needed to be done. I wish I was still there, but Gilda comes highly recommended."

I wish you were here. Too much. "She's a treasure, but I'm sending her home tomorrow morning. I feel much better, so don't argue," she said, using his own words.

"I'm too far away to argue successfully, and I don't like to lose. I hope to be back in Chicago sometime next week. I'm eager to check on you and our rosebushes. How are they doing?"

"Still enjoying themselves."

By the way he chuckled, she knew he'd understood her unspoken message.

"I'm making sure they get all the TLC they need. You, too. Don't go back to work until you're a hundred percent. We'll talk soon."

After he rang off, she realized it had been a very long time since she'd thought about David in connection with the *Daily Mail*. She'd started out thinking she could change his mind about her job and the paper in general, but *he'd* changed her. Now the thought of business intruding on her feelings for him left a bad taste in her mouth.

She snuggled down in her covers, thinking of David sharing this bed with her. She smiled, remembering all the playful "Ask Becky" moments. She got out her scrapbooks of old "Ask Becky" columns and read through them, laughing at how young she sounded, yet surprisingly wise at times. Unfortunately, she didn't come across any advice that might remotely help her with her dangerous feelings for David. How to protect herself from the inevitable ending to all this joy.

On Wednesday, Gilda refused any money whatsoever, saying Mr. Sumner had already been more than generous.

On Thursday, the same two burly men wearing "The Farmer's Market Nursery" T-shirts who had brought the rosebushes arrived to administer TLC on David's behalf.

Rebecca, dressed for the first time in days, put a coat on over her cashmere Juicy Couture sweat suit to stand on the terrace to watch them prepare the bushes for winter.

They placed a quilted blanket like movers use to wrap furniture around the planters.

"Aren't you supposed to put a house over the rosebushes? That conelike thing I've seen?"

The taller man looked up at her. "Nope. We found out when it gets warmer the house causes mildew inside the cone. It's bad for the roses."

When they pulled out clippers, fear clutched at her heart. "What are you doing?"

"Gonna cut 'em back to eight and one-half inches. Then we mulch over the top," the shorter one said and snipped the first bush.

"They'll grow again. In the spring when the conditions are right," the taller, kinder one promised when he saw her face.

Once they were gone, she looked at the rosebushes. Thanks to David they were tucked up safe and snug for the harsh winter. Thanks to David she felt swaddled in a warm glow of care herself.

She was so far past merely *enjoying herself* and dangerously, terrifyingly close to *falling in love with him*. *Not* that she'd allow such feelings to flourish, because then she'd lose control and open the door to pain. Yet *something wonderful* was happening between them, and she was bursting to share it with someone.

She knew the only safe place to do it.

CHICAGO DAILY MAIL
WEDNESDAY FOOD

OYSTER AND COCKTAIL

Oysters on the half shell
1 cup ketchup
2 heaping tablespoons of horseradish, very fresh;
  adjust to taste
Dash of Tabasco
1 teaspoon fresh lemon juice
1 teaspoon tarragon

Mix and serve with oysters, shrimp, or crab.

A Note from Rebecca Covington

Darlings, that's not snow in the air, it's love! I know I've been sharing stories about men getting it so *wrong in the romance department. Now I'm thrilled to tell you about a divine husband who got it* so *right I wept when I heard the story.*

This enlightened male knew how much his wife of fifteen years was dreading her fortieth birthday, so he planned a party for two at their favorite restaurant.

First came the oysters on the half shell, in which she found two-carat diamond studs.

Second came the filet mignon, wrapped with a diamond bracelet.

Third came the crème brûlée, with a diamond necklace sparkling on the rim of the cup instead of sugar.

The pièce de résistance was the small birthday cake on a plate sprinkled liberally with tiny pieces of what looked like confetti but was actually their prenup, which he had torn up out of overpowering love for her.

Finally a man who knows the definition of true romance.

Sigh.

Good luck in finding your own Prince Charming. These oysters might help.

Enjoy!

Xo Rebecca

Chapter 19

On Wednesday, Rebecca closed her office door and sat in her favorite chair, waiting for the clock to finally reach the bewitching hour when David always called. She felt overheated, flushed by her ever-present excitement.

At the stroke of twelve, the phone rang. To prove she still retained some control over her feelings, she forced herself to wait for three rings before picking it up slowly.

"Rebecca, it's David."

"Hi." Happiness bubbled through her, but she tried very hard to keep it out of her voice. "What part of your far-flung empire are you ruling today?"

"Iowa." She'd learned to recognize the amusement in his voice. "I'm acquiring two small local TV affiliates. I read your column today."

She smiled at his change of subject. "Yes?"

"I'm pleased you wrote something positive about men. Did I have anything to do with your change of heart?"

David *knew*, but she couldn't help sparring with him. It was too much fun. "My god, your ego is as big as Lake Michigan!" She laughed through the pleasure burning in her stomach.

"That's my Rebecca. Back to normal."

"Yes. Thanks to you and Gilda." She took a strengthening breath to say what she thought she should. "All better. So you don't need to check on me every day."

"Evidently I enjoy it. Do you?"

"Evidently." The word came out soft and fluttery because she'd been holding her breath.

"Then I'll call you tomorrow."

Basking in the tingling, pulse-racing afterglow of David's daily call, Rebecca knew she was in a new "life stage." The consulting firms' latest buzzword for baby boomers could now be applied to her.

Since she was ten, she'd feared people deserting her, or even worse, that she might desert someone who needed her. But when she'd finally let her guard down, Peter's betrayal had reinforced why she needed to protect herself, and that launched her into the commitment-phobic years. *Don't love 'em, just have fun and leave 'em.*

Rebecca wasn't sure what label to place on her newly evolved stage. Maybe it should be called the "I want to take a chance on happiness stage" or, probably closer to the mark, "I'm being a complete fool stage."

Whichever it turned out to be, it was fraught with so many contradictions it made her head spin. Like now.

At the heart of the contradictions was David, whom she had thought she could charm into giving her column back. Instead he made her understand how cleanly and completely one's personal and professional life *could* be separated. There was nothing left of the silly idea of David being "dough" in her hands, as she'd so long ago bragged to Harry.

David had changed everything. He made her hope "as long as you and I are both enjoying it" would last forever.

She knew she should be terrified of these feelings. She knew David would leave her. He'd been honest from the beginning. But like a moth to the flame, she couldn't pull back from this.

Maybe it was her recent birthday and the fact everyone knew she was smack in the middle of her forties, not just past her thirty-ninth birthday or even fortyish. Maybe the fact she'd never felt better made her believe she could handle the end of their affair. She was already building up her defenses against it. Just as she was building up her courage to leave the *Daily Mail* at the right time and accept Charlie Bartholomew's offer.

By Sunday, six calls later, Rebecca was so mellow she practically floated to Harry's brownstone. He was waiting for her in his kitchen.

"You're glowing, sweet pea. And all from a few phone calls." He stuck out his perfectly shaped lower lip in a pout. "I wish the same happiness for all of us."

"So do I. But David's not going to be back in Chicago until the night before Thanksgiving. They're all flying in together from California on the jet."

"Lucky you." He kissed her forehead. "Just imagine the sizzling sex you'll have once he returns."

She smiled dreamily at the totally X-rated images Harry's remarks made race through her head, sending a shiver over every part of her David had touched.

"Stop!" Harry demanded. "That sex-crazed look is making me envious. Take your mind off your sex life and go to Whole Foods. Remember you have to feed him before you can ravish him on Thanksgiving Day. We have recipes to try. Here's the list."

*   *   *

The Whole Foods at Huron and Dearborn had a shopping cart traffic jam in every aisle. Customers, Starbucks in hand, strolled the aisles like Sunday drivers out for a relaxing afternoon. This might be fun for some, but Rebecca was on a mission.

Checking her list, she slowly walked along the meat section. She stopped to look down at the chicken breasts. Harry didn't need any, but for some reason they reminded her of David and their first dinner. Disastrous on so many levels, but oh-so-stimulating and sexy on others.

In the liquor section, she picked up the sherry on Harry's list. It was across the aisle from the champagne. She felt light-headed, warm and tingling, the way she had the night she and David had drunk Cristal to celebrate the twinners.

As she ground coffee, its aroma drifted around her, rich and full. It smelled great, but she'd always preferred tea. Her gaze fell on the boxes of English breakfast tea. The kind David had brewed for her the morning after.

This place is practically an aphrodisiac. No wonder people hang out here.

In the next aisle, the Belgian chocolates sent her thoughts racing to her birthday party and David bringing the rosebushes. In the middle of the delicious memory, she glanced up to see Shannon and a tall, slim-hipped, dark-haired woman pushing a cart around the corner at the end of the aisle.

There was something familiar about the other woman. Rebecca's instincts sent out the alarm to follow that grocery cart.

She found the woman looking over the organic strawberries, but Shannon had disappeared.

Why does she seem so familiar? Trying to place her,

Rebecca studied the perfectly made-up face, the trim body, the long legs encased in the newest narrow-cut pants.

The woman glanced up and spotted Rebecca.

The expression of distaste on her face warned Rebecca to brace herself. Years of professionally dealing with people, eager and not so eager to talk, had taught her how to single out foe from friend.

The moment she'd seen the woman with Shannon, Rebecca's antennae told her she was on to something. "Hello. Have we met?" Smiling, Rebecca extended her hand. "I'm Rebecca Covington."

The woman cut her off, pushing her cart past Rebecca and moving as fast as possible to the checkout counter.

Rebecca threw the last few items into her cart and followed. She needed the final piece of the puzzle to explain this circle of events that had so changed her life, and she had a hunch this woman was the answer.

The woman got out of the store faster than Rebecca. Finally done checking out, Rebecca raced after her.

In the parking lot Rebecca looked wildly around. Panic set in when it seemed she'd lost her. Then she spotted the woman loading groceries into the trunk of a navy blue Lexus.

Rebecca approached her again, this time blocking the door to the driver's seat. "I'm sorry to bother you again. I'm—"

"I know damn well who you are," the woman interrupted. Her disdainful glare and cold voice should have sent any sensible person racing for cover.

Rebecca dropped her hand but held her ground. "I believe we have a mutual friend. Shannon Forrester."

"Friend?" the woman barked in a harsh intake of

breath. Her glare and voice left no doubt she had an ax to grind.

The elusive memory of this woman's patrician features and short, wavy dark hair finally clicked together.

"You're Charlene Jones. You're on the Culinary Institute Board. And I believe you live at Eagle Towers." She nodded, putting the last piece of the puzzle together. "I understand now."

"You don't understand anything." Hatred blazed out of Charlene's cornflower blue eyes. "You ruined my life. I'm glad I made problems for you!"

Other shoppers were staring curiously at them as they walked by into the store. Rebecca tried to stay calm, but something nasty and hot was filling the back of her throat. "I don't understand. *Why* do you think I ruined your life?"

"Think." Charlene's hands gripped the handle of the grocery cart so tightly her skin turned chalk white, making her nails look like bloodred talons. "You wrote one of your so-called blind items about what socialite on the Gold Coast is having an affair with her yoga instructor. Who knew my husband read your stupid column?"

A sense of needing to make retribution washed over Rebecca, and she steeled herself to take whatever tongue-lashing Charlene gave her. "I never mentioned names when I dropped in a blind item. I'm sorry if it caused problems in your marriage."

"He divorced me. After having me followed and drawing his own conclusion." A tear trickled down Charlene's smooth, flushed face. "The irony is I hadn't even had an affair. I'd only fantasized about it with my friends."

Rebecca's whole gossip column career flashed in front of her eyes. How many others had been hurt like this?

Some images brought the bile back up in her throat. "I'm sorry," she whispered.

"Go to hell and get out of my way!" Charlene snarled, shoving Rebecca aside to get into her car.

Rebecca felt like she was descending into guilt hell with every step she took back to Harry's brownstone. By the time she reached the kitchen and put the grocery bags down, she had entered whichever circle of Dante's *Inferno* was reserved for doomed souls who had hurt others. Harry found her sobbing into the sweet potatoes.

"What happened to you? Come here and tell me all about it," he coaxed.

She stepped into his comforting arms and sobbed out Charlene's story. At the end, Rebecca sniffed and stepped away to wipe at her wet face with the back of her hand. "I think she's right about me. What gave me the right to decide who deserved to have their secrets revealed?"

"Sweet pea, stop beating yourself up over this. Trust me. There's more to the story than this woman is telling you. If her husband decided to divorce her after having her followed, then there was something more than mere lusting in her heart."

She could hear the anger in his voice on her behalf. "I know. You're probably right. But if the columns I intended to be witty and provocative had *anything* to do with ruining someone's life, then I have to think seriously about whether or not I want to do it again."

On Monday morning, still agonizing over what part she might have played in the dissolution of the Jones' marriage, Rebecca walked into Shannon's office and shut the door behind her.

From the stony look on Shannon's face, Rebecca knew Charlene had called her about their Whole Foods confrontation.

"We need to talk, Shannon," Rebecca said warily, exhausted to her bones with her soul-searching weekend.

Shannon relaxed back in her chair, swiveling it gently to and fro. "It's about time someone told you what they thought of your irresponsible journalism. You cost Charlene Jones the love of her life."

"I understand you plotted with her to get even with me by planting that false tip about the senator at Eagle Towers and rigging the Culinary Institute auction."

Shannon tossed her hair over her shoulder. "I admit to nothing."

Feeling sick at the way Shannon was looking at her, Rebecca perched on the edge of the chair in front of the desk. "I deeply regret any pain I caused Charlene, and you with George."

Something flickered in Shannon's slightly bulgy blue eyes. "I'm not discussing my personal life with you, of all people."

Still vulnerable from guilt, Rebecca hesitated. "Shannon . . . I'm truly sorry. I didn't know you had feelings for George when I started seeing him."

Shannon jumped up, slamming the chair back against the wall. "Charlene's right. Your egotism is appalling. You don't know anything about my feelings for George." Shannon blinked several times, like she was fighting back tears. "George didn't mean anything to you, but we were perfect for each other. All our friends said so." She glanced down at the goldfish swimming in the bowl. "Chris and Kara were even setting us up before George started seeing you." She curled her lip.

"But you ruined it. I'd die before I'd stoop to take your rejects."

Her fingers hidden in her lap, Rebecca twisted them together, struggling to find the right words to calm Shannon's near hysterics. "George isn't my reject. We were simply two consenting adults who shared a brief fling. End of story."

"You're eleven years older than he is!" Shannon shouted, her face turning a molten red. "You're nearly old enough to be his mother!"

Shannon's behavior over the last several months had caused Rebecca pain and sadness, but this last remark made her laugh. "Hardly. I was a late bloomer."

"Don't you dare laugh at me." Shannon slammed her palms flat on the desk. "You're the laughingstock, hanging on here when no one wants you. Why don't you admit you're over the hill? Finished."

Rebecca found herself on her feet. "Shannon, calm down. Of course I'm not finished at forty-five. I'm in my prime. I've never felt better, sexier, or more alive."

"The rest of the world doesn't think so. Look at the tabloids and television. It's youth they want." Shannon pushed herself up and took a deep breath. "I admit I didn't want your job until I realized it would be the perfect intro into print, radio, and television. It's the perfect start to becoming a media personality. At thirty, I'm ripe for it. You're too old. I simply helped your inevitable departure along. It was time."

Rebecca shook her head in disbelief. "You silly girl. Don't you know things have changed? Look at Diane Sawyer. At forty-five, if I choose, I'll be the one doing print and television. I'll have it all because *I paid my dues.* I earned it." Heartsick at all the pain they'd caused each other, Rebecca tried again to reach Shannon. "I'm going to give you some advice I wish I'd gotten when I believed I'd lost the only man for me. Learn from the pain and move on to discover who you really are and what you truly want out of life."

"I wanted George, but you made it impossible." Shannon flicked something suspiciously like tears out of the corners of her eyes. At this moment, she looked very young and very confused.

Rebecca's feelings of guilt were gone, replaced by a deep sadness. "Nothing is impossible at any age if you want it badly enough to work hard to get it. I hope you understand that someday."

Chapter 20

On Thanksgiving Day, Rebecca woke up feeling like it was Christmas morning. There was an urgency in the air. The possibilities for wonderful surprises stretched endlessly in front of her.

Yawning, she glanced at the clock next to her. "No!" she screamed, nearly falling out of bed in her eagerness to get to the kitchen.

Harry's written instructions were right where he'd left them last night after they'd finished making the mushroom and water chestnut stuffing. It was already fifteen minutes after the estimated time Harry had calculated for her to begin preparing the turkey to be done for dinner at five.

She flew around the kitchen, the floor tiles cold on her bare feet. She shivered in her "There comes a time in every woman's life when the only thing that helps is a glass of champagne" sleep shirt, which fell only to her midthighs.

She lugged the turkey to the sink to rinse, salt, stuff, and baste. Huffing from hefting the twenty-three-pound bird, she shoved it into the oven and glanced at her watch. She'd cut her losses to eleven minutes.

Mission accomplished, she collapsed at the kitchen table. Now she had six hours of basting to fill before Harry arrived with the rest of dinner and eight hours to count off until she saw David again.

Another eight hours to worry whether or not he'd have the same erotic look in his eyes when he saw her. Another eight hours to live in fear that his children would loathe her on sight.

David time, minus eighty minutes, Kate stood at the door balancing a long, low, lush arrangement of russet roses, cockscomb, sedum, eucalyptus berries, and chocolate cosmos. "This is quite beautiful, but also quite heavy."

Kate gladly relinquished one side of the open florist box to Rebecca, and they carried it into the dining room. With Harry's help they positioned the flowers in the center of the table Rebecca had spread with her granny's heavy lace cloth.

Stepping away, he nodded. "Perfection. And I must say, Kate, you are looking quite fetching. Join me in the kitchen for a glass of wine while I cook?"

Blushing, Kate pulled at the turtleneck of her black cashmere sweater, which perfectly complemented her long red and black plaid skirt. "I believe I will. Are you joining us, Rebecca?"

"No. Go ahead. I'll be hovering by the door in stomach-churning fear, which is what I've been doing all day."

Chuckling, Kate left her to it.

Rebecca wished she hadn't given Malcolm her guest list so he wouldn't have to call her every time someone arrived. Each time the doorbell rang, her heart leaped into her throat.

David time, minus thirty-five minutes, Pauline walked in, followed by the girls, each carrying a pie.

"Mine's apple crumb," Polly declared, holding it up for Rebecca to admire. "It tastes better than Patty's pumpkin one."

"Does not!" Patty shouted.

"Take them into the kitchen, girls." Pauline rolled her eyes. "I brought along the DVD of the third *Pirates of the Caribbean* movie to watch in your den. It's our bonding moment together. Me drooling over Johnny Depp, and them screaming for Orlando Bloom." She gasped. "Rebecca, I love that outfit. It's wonderful on you. New?"

"Yes." She played nervously with the sash on her red Carolina Herrera silk dress. "Wearing this color always gives me courage. What if they don't like me?"

"Oh, Rebecca, they'll love you. We all do."

The doorbell rang, and every muscle in Rebecca's body froze up. "They're fifteen minutes early!"

On the second ring, Pauline looked ready to pounce. "Aren't you going to let them in?"

"Of course!" Taking her time so she could steady her breathing and compose her face into merely warm interest, Rebecca opened the door.

The first thing she saw were David's blue eyes blazing with restrained passion. His soft, smooth mouth curled the way it often did right before he kissed her. She was sure that instead of looking warmly interested, she was smiling like a lovesick adolescent would over Orlando.

Beside David stood a sharp-featured, exotic beauty who had to be Jasmine. Looming behind her were two tall young men, softer, baby-faced versions of their father.

"Welcome. Please come in." Pleased at how normal she sounded, she pulled the door open and stepped back.

The foyer was so small and narrow they had to pass through nearly in single file.

David bent to kiss her cheek. "I've missed you, Becky," he whispered so low only she caught his words. Unappeasable desire, more intense because it was forbidden, at least until dinner was over, fluttered through her.

David straightened and gently urged Jasmine forward. "I'd like you to meet my daughter-in-law." Jasmine smiled at David before he moved on into the living room.

Rebecca wasn't tall or large in any way, but she felt like a giant next to this dainty young woman in black velvet ballet flats and a black stretch velvet dress that proudly hugged her small bump.

"Thank you for having us to dinner, Rebecca. I'm a horrible cook, so this is a real treat. Especially for my Ryan." She cast a loving look over her shoulder at the twin in the blue cashmere sweater. "You can tell this is Ryan because his ears are so much larger than Michael's."

Her besotted husband devoured her with his eyes and laughed. "Jasie is right on all counts." He held out his hand. "I'm thrilled to be here, Rebecca. And to meet you."

Michael, wearing a light blue shirt open at the neck, under a navy blazer, nudged his brother aside. "Sorry we're early, but Dad couldn't wait any longer to see you. Now I can tell why. You're beautiful."

The mischievous gleam in his eyes was so reminiscent of David's she had to laugh. "You're a chip off the old block, aren't you, Michael?"

Michael's dimple was exactly like his father's, only on the opposite cheek. "I hope so," he said before following the others into the living room.

By the time Rebecca got there, David had made all the introductions and the girls were staring up with wide eyes at both Michael and Ryan.

"You're twins!" Polly shouted. "You look 'xactly alike."

"We look like twins." Patty shook her head. "But I'm eleven months older."

Michael knelt down to their level. "I can see that. You look much older, Patty."

"Want to watch the third *Pirates of the Caribbean* movie with us?" Polly asked. "We like the monsters in it and Orlando."

"Monsters work for me. Lead the way, girls." They each took a hand to pull him toward the den, and Michael winked back. "Call us when dinner is ready."

Patting her bump, Jasmine strolled to Rebecca's side. "Michael genuinely loves kids. He's already bought these little ones swimming trunks and books on marine life. I drew the line at matching baby snorkels."

An outrageous thought threaded through Rebecca's head as she watched Pauline follow the laughing trio into the den. "How old are the twins?"

"We're all the same age. Twenty-eight. Ellen and Dad Sumner were married in college. The boys were born on his twenty-first birthday."

Rebecca gazed hungrily across the room to where David stood, talking to Kate. "Ellen was his wife and the mother of his children. No wonder he doesn't want to move on. Excuse me. I'd better check on dinner." Nearly overcome with emotion, she fled before she burst into tears.

My God, I have been writing fantasies in my head about David. I needed this reminder that whatever we have won't be forever.

An hour later, outwardly calm but inwardly a wreck, Rebecca sat at one end of the dining table, blushing at all the praise for the squash soup. "Thank you, but I couldn't have done it without Harry. He's the *really talented* chef."

All eyes turned to Harry at the other end of the table. He bowed his head. "It is my pleasure."

"Any tips for cooks who aren't really talented?" Jasmine asked.

David glanced back at Rebecca and shifted his foot so they were touching under the table. Rebecca always prided herself on her self-control, but now it failed her. She tuned out all talk to study David's profile next to her. So close she could touch him if she dared. Watching him made her feel the same way she did looking over the edge of a precipice. Her body trembled, her stomach felt hollow, and the urge to jump was overpowering even though she knew it would kill her. Every time, self-preservation pulled her back from the edge. Just like it did now.

Over turkey and stuffing, David kept casually rubbing his thigh against hers under the table. With a seductive smile, he touched her arm. "Please pass the salt and pepper."

Beginning to feel aroused, she fanned herself with her napkin. Since it was warm in the dining area, she hoped no one would think it was unusual.

By the time she needed to clear the dishes for dessert, David had her in a sensual near-frenzy. She jumped up. "Everyone relax. I'll get the dessert." She gathered up a few dirty dinner plates and fled to the kitchen.

Pauline followed her, balancing dinner plates in her hands. "Oh, let me help you."

Kate appeared and pushed up her sleeves. "Six hands are better than two. Where are the dishcloths?"

While doing dishes, they kept bumping into one another, laughing and taking last tastes of food before they wrapped it up and put it in the refrigerator.

"You sound like you're having fun in here. Let me join the party," Jasmine called from the doorway.

Pauline gasped. "You should be resting."

Jasmine shook her head, sending her thick dark hair swinging around her shoulders. "No way. I want to help."

Kate thrust a pie into her hands. "Make the slices small. We're all on diets."

With all four of them working, the pies were on the buffet in record time. Pauline and Kate took in cups and saucers. Carrying the teapot, Jasmine hesitated in the doorway and then turned back.

"Thank you for making Dad so happy, Rebecca. It's changed him." A smile broke across Jasmine's narrow face. "FYI. We approve. You have our blessings."

After Jasmine went back into the dining room, Rebecca's knees felt weak and she dropped down onto a chair. Her eyes got hot and stingy like she might cry, so she patted cold water around them for five minutes. All the while she was letting a little seed of hope grow. If David had really changed, as his family thought, then maybe it was possible for him to make a commitment. Her mind couldn't quite wrap around that blissful possibility yet, for fear of deeper disappointment. She plastered on her most confident smile and, carrying more pies, sailed into the dining room.

After dessert, once Patty and Polly were happily back watching their movie, David turned the conversation to business. He stroked Rebecca's inner thigh under the table and threw her such a blazing smile she thought she was melting.

I hope this isn't my first hot flash!

"Since my first dinner with Rebecca, I've been reconsidering my plans for some network programming." Under the lace tablecloth, David clasped her hand. "Instead of a daytime version of the reality show *Defeat Your Demons,* I want to do a program on personal financial empowerment for women. Kate's finance columns have been so well received I can't think of anyone better qualified to host it."

Kate's cheeks bloomed roses, and her eyes sparkled as everyone at the table applauded. "Thank you. I'm excited about the project."

Kate looked thrilled, and Rebecca shared her excitement. David was capable of changing his mind. The idea that he might do the same about committing to her made it impossible to concentrate on anything else.

She'd told Shannon anything was possible if she wanted it badly enough. And Rebecca wanted David.

She *was* having a hot flash. Everything she'd heard about menopause was true. She *did* want to rip off all her clothes. But she didn't want a cold shower. She wanted to rip off David's clothes, too!

Guilt washed over her in hot waves for wishing their loved ones would leave soon so she and David could get to it. At last those Très Treat pillow covers would come out of her hope chest. She was overcome with such a glorious feeling of being alive.

I'm not too old, or too jaded, or too afraid to fall madly in love!

At last Harry suggested having after-dinner drinks in the living room. Everyone followed except for David.

"I'd like to see how my rosebushes are doing," he said quietly.

"Of course." Desperate to get him alone, Rebecca abandoned her other guests to lead him out onto the dark terrace. Once in the darker shadows by the rosebushes, she turned to cup his face with her hands. His lime aftershave and clean-male scent engulfed her. She loved how firm and dry, yet smooth, his lips felt. He pulled her closer, his hand cradling the back of her head. The kiss hardened and deepened, the heat of their mouths contrasting with the cold Chicago night, making it more secret and delicious hidden here on the terrace.

"I couldn't wait," David sighed, his breath warming her cheek.

"I know. Let's send the children home to bed early."

In an agony of waiting, Rebecca said good night to her guests. The expressions on everyone's faces, except Patty's and Polly's, told Rebecca they knew *exactly* why David had rolled up his sleeves, declaring he was staying to help clean up.

Jasmine looked particularly pleased, giving Rebecca a thumbs-up on the way out the door. At last, they were alone.

"Come here," David said softly.

He pulled her toward him, and nurturing hope, Rebecca watched the intimate, meaningful look as he lowered his face.

I want this always. In time I'll convince him he can trust me with his heart. I know it. I feel it in his touch.

She closed her eyes and opened her mouth to his kiss, her body blossoming, like the rosebushes would when conditions were perfect.

This is perfect.

David pulled slightly away, looking down at her. "It was a wonderful evening. They all think you're great."

"Ditto," she muttered, trembling in anticipation.

"You're tense," he murmured. His hands moved to her shoulders to knead gently. "You need a hot bath to relax. Let's go."

He led her by the hand to her bathroom. The Jacuzzi tub was built for two, but Rebecca had only used it alone.

Silly, but I'm glad David is the first and only.

They undressed like comfortable lovers, lazy and sensuous. He settled down in the water first before reaching out to help her step in. She settled between his thighs, her back resting against his hard chest.

"Close your eyes and relax. You deserve this after all your hard work," he whispered in her ear.

Mesmerized by his voice and his caressing hands, Rebecca leaned her head back and closed her eyes.

The sensation of David slowly rubbing the soapy washcloth down her neck, lingering on her nape, curled desire low in her abdomen, like the hot, moist air swirling around them. She felt him massage the soft cloth across her shoulders and down her arms. All the while, his lips brushed her ear over and over.

Her fingers curled in anticipation when he reached her stomach and swept up to her rib cage. He stroked beneath her breasts and then to the sides.

Pleasure rippled through her. She felt his erection at her back, loving that touching her gave him this same pleasure.

Instead of relaxing, she was finding it hard to breathe, waiting for his hot, soapy touch on her breasts. She wanted to scream at the way he gently massaged her breasts in slower, smaller circles to their burning center. At last he reached her nipples, rubbing ever so gently.

Desire exploded inside her. She twisted around, straddling his hips, found him beneath the soapy water, and settled herself over him.

She kissed him deeply, passionately, pouring all her feelings of love and desire into her mouth and the movement of her body over his. She wanted to show him that he could trust her with his heart.

He held her hips, helping her lift and glide over him, short and long, deeper and harder. Until she became so weak she sobbed for help to prolong it, to keep the spiraling pleasure building higher and higher. Then it was only David's hands holding her, lifting her over and over and over again. Her breasts crushed to his chest, she clung to his shoulders, lost in the movement, in the sensations ripping through her.

He arched up hard and tight against her, and throwing back her head, she groaned with the intense, sweet pleasure flowing from him.

She collapsed on his chest, his heart thudding beneath her ear. Both too exhausted to move, their hot soapy bodies cooled in the tepid water.

As breathless as she was, David lifted her hand to kiss it. Her fingertips were white and puckering.

"We should get out," she sighed. "We're shrinking into prunes."

"Not all of us," David chuckled in a little gasp.

She felt him swelling again between her thighs. "My God, you're insatiable!" She laughed, excited again herself.

"It's your fault," he murmured, running his fingers down her spine. "You're irresistible."

"If you want me, you'll have to catch me. I'm freezing!" Splashing water all over them and half the bathroom, she scurried out of the tub, dashing to her bed.

Laughing, he followed and caught her, like she'd planned. Kissing, they rolled across the silky bedspread.

She loved David's long, probing, burning kisses. She could kiss him for hours. She loved him half on top of her, the weight of his body delicious, and his leg thrown over her, his hand caressing her.

I love him. I won't live without this ever again.

❦

I love her.

The three simple words his mind imprinted with firmness and conviction penetrated David's brain and his battered heart.

Blindly, he reached for Rebecca, cradling her in his arms, stroking her hair, watching her sleep like he'd done when she was ill.

He loved watching her. The way her hair fell across her high forehead and the way her lips parted the tiniest bit, like they did right before she kissed him.

Her lids drifted open, her eyes luminous in the moonlight. "Why are you smiling?" she whispered.

"Thinking of you." He kissed the tip of her nose.

"That's good," she sighed, snuggling closer, her breasts pressed against his side. "Remember the first night we were together?"

"Yeah. Rough start. Spectacular finish." He heard the huskiness in his voice.

She tilted her head back against his shoulder and looked up into his eyes. Hers were filled with anguish like they'd been then. "I'm so sorry I hurt your feelings that night."

He couldn't bear to see her sad. He kissed her eyelids closed. "You kissed it and made it all better."

"I did, didn't I," she chuckled, then pressed her lips against his chest and rested her cheek there.

He could tell by her even breathing that she'd fallen back to sleep.

Every promise he'd ever made about his future alone cracked inside him, like an iceberg breaking apart under a brilliant sun.

He wished he could say the words to her. Maybe someday. For now, being happier than he'd ever been was enough.

Chapter 21

Rebecca moved through the weekend in a daze of joy. If David's armor was cracking, like hers had done, then they were both capable of letting go of the past. There was nothing stopping them from being together except their own fears and misplaced guilt. She'd help David understand they could have it all together.

On the phone, she gushed so much about David to Harry he demanded she stop or he'd have to go take a cold shower. Pauline was more eager to know everything Rebecca wasn't too embarrassed to share. Long ago, Kate had given Rebecca her number and her address. Rebecca tried several times to reach Kate but only got her voice mail, so she left messages until the mailbox was full.

On Monday, Pauline told her Kate had phoned in sick.

An alarm bell went off in Rebecca's head, sending an uncomfortable tremor through her new romantic daydream world.

"Did she say what was wrong?" Rebecca asked.

Pauline bit her lip. "No, darn it! I tried to find out, but I couldn't get anything out of her. She had an important meeting scheduled with Mr. Sumner at eleven that I had to cancel. He's meeting with all the key people individually because he's been gone for weeks. You're at five."

"Me?" David hadn't left her condo until Saturday morning, and when they'd spoken on Sunday, he hadn't said a word about a meeting. "Are you sure?"

"Sure. There's a memo on your desk." Pauline threw her a sweet, knowing smile. "Except yours is in a sealed envelope." She waved a sheet of paper in front of Rebecca's eyes. "I know you're at five, because he gave me this master list in case anyone calls about their time."

The thought of a love note from David sent her hurrying upstairs to her office. She tore it open and gazed, enchanted, at his small, neat writing.

Becky,
It occurred to me I might be able to bear all these meetings today if being with you is my reward. Business meeting at five. The rest of the evening belongs to us.
David

Reading the note again, it occurred to her that lately she was living in constant anticipation of seeing David. That thought led to another rush of delicious, fearless excitement. *Soon, very soon, maybe even today, David will see that anything is possible with us now.*

She looked at her watch. *David time,* eight hours. She couldn't wait.

But the little alarm bell of concern for Kate went off again. She glanced at her watch. Nine-thirty. Not too early to call.

By eleven-thirty, when she still hadn't been able to reach Kate, she made her decision. Her worry had intensified to an icy-cold, huge knot in her stomach. Time to take action.

By noon, she stood in front of Kate's town house. Built in the sixties, it was one of the oldest on the Kinzie Corridor along the Chicago River, splitting North Michigan Avenue from downtown.

Rebecca rang the doorbell and turned up the collar of her navy cashmere coat. She shivered in the damp, cold wind off the lake. It felt and looked like it could snow any minute.

When Kate didn't answer, Rebecca rapped on the glass window of the door.

Nothing.

Beginning to panic, she punched the doorbell again and again. She needed to make sure Kate only had the flu or a cold or a million other things that had nothing to do with her former depression. Rebecca felt a sickening guilt bubble up through her chest. Had she ignored Kate by spending nearly every waking moment thinking about David? Had there been glaring neon signs to warn her that something was wrong with Kate and Rebecca had blithely overlooked them because she was too busy falling in love at the ripe age of forty-five?

Consumed by guilt and worry, with horrible, unspeakable visions racing through her mind, Rebecca banged on the door again. "Kate, I know you're in there!" she shouted, hoping her voice would carry through the wood and glass and the white plantation shutters covering the window. "Open this door. I'm not leaving. Kate!"

She yelled until the back of her throat was dry, and when she called Kate's name, it sounded strained and thinned.

The longer she pounded, the clearer and more unspeakable the images in her head became. Shaking, she reached into her leather tote for her cell phone. She was calling the police.

So slowly Rebecca at first thought she was imagining it, Kate opened the door. There were no lights outlining her, but even in the dim grayness, Rebecca clearly saw how tired Kate looked and how shrunken in the thick black fleece robe.

"Thank God you're all right!" Rebecca rushed in before Kate could slam the door in her face.

The rooms were dark, gloomy, and cold. "I'm turning on some lights before I fall and kill myself in these heels."

Groping along the wall, Rebecca found the switch. The ceiling light flooded the hall and threw enough illumination into the living room so she could see to turn on two lamps.

Once Rebecca turned on lights, she could see the town house was classy and efficient, like Kate. No frills. Not quite spartan, but close.

Rebecca wrapped her arms around herself for warmth. "Where's the thermostat? It's freezing in here."

"Back in the hallway," Kate said dully. She lifted her hand to point and then dropped it like she didn't have the energy.

"When did you eat last? Not Thanksgiving at my place?" Rebecca couldn't keep the horror out of her voice.

"No. On Saturday I had the leftovers you sent home with me."

"Kate, this is Monday! Where's the kitchen?"

"This way." Kate walked away, and Rebecca followed her into a modern kitchen, obviously recently remodeled.

The refrigerator was empty except for a turkey drumstick and a slice of pumpkin pie, both dried out.

"Sit down, Kate. I'll fix you a cup of tea." She didn't know if Kate even *liked* tea, but it had been Rebecca's granny's cure for everything. Often it actually helped.

While she waited for the water to boil, she sent a text message to Harry. Before the kettle whistled, he replied, *Have food. Will be there in fifty minutes.*

She checked her watch and breathed a sigh of relief.

Afraid to push too hard, Rebecca let Kate sit in pensive silence, sipping her tea. She sat across from her at the chrome and glass table to watch every movement Kate made, in the hopes of getting some clue as to how to help.

The door chime made them both jump. It sparked interest in Kate's blank eyes. "Reinforcements?" she asked dryly.

"Harry. I'll be right back." Rebecca rushed down the hall and flung open the door. "I've never been so glad to see you in my entire life," she whispered with real feeling.

Harry, bundled up in a gray cashmere overcoat with a gray plaid Burberry scarf wrapped around his throat, walked in and in one long look swept the hall and living room.

"This place is nearly as sterile as my operating room. Where is she?"

"The kitchen. At the back." Rebecca had to run a little to keep up with his long strides.

He studied Kate as he unwound his scarf and took off his coat. He placed them both neatly on the metal stool at the tiny bar. "Kate, when did you stop taking your medication?" Harry spoke loudly and firmly.

Kate looked up at him. "A month ago."

The uncharacteristic confusion in Kate's eyes was so painful to watch, Rebecca couldn't hold back tears. They rolled, hot and salty, down her cheeks and onto her lips.

"Harry, I've been in remission for almost two years." Kate sighed. "Six months ago the doctor suggested I could stop my medication."

"Is this your second or third episode of depression?" All the time he was talking, Harry continued to unload containers of food from the two large bags he'd carried in with him.

"My second. Is this another episode?" She shook her head. "It's different than the first. Then I couldn't get out of bed for weeks. My doctors told me I should seek treatment if any problem lasted more than two weeks. It's more likely I've been frightening myself into a stupor this weekend."

Rebecca scrubbed her cheeks dry and again sat down across from Kate. "What's frightening you?"

"My future." Kate ran her fingers through her hair, and Rebecca felt encouraged by the little mini-spikes that sprang up. "I very much want my old life as a finance guru back. To feel fully alive again."

"Here, eat. Doctor's orders. You'll feel stronger."

The artistic way Harry had arranged the cold shrimp—drizzled with a thin cocktail sauce—cold asparagus, and perfectly prepared beef tenderloin covered lightly in béarnaise on the plate looked too tempting to resist.

When Kate picked up the first shrimp, Rebecca met Harry's triumphant eyes.

"Thank you, Harry. I am starving." Kate's face looked less strained by the time she finished the beef tenderloin. She laid down her fork and looked up at them. "Do you know how old I am?"

"No. But if you let me do Botox on your forehead and around your eyes, I'll take off ten years."

Harry's declaration brought a smile to Kate's thin lips. "I am fifty-one years old. Some segments of society might think I'm a failure because I never married or had children. I never saw it that way. I fully enjoyed my life and my career." The fresh fierceness in Kate's voice gave Rebecca hope.

"You can again." Rebecca leaned across the table, desperate to convince her. "You have this second chance to be right back at the top of your game."

"Rebecca, don't you see? That's the crux of my fear." She stared Rebecca in the eyes like she had in the cab months ago, when she'd warned her about the danger of challenging David. "I'm not brave like you. I'm afraid to fail again. There won't be another chance for me if I can't take the pressure and I break down."

"Your depression has already been well treated with meds. Recurrences can be prevented for extremely long periods of time."

Harry sounded so sure of himself, Rebecca felt reassured herself and nodded enthusiastically. "Think of all the new, exciting opportunities right around the corner for you. Right, Harry?"

"Kate, I personally feel you are one of the most intelligent people I know. Your television show will be a tremendous success. And if you're as smart as I think, you will bring the two of us on as guests." He lifted his chin in a movie star pose. "I, as the plastic surgeon chef extraordinaire. Rebecca doing what she does best. Being bright and lovely and charming us all with the latest gossip about the rich and famous."

"Thank you, darling." Rebecca blew him a kiss.

Kate sat up straighter. "That's not a bad idea to do more than a strictly finance format."

Taking her cue from Harry, Rebecca helped Kate brainstorm her new show, warming to the idea. "I told you, you're the baby boomers' finance guru! Why not open their minds to all the possibilities still in life? Second. Third. Fourth chances. How to make the most out of all of them. Finance. Cooking. Personal advice."

I said advice. Not gossip. Struck numb by her epiphany, Rebecca sat utterly still, not hearing what her friends were saying to each other.

Clearly, somewhere back in her subconscious the idea had been fermenting, and it had finally spewed out. If David liked the format they'd come up with for Kate, and if Rebecca was ever Kate's guest, she wouldn't want to promote gossip. It would be to promote a column like . . . "Ask Becky." Or, now that she was more mature, "Ask Rebecca."

"Sweet pea, did you hear me?"

She blinked up at him. "Sorry, what did you say?"

"We need to let David know Kate is fine and will be in the office tomorrow to discuss all her options."

"Of course, I'll tell him." She sensed something magical would happen. It always did with David now. "I'm meeting with him in an hour."

❧

While David waited for Shannon to appear for their meeting, he stared out his office window, watching sunlight wash over Lake Michigan. He always thought of Rebecca as sunshine. Bringing him back to life.

Again he glanced at his watch. Only an hour until

he saw her. There was an aching throb in his head. A part of him still held back. Afraid to take the final leap. Afraid to believe such happiness was within his grasp again.

He shouldn't have written the note setting up their five-o'clock meeting. He should be putting some distance between them. Protecting himself from the emotions whipping through him whenever he thought of her.

Shannon knocked at the open door before walking in.

Glad for the diversion, he glanced around and noticed she looked especially pale and tense.

He sat down behind his desk, consciously trying to appear relaxed in an effort to make her feel at ease.

"Is something wrong, Shannon?" he asked quietly.

"I'm concerned about my job." She looked away, avoiding David's steady gaze.

He tensed in his chair and leaned forward, his arms on the desk. "What makes you concerned about your job?"

"Because of what Rebecca told me . . ." Shannon broke off. Her voice sounded shaky, and tears filled her eyes. "No, that's not fair," she whispered. "In a . . . discussion Rebecca and I had, she said she would be doing TV and print because she'd earned it." She cleared her throat. "I mean, Rebecca is an experienced journalist, and everyone in the office knows how badly she wanted her column back. Since the two of you have become close, I thought perhaps she'd convinced you to change your mind and give it back to her." She shook her head. "No, wait. I honestly didn't mean to imply that you'd give it back just because you're personally involved, but because . . ." She broke off again, to bite nervously at her lower lip.

David sat so still he might have turned to stone. His

mind raced back to the day Joe had told him about the betting pool, and how he'd rejected the whole idea of Rebecca betraying him. Now here it was back again, filling his world. Flooding him with pain.

Christ, he couldn't believe it. How could she be so cold and calculating and him not see it?

The part of him that had held back out of self-preservation believed it could be true.

Pain was displaced by anger of such icy ferocity it propelled him to his feet. "My relationship with any member of this staff is not a subject for discussion in the office, Shannon."

"David, I'm sorry." Tears streaming down her face, Shannon shook her head. "Everyone can see how happy Rebecca has been lately, and she talks about it with Pauline all the time. I thought it could be because she'd succeeded in getting her column back." Shannon took a deep, ragged breath. "I need to know if I still have a job. I don't want to cause any trouble."

"I'm sure you don't," David said with heavy sarcasm. "Don't worry. Your job is safe."

Shannon covered her mouth and sobbed. "No, I mean it, David. I don't want you to misunderstand. I really don't want to cause Rebecca more problems."

He held up his hand, not wanting to hear any more. "Keep your emotions out of the office, Shannon. And take the rest of the day off."

He watched Shannon flee the room before he stood and walked to the window. He pressed his aching head against it and closed his eyes, thinking of Rebecca.

The feeling of his body being bludgeoned slowly drained away, leaving him cold. Somewhere in the recesses of his mind he knew what he was about to do was wrong. But there was no other way out of this pain and confusion.

❧

When Rebecca ran into the *Daily Mail* lobby half an hour late, Pauline stood beside a red-faced, weeping Shannon.

Pauline shrugged her shoulders and looked bewildered.

"Shannon, what's wrong?" Rebecca asked quietly. Her instincts to help moved her closer.

"I think David misunderstood. All I wanted was for this to be finished," Shannon sobbed. "I honestly didn't mean it the way it came out. I just wanted to know if I still had my job. Not to hurt you any more."

Shannon thrust the framed poster of the Chicago skyline that had hung in her office into Rebecca's hands. "I understand it never belonged to me. I don't know what else to do. I'm sorry for everything." Covering her quivering lips with one palm, Shannon bolted out the door.

"Did that make any sense to you?" Pauline asked, shaking her head.

Rebecca nodded. "A little. I think Shannon is moving on personally."

"But what was she talking about with David? He has been in a terrible mood since his meeting with Shannon."

"Don't worry, sweetheart. Everything is fine." Once she might have worried about David's bad mood, but now she knew she had the power to change it.

But the instant Rebecca walked into David's office, the buoyant, enthusiastic feeling of being on a new, exciting path crashed and burned.

"Hello, Rebecca." He stood when she came in, like

he always did. And like he always did, his face and eyes changed when he saw her. But today was different.

The light didn't come on inside him. Instead, his eyes were cold as he stood, hands rammed into his trouser pockets, and stared at her.

Fear clasped its icy hand around her heart, but then reason took hold.

This is a business meeting.

Of course, that was the reason the usual sexual tension wasn't crackling in the air between them.

She told herself not to worry. Even though all the other executive offices were dark and empty, she pretended to be discreet and sat in the chair on the other side of his huge desk, instead of *on* the desk as he'd once teased. Or on his lap or in his arms, where she wanted to be.

Her mouth curled thinking of the incongruity of this stiff formality when a few days ago they were passionately involved in acts she *knew* must be illegal in several states.

"I tried to reach you earlier today, Rebecca."

Why was he looking at her in such a strange, remote way? Was this the business glare he'd perfected to intimidate and conquer the competition? She wasn't sure she approved.

"Are you upset about something?" Throwing discretion away, she stood and moved around the massive desk to his side.

"It's been a . . . challenging day." He looked up at her, his eyes searching her face, like he was looking for something he'd lost. "Perhaps we should go somewhere else to talk." He swiveled the heavy stuffed black leather chair to the other side and sprang up.

Watching him move quickly to the small built-in bar,

she was struck by the same sort of panic she'd felt earlier when she couldn't reach Kate.

David wasn't *accessible.* For some reason he'd distanced himself, closed her out, and she didn't like it one bit.

"I was visiting Kate," she called out to him in the hope of lightening his mood.

He turned, a martini glass in his hand. "How is she feeling?"

"Great! Actually we were busy . . . brainstorming her new show when you couldn't reach me. She'll be back in tomorrow to talk with you about it."

"Good. I'm glad she's feeling better." He took a long drink and rolled his shoulders like he was tense and trying to unwind.

Maybe he was just tired. He looked tired. He looked like he had the weight of the world on those broad, wonderful shoulders. She could help him.

Smiling, she walked slowly toward him, trying to be provocative, trying to charm him into a good mood. "I think you'll be very happy with Kate's ideas for the new show."

"What kind of ideas?" he asked, the same watchful look in his eyes.

Excited for Kate and hoping it would take the edge off whatever bad news was wearing him down, she decided to tell him.

"Kate has come up with a brilliant new format. She wants to combine finance with cooking and . . . a personal advice segment." She'd hesitated before adding the last, because she wasn't ready to share her new career path with him. She didn't quite believe it herself, and he was acting so . . . removed.

He ran his fingers through his hair. "What? No Chicago society gossip? No place for you?"

He'll love the idea of "Ask Becky" giving advice. I will tell him. "As a matter of fact, Kate does think there might be a place for me." She smiled and swayed closer, to put her palms on his hard, warm chest.

He took one step back and turned to set his glass carefully on the bar. The separation might be mere inches, but it was more like Lake Michigan lay between them.

Rebecca wished she could disappear right out of this room. Be back at Kate's still believing the magic of Rebecca and David was in the air. She stared at him, needing to understand. A hot wave of fear hit her. "What has changed? Please tell me. I can fix it."

David crossed his arms over his chest, his eyes heavy and watchful. "When I had my meeting with Shannon she told me about your . . . discussion in her office. You telling her that you would be getting your column and a television show out of me because you'd earned it." He shrugged and then threw the dregs of his martini down his throat. "The implications are clear. I didn't appreciate the unprofessional way she sobbed out the story, and I told her she'd have to make some changes. But that doesn't change the facts. Evidently, it's common knowledge you'd do anything to get your gossip column back."

His words stunned her. Little tremors of fear rolled up from her core while she struggled to find the right words. Shannon had tried to warn her, but she'd been so sure of herself she'd not paid attention. "Shannon is very upset over a personal matter between us that has nothing to do with you. It's all tied up in her feelings for George and her belief that I stole him away from her. It has nothing to do with us. You misunderstood her."

He dropped his arms to his sides, looking so vulnerable she ached for him. "I'd like to believe that this is nothing more than my overreacting to her hysterics. But here you are with an idea for programming that somehow includes you. How can I believe what we're sharing had nothing to do with business?"

"My choice to become lovers with you was a personal decision," she said softly, closing the space between them. "Not a business one. Remember, you taught me separating one from the other is possible."

His eyes lightened, and his lips began to curl in his irresistible dimpled smile.

It's all right. I've fixed it.

"So you never bragged to anyone that you'd charm me into giving you back your job?"

She heard herself declaring to both Harry and Kate that she'd do anything to get back her column. She wanted, *needed,* to be honest with him.

"I can't . . . *exactly* . . . say that I *never* planned to try to convince you to give back my job." She could hear nervousness in her voice, feel her face flush, and it scared her.

His lips curled into the cold, steely-eyed smile of the David Sumner who had taken away her job that first day. "Christ, Rebecca, I'm sorry you felt like you had to sleep with me in the hopes of getting your job back. Although it was my pleasure. Can we consider a role on the new show payment in full for . . . services rendered?"

Images flashed in front of her. Her heart breaking as her parents drove away again and again, leaving her with Granny. Her pride shattering when she caught her husband betraying her in their marriage bed. Each time she'd done nothing. Felt powerless. She'd shut down her anger and the soul-searing pain, hiding it from the world.

This time the pain was too much. Her self-control dissolved into rage, giving power to the upward swipe of her hand.

The contact of her flat palm against his cheek rippled through her arm. "How dare you say such a thing to me!"

His derisive laughter threw her off guard. She stepped back, but he jerked her to his chest.

"Now that we're both on the same page, Rebecca, we can still enjoy each other." His mouth swept down in a hot open kiss that made her dizzy and sick. There was nothing in this kiss of the David she loved.

She pushed hard against his chest until he let her go. She stumbled back, the hard knot of pain in her throat strangling her. "You bastard!" Her voice quivered. "You finally get your wish. I quit!"

Chapter 22

Rebecca stood on the sidewalk outside the Daily Mail building, looking blindly up and down Michigan Avenue. She couldn't remember how she got out here.

Shooting her curious looks, Christmas shoppers and tourists walked around her. She blinked several times, her eye sockets drained of all tears. The millions of twinkling lights strung along the Magnificent Mile were hurting her eyes. The cold late-November night air stung her wet, raw cheeks and the still-burning palm of the hand she'd used to slap David. It told her she was still alive.

I jumped, and it killed me.

Killed the secret little hope buried deep inside her that with him she could *have it all.* She'd clung to that fantasy about true love, hiding it under layers and layers of sophistication and witty cynicism for years. Now it was gone.

She felt hollow without it. Cold, like the part of her that fueled her to work harder, play harder, and be bigger than life had been partly extinguished.

Like a zombie, she turned to walk north on Michigan Avenue, to her condo. She knew people didn't really die of broken hearts. She wouldn't dissolve into a pool of despair in front of Neiman Marcus or Water Tower Place. Only in period movies did heroines succumb to such drama.

She remembered writing about a beautiful socialite who threatened to starve herself to death when her husband left her for an emaciated model. But it wasn't long before she fell in love with her divorce lawyer, who was richer and more handsome than her ex. Now she was a pleasantly trim suburbanite in Winnetka.

I'm already spinning the truth. Already hiding from it. Hiding from myself like always.

A dark, ugly robe of pain wrapped around her chest, tightening.

How could David walk away so easily? How could he have believed, *said,* such horrible things?

Because I'm so eminently leaveable, like I've always been.

How could he have fooled her so completely? My God, she was a mature, successful, worldly woman!

She'd wanted to believe the fairy tale could come true. David had touched her in such a way that she yearned to open her heart to him and share a life together.

Four blocks from her condo it started to snow big, wet flakes that wrecked her hair and soaked through her coat. She thought of hailing a cab but kept walking. The cold, wet, blowing snow seemed like the icing on the cake of her misery.

Just inside her condo door she shrugged out of the soaking-wet cashmere and let it fall, damp and heavy, onto the floor. In the bedroom she kicked off her heels and threw her tote onto the bed. She lay down next to it. On her side, the way she always slept, her cheek rested on the silk pillowcase. Quickly, it grew damp from her hair and her tears.

I will not cry anymore. A sob burst out like it had been heaved up by emotion so strong even her iron will couldn't stop it.

I'll let myself cry for five minutes. She curled into a fetal position, rocking back and forth with the power of her painful sobs. It wasn't just her heart breaking, it was her body ripping in two parts.

How had it all gone so wrong when it had seemed so perfect? Only hours ago she'd marveled at how she'd ever lived without David, without the emotional explosion love brings, lighting up her life like fireworks on the Fourth of July. It was worse now because she'd had it for an instant and knew what she was missing from her life.

Exhausted, sucking in a hiccupping breath to try to stop her fading sobs, Rebecca turned onto her back to stare up at the ceiling, her eyes tired and burning.

She knew she could never go back to the *Daily Mail*. That was finished. A part of her life she must cut away. Like David had cut her off. *Why?* She hadn't seen it coming. Could it have anything to do with his promise? Did she underestimate the depth of his commitment to that promise? Had he been looking for an excuse to break it off with her because the force of his feelings frightened him, like they once had Rebecca?

Or am I spinning the truth again to make it less painful?

Her eyes open, she faced the truth. She was alone again. But this time she felt so desolate, she couldn't move or think beyond the pain. Life had taught her not to wallow in self-pity but to take action.

I have to do it again.

She forced herself up off the bed to stand in front of the mirror and stared into her pain-ravaged face. She knew she'd been a fool to risk this heartbreak, but it was too late now.

She pressed her palms into her eyes, blotting out the world and wiping away her tears.

With a ragged sigh, she dropped her hands and looked in the mirror to see the slight difference in her eyes. She was ready to do what had to be done.

Charlie's business card was tucked safely in the back of her small purple Symthson Panama diary. One glance at the clock confirmed it was past the dinner hour.

"Charlie Bartholomew here!"

A little frisson of shock ran through her at the sound of his voice. She couldn't believe she was making this call. Yet she knew it was the right thing to do. This must be the true definition of courage.

One part is the primal me howling in the wilderness. The other is the me that says get a grip on yourself and do something about it.

"Charlie, it's Rebecca Covington."

"What a nice surprise! I've been hopin' to hear from you before the end of the year."

Her time had been nearly up. "Here I am!" She forced a laugh, a half-baked one, but at least she wasn't crying. "I'd like to meet with you as soon as possible."

"Well, now, I've got a busy schedule tomorrow. Could we do breakfast? I have it served in my office every mornin' at eight a.m."

"I'll see you at eight. By the way, I like my eggs over medium."

His belly laugh sounded deeper than usual. "Always liked your spunk. Lookin' forward to seein' you tomorrow."

She slowly hung up, closed her eyes, and counted eight beats of her heart, relishing the feeling of coming back alive. That extra little spurt of energy she depended on to see her through flickered back to life.

The phone by her bed rang, and her heart seemed to skip a beat. *David?* Hope and dread made her hand shake as she answered. "Hello."

"Rebecca, I've been trying to track you down." Kate's worried voice cut through her like a knife. "Your cell phone is off. I was concerned when you didn't call about your meeting. Are you still with David?"

Rebecca willed herself to ignore the nearly overwhelming urge to wail out her pain. She couldn't burden Kate. Certainly not tonight. "No, I'm alone. I need to talk to you tomorrow. But I won't be at the office."

"Something's wrong. I can hear it in your voice. If David didn't like our ideas for the program, I'd prefer to hear it from you first tonight."

"No, it has nothing to do with you. I promise."

After a short silence, Kate sighed. "If you're not going to be at work tomorrow, then come to my place at twelve-thirty for lunch. Harry has arranged for a delivery, and I must be home to sign for it. Something about a holistic approach to my recovery."

"That's my darling Harry. I'll see you then."

It felt good to have a plan. Some reason to get up and face the lonely day. She'd call Harry next. Then Pauline. By noon tomorrow, everything would be in place for her to start fixing herself.

The next morning, Rebecca took a last look at herself in the foyer mirrors. She'd learned about survival over the years. Brick by painful brick, she'd walled in her feelings for David. Only when she was stronger and could bear examining her feelings would she risk little by little taking the wall down.

It had been a lot easier to fix her red, swollen eyes with hourly applications of soothing masks. To be absolutely, positively sure she could pull off this meeting with Charlie, she put on what she fondly called her "drop-dead gorgeous suit." The red Valentino suit people were so busy admiring that they didn't notice if she looked a bit haggard around the edges.

Twenty minutes later, with her leather portfolio of "Ask Becky" columns under her arm, she strolled confidently into the Chicago Journal and Courier building. It was a Gothic structure, older than the Daily Mail building. The heavy wood moldings and fine glass fixtures in the lobby harkened back to the days Colonel McCormick ruled his newspaper empire.

The security guard checked her name and showed her the private elevator to the executive offices. There the doors slid open to a walnut-paneled foyer with a thick, rich ruby-colored carpet.

There was such an air of quiet elegance she felt she should whisper to the older, austere-looking receptionist who was looking sternly up at her.

"I'm Rebecca Covington. Mr. Bartholomew is expecting me."

"Beautiful suit," the woman said coolly. She stood and, with a glance that indicated Rebecca should follow her, walked down a short hallway. She had the best posture Rebecca had ever seen.

At the end of the hall, the woman rapped once on

thick double doors topped by a magnificent carved lintel. Without waiting, she opened one side for Rebecca to walk through.

In front of large windows with a view of Lake Michigan and the Chicago River, Charlie Bartholomew sat behind an antique desk of mammoth proportions. Everything about the room was scaled to match. Bookcases lined two walls, and a built-in bar ran the length of another. In front of the second set of windows, a small round table was set with china and crystal for breakfast.

She saw all this in the minute it took Charlie to get up from behind his desk and meet her in the center of the room.

"Beautiful suit, Rebecca. Martha would love it. Yes, indeed, she would."

"Beautiful office!" Rebecca said. "Quite frankly, I've never seen anything like it."

He looked around, a proud smile splitting his round, ruddy face. "I spend most of my days here. Needs to feel like home. I told you, we're family here at the *Courier*. Are you hungry?"

"Starving," she lied. Her nerves were strangling her at the magnitude of what she was about to do.

She sat down at the table, placed the portfolio on the floor beside her, and gripped her fingers tightly together on her lap to hold herself together.

Two waiters walked in carrying plates covered with silver domes. One was set in front of her. She looked up and smiled. "Thank you."

With a timed flourish, the waiters lifted the domes.

Feeling slightly queasy, she gazed down at two over-medium eggs, asparagus spears, half a grilled tomato sprinkled with Parmesan, and breakfast potatoes.

"Hope you enjoy your breakfast, Rebecca. To me it's the most important meal of the day." Charlie tucked the huge white linen napkin under his chin and spread it across his heavily starched shirt and conservative striped tie.

Since she started writing about food, she'd spent more time than ever in her life eating, buying, and thinking about food. Now she had to wait in agony over her professional life while Charlie ate his breakfast with gusto and she picked at hers.

Her heart was already broken. She honestly didn't know if she could stand up under another nearly lethal blow should Charlie withdraw his offer.

"What do you have in your portfolio, Rebecca?"

She nearly fell off her chair in shock at Charlie's abrupt switch to business. She was still pretending to enjoy her asparagus.

He pressed his napkin to his lips, his white beard still pristine, while she fumbled for her portfolio.

This is it. Do or die.

She handed the scrapbook across the table. "Here are copies of an advice column called 'Ask Becky' I did for my college newspaper. If I join the *Courier* family, I won't be bringing 'Rebecca Covington's World.' I want to do four advice columns a week. There's been a void since Ann Landers passed away. I believe I can fill that niche."

Charlie looked at her long and hard and then opened the portfolio.

Since she had nothing to lose, she felt oddly reckless. "I think the columns have a certain grit and spunk to them. Isn't that how you've described me the last few times we talked?"

Not looking up, he nodded. She couldn't see his eyes, so couldn't gauge his reaction as he shuffled the pages, reading.

Stress. I need to feed it. She took another bite of cold asparagus.

He glanced up, and she dropped her fork. It clattered on the edge of the plate and landed in her congealing eggs.

All traces of the good ol' boy persona wiped away, he looked her steadily in the eyes. "These advice columns would need to reflect your unique style."

"Of course." She was trembling with excitement. "It will be me imparting my worldly wisdom with humor. My Rebecca Covington philosophy that we're all on this journey together. We need to deal with one another with as much grace, humor, and compassion as we can muster."

"Five days a week."

She'd planned for five but hesitated for effect before nodding.

"Sunday you'll do a big gossip page like 'Suzy' in *W*, or 'Page Six.'"

She could taste victory. "More like 'Suzy' than 'Page Six.' I want to give good press to the movers and shakers who are making the arts and charities work in Chicago. I'll need at least two pages of colored photos. Readers like to see their pictures in the paper. They clip them. Send them to family and friends. Often they need to buy extra copies of the paper. Advertisers like that."

"We need to agree on the television segments. It has to be both gossip and advice."

"Of course. Advice and gossip. Plus guests. I have some ideas that will put *Oprah* on alert."

He rubbed his hands together. "Should those fine gals on *The View* be worried?"

"You never know." She met him eyeball to eyeball, exhilaration coursing through her veins. "Do we have a deal?"

"Three-year contract. I'll match your salary from the *Daily Mail*. Plus a ten percent signing bonus."

I need to show some grit. "Six years. My present salary. Plus fifty percent more for the television spots and the Sunday feature. Twenty percent signing bonus."

He lifted his bushy white eyebrows and crossed his arms across his barrel chest. "You put a mighty high price tag on yourself, Rebecca."

He wants spunky, I'll give him spunky. "We both know I'm worth it, Charlie."

His belly laugh echoed off the thick crown moldings of the high ceiling as he spread out his arms. "Welcome to the family, Rebecca."

After three hours filled with a tour of the newspaper, seeing her new truly spectacular office, and talking to Martha, who was ecstatic at the news, Rebecca finally arrived at Kate's. She still hadn't decided how to tell her friends.

They were all sitting in the dining room, laughing and playing poker. Most of the chips were in front of Pauline.

Pauline looked up and smiled. "Beginner's luck. Kate is teaching us how to play."

Rebecca gazed around, noticing the town house felt warmer and looked more inviting. Green plants, a ficus tree, and several large poinsettias were now placed artfully in all the rooms she could see. In the long hallway, two electricians were working on new larger light fixtures.

"The place looks great." She slid into the empty chair at the table.

Kate nodded. "Harry believes I need to add brighter lights and vegetation into my environment. It's a holistic approach to dealing with my condition. I rather like the greenery."

They were all studying Rebecca, which made her try harder to be *upbeat*. "Love it!" She smiled around the table.

"You look feverish, sweet pea." Harry reached across the table, and before she could stop him, he was feeling her pulse. "Racing."

"Oh, I knew you called this meeting to tell us the good news! You and Mr. Sumner are getting married! Right?"

Pauline's enthusiastic outburst kicked in Rebecca's protective wall with one shout of joy. All the primal feelings rushed out to swallow her.

How will I ever get through this? The ache of loss again scalded her throat. "No . . ." she squeezed the word through the burn. "We . . . we . . . actually . . . it's over." She rushed the last words out while she could.

Thank God, no one spoke. Before she lost control and starting wailing again, she needed to tell them. "I've left the paper. I'm moving to the *Journal and Courier*." She stared into Kate's shocked face. "I feel like the worst friend in the world leaving you right now, but I desperately need you to understand. This is a tremendous opportunity for me. I know the timing is appalling. Please forgive me."

Her mouth firm and hard, Kate shook her head. "I can't tell you this isn't a blow."

Harry lowered his eyebrows, watching her. And Pauline's lip began to quiver.

Wanting them all to understand, she stared pleadingly into each of their faces. "I'd like you all to understand that this change is good for me." She smiled hopefully around the table. "I may not be at the paper, but I'll still be here for you, even when you don't need or want it. Kate, you should have celebrity chefs do the food columns, starting with Harry. He's a great cook. Plus he has a huge fan base."

Tears of relief pooled at the back of her throat when Harry's frown curved into a cocky smile worthy of his hero, Rupert Everett.

"It's true, I have freshened the faces of much of Chicago."

Rebecca turned to Pauline. "Sweetheart, I'm not deserting you. We can do secret dinners where you can tell me what the competition is doing."

"Mr. Porter will die when he finds out Mr. Bartholomew stole you away. So will Maybella and Shannon." At that, a smile brightened Pauline's face. "The place will go to Hades without you. We'll miss you so much, won't we, Kate?"

Knowing she was burdening Kate when she was so vulnerable made Rebecca feel small. She wished there had been another way out.

"Don't look like you failed, Rebecca," Kate said briskly. "You've seized your personal power. As I must retrieve mine. I have your Christmas recipe scheduled for next Sunday's edition. I'm still running it. Moving forward, I believe I will take your excellent advice and use celebrity food columnists. Harry, are you interested?"

He bowed his head. "It will be my pleasure. I can't

imagine why you'd ever want another celebrity besides me."

Their laughter broke something free inside Rebecca. Their worlds were spinning in new, exciting ways. New challenges. New choices. Fresh beginnings. Good at any age.

"Sweet pea, now tell us what happened with David?" Harry asked in his kindest voice.

She didn't want to think about David. She wanted to think about her new job. Moving into her new office. Christmas shopping. Anything and everything except David.

"I really, truly don't want to talk about him," she said at last.

They looked at her with such compassion she was afraid in another few minutes she'd start crying on *all* their shoulders.

"I *will* say I'm now ready to embrace a *real* relationship if I get the chance. Even though David isn't 'the one' for me, he did open my heart to the possibility there may be someone out there. I realize my chances of this happening at forty-five are slim, but you never know." She shrugged, struggling before their pointed silence. "Of course we all know there's not just *one* person for anyone. I'm talking about someone I connect with. Not someone I think might complete me. Because God knows I have to be a whole person to even know how to really love. But someone who complements me. Together we're more powerful, more alive than apart." Realizing she was babbling, she shut her mouth.

"Are you sure Mr. Sumner isn't 'the one'?" Pauline asked softly.

Desperate not to answer so she wouldn't be forced to lie, Rebecca looked wildly to Harry for support.

"I wonder the same thing, sweet pea."

Kate nodded. "I must agree with them, Rebecca. What I observed between you and David seemed real."

Looking into their determined faces, she knew the time for hiding was done. Only the truth would end this. "All right! The truth. I love you all to death and know you love me. But David doesn't. Told me so in his own inimitable way. End of story. Satisfied?"

It was strangely comforting in her fragile state to see the disbelief on their faces. She'd felt the same way last night.

But they were all wrong.

CHICAGO DAILY MAIL
SUNDAY FOOD

GROT
(A FAMILY HOLIDAY TRADITION)

1 quart whole milk
½ cup long-grain rice
Salt to taste

In a double boiler, add milk and rice. Keep on low heat and cover. Stir occasionally and add more milk when necessary. Heat must be kept very low so it does not burn at bottom. Cook for about 3 hours so that rice is very tender. Add salt to taste. Serve with cinnamon and sugar and cream. Serves 8.

A Note from Rebecca Covington

This incredibly rich, sinfully delicious rice dessert was served every December 24 at my grandmother's house, when the entire family of cousins, aunts, and uncles, plus friends, was present.

A faux gold ring was placed in one bowl. The lucky recipient was destined to be the next bride or groom in the coming year.

My cousin Brandon was so enchanted with the legend that he arranged to place the diamond engagement ring for his beloved in her bowl.

Unfortunately, she swallowed the small gem with her first spoonful of grot.

Never fear, all ended happily with a beautiful wedding. Although the ring had to be retrieved in a way that does not bear mentioning.

May your holidays be as happy.

Enjoy!

Xo Rebecca

Chapter 23

The next day, Rebecca sent her letter of resignation to the newspaper by courier.

Later in the afternoon she received back all her personal belongings from the office and a formal severance letter signed by David. The letter and the mementoes represented the end of another life stage. Should she label the last fifteen years at the *Daily Mail* the "maturing stage"? Getting her to the point she wasn't afraid to take a chance on a new life?

She looked down at David's small, neat handwriting and remembered the last memo from him.

She cried for ten minutes.

Her mood had been shifting back and forth since the lunch at Kate's. One minute she felt happy with her choices. The next moment guilty and scared. Then the next, eager to start her new job on January 1. New year. New life.

Now, as she looked down at David's signature, the bright future dissolved into a barren stretch of meaningless days for the rest of her life.

She felt hot. Cold. Happy. Sad. Who would have thought a broken heart would have the same symptoms as a midlife crisis and perimenopause?

She was saved from utter misery by the rapidly approaching Christmas holidays. She indulged in an orgy of shopping every day for everyone she knew. Butcher, baker, gourmet food maker, all benefited from her burning need to stay super busy so she wouldn't have time to think. Every night she arrived home laden with packages to fall exhausted into bed.

Three days before the Chicago Media annual black-tie holiday dinner, she treated herself to a long strapless gold silk beaded gown she'd admired in the window at Luca Luca, thus keeping her promise given so long ago to Simone, the manager, that they could dress her for her television show. That day on Oak Street, she'd been spinning stories to save face. Now it had come true. This media party was to be her *unofficial* launch as "Ask Rebecca" and Sunday's "Talk of the Town" for the *Journal and Courier* and the television segments. She wanted to dazzle. She *needed* to dazzle to keep her courage up. After all, David was invited to the party.

For the last few weeks she'd lived in constant anticipation of running into him. In some ways, Chicago was a small town at heart. Often the same people went to the same places at the same time.

Whenever the phone rang, she felt a rush of fearful excitement. Was it David? If he called, would she answer?

But his call never came.

❧

At the end of every day while David pored over balance sheets, stock reports, and legal documents, he was wracked by such a need to hear Rebecca's voice he had to get up and pace the room to keep from picking up the phone. His mind froze in panic. How could he hang on to his protective armor when he searched for her face everywhere he went?

Then the need would pass and he'd go back to work with speed and diligence, using it like he always had to cover his pain.

Tonight, staring at himself in the mirror, fumbling, trying to adjust his tux tie, the pain was razor sharp again.

For weeks he'd beaten himself up with the knowledge that there was no future for them. But tonight was the true test.

Tonight, he'd see her.

It scared the hell out of him.

❦

The night of the media party she had her glossy and elegant look down pat, her cool and in-control attitude in place.

The Ritz Carlton at the holidays shone like a gaily trimmed Christmas tree. Lights. Flowers. An array of beautifully wrapped partygoers.

The split-level ballroom was one of the smaller ones in the pecking order of hotels vying for social events, making it perfect for this more intimate party. There couldn't have been more than a hundred people drinking and talking and milling around when she walked in.

As she stood on the wide upper level, Rebecca's gaze immediately found David, dressed in a tux and standing across the floor in front of the orchestra. She looked away, feeling dizzy, terrified, excited, confused, and guilty all at the same time.

She sneaked another peek at David's face. At some

point in her life she would have to apologize for slapping him, but she didn't have the strength to do it now.

Watching David talking and laughing, she was reminded of every kiss those smooth lips had given her.

I'm not sure I can do this tonight. She turned to walk out and get some fresh air or hide in the ladies' lounge for a while.

In her rush to leave, she nearly stepped on the hem of Martha Bartholomew's purple gown. She and Charlie were blocking Rebecca's escape.

"You look lovely, Rebecca. Doesn't she, Charlie?" Martha gushed.

The red plaid vest barely containing Charlie's stomach shook with his chuckle. "As befittin' our new star. Everyone here tonight already knows our news. Big things start happenin' tonight for you, Rebecca."

Charlie, who was known to never look away from the person he had engaged in conversation, shifted his eyes to a point over Rebecca's shoulder. "David, my boy, how are you?"

They were standing in the middle of the landing, so there was no way for David to pass them unnoticed or ignore Charlie's greeting.

Rebecca's knees began to shake under her gown. She pressed her thighs together to keep her body still. She struggled to appear cool and confident. With a last hope she could get through this with her pride intact, she turned to him.

"Good evening, Charlie. Martha." David's voice was as formal as his expression. He glanced briefly at her. "Rebecca."

"Hello, David," she said softly. She was holding herself together so tightly she trembled from the effort.

Could he tell?

Martha's sharp, small eyes darted from her to David.

Charlie clasped David's shoulder. "No hard feelings that I snatched Rebecca away, is there, my boy? You understand good business."

Through narrowed eyes, David finally looked fully at her, his face still expressionless. "I found Rebecca to be all about business."

"Yes, indeed. She's quite the businesswoman. Don't mind tellin' you, now. She kept me danglin' for months." Charlie sounded pained but looked extremely pleased with himself. "Thought I'd lost out. I offered her the moon! Her own column and television show. But she turned it all down out of loyalty to you and the paper. Made me more eager than ever to have her join us."

"Interesting." David's eyes widened and became strangely watchful. "So, Charlie, how long ago did you start trying to steal my staff?"

Rebecca felt like a specimen they were discussing. Like a social butterfly. Pinned through the heart.

"You remember, my boy. The night of the Culinary Cook-off I warned you I was mighty impressed with Rebecca. I contacted her shortly afterward."

The change that came over David's face made it hard for her to breathe, and the sound around her faded into the distance. Like so many other times, she felt they were the only two people in the room.

I need to get out of here before I make a fool of myself. She hoped her smile didn't look as awkward and stiff as it felt. "Please excuse me. I see someone I must say hello to." Before anyone tried to stop her, she bolted toward the door.

~~❧~~

Her eyes flashing, Rebecca swung away. To David, she looked scared, and his chest tightened with tenderness.

He had been right to be afraid to see her. His mind reeled with reaction after weeks of fighting his feelings for her. Accepting that there was no future for them had been wrong. Just as he'd been wrong to push aside his emotions, pouring his energy into his work to keep from living his life to the fullest.

He'd made a terrible mistake that day in his office. He didn't need Charlie's confession to tell him he'd been a fool to doubt Rebecca. All his actions had been his last-ditch effort to protect himself. Seeing her again made it impossible to hide from the truth any longer. The last vestige of his armor fell away.

He might be a stupid, frightened fool who didn't deserve this beautiful, strong, courageous, loyal woman. But she was his, and he would fight to make her see it was true.

"Rebecca!"

He knew she heard, but she ignored him, walking quickly out into the small hallway. He could see the defiance in the way she thrust up her chin.

She dashed into the closest open door, and he followed. It was a small room with a bar for the overflow during cocktails.

"Rebecca!" At last he was able to touch her bare shoulder. She looked up, shock darkening her eyes. He knew he had this moment of grace, here in public, with half the media in Chicago watching.

"We need to talk." His fingers slid down to her arm, holding it gently, determined never to let her go. "We need to go somewhere private. I need to explain so much. I'm so sorry I hurt you. I—"

"Stop, David!" Rebecca demanded.

She looked vulnerable and hurt. David ached with love for her. He deserved whatever anger she threw at him. He'd take it. They had the rest of their lives to make up.

～✦～

She had to stop him before it was too late. His serious, sensual expression and his words sent such heat rising up from her tight chest she felt weak, light-headed, and breathless.

Escape was the cure. But first she needed to apologize, too, and then they would both have closure.

She thrust her chin higher in the air. "I want to apologize, too. For slapping you. My loss of control is inexcusable. If you'd struck me, I would have had you arrested."

A faint smile curled his mouth. "You don't pack much of a wallop. Your angle was too low—I barely felt it. Is it true you originally turned down Charlie out of loyalty to the paper and me? It's everything professionally I could offer you and more."

His abrupt change of subject threw her even further off balance.

She looked around to see if anyone was observing them standing too close, David's hand possessively on her arm. It gave her a few precious seconds to compose herself. "It's none of your business why I turned down Charlie." She tried to pull free, but he wouldn't let her.

Worse, he grabbed her other hand so he was holding both and staring intently down into her face.

She turned her head away, hoping it looked as if they were merely having a friendly conversation. "David, you're making a scene."

"I don't give a damn! And I don't give a damn about why you turned down Charlie. I was a fool to ever have doubted you." His wide, vulnerable sapphire gaze held her.

She refused to be taken in again. "Yes, you are a fool, David."

"I wanted to call you a hundred times, but my pride and fear wouldn't let me. You have to forgive me," he demanded.

"No, I don't! Now everything is fine because *Charlie told you so?* Why couldn't you believe me? Trust me? How could you have hurt me so much?" She looked away from the intensity of his eyes and straight at Charlie, who was staring curiously at them from the doorway. Beside him, Martha's rosebud mouth curved in an encouraging smile.

I must end this. "It's too late, David," she whispered.

"No. It's never too late for this." He swooped down and covered her mouth with his lips. Traitorous desire curved her body into his for what felt like minutes but was mere seconds.

She pulled away, taking one step back. She looked around at the people staring at them, including a shocked Charlie and a misty-eyed Martha. Rebecca shrugged, trying to give the best performance of her life. "Mistletoe! Everyone be careful where they stand!"

David didn't seem to notice the laughter surrounding them, or Martha and Charlie, watchful from across the room. His eyes kept searching her face. "You have to give me another chance to show you how I feel."

I can't. I can't take that leap again.

She shut her eyes tight to hold back the tears. She shut her eyes like she had as a child when her parents deserted her. As she'd done when Peter had betrayed her. When Tim fired her. Each time she hoped that when she opened her eyes the pain would be gone. As always, it was still with her.

The Ask Becky part of her wanted to believe anything was possible, but the Rebecca Covington sense of self-preservation was too strong.

"Why give you another chance, David? My granny always told me actions speak louder than words. If you *really* cared about me, you couldn't have said or even thought those horrible things. You couldn't have been so cold. So unfeeling. You couldn't have let me go."

He looked grim and determined, and his grip on her hands was numbing her fingers. "I'm not proud of my actions that night in my office. I was afraid to believe in you. In us. You need to understand how finding you has changed my life."

She was too terrified to believe him. It wasn't that she didn't still love him, but she had to protect herself.

"I meant it when I said it was too late. I'm forty-five years old, David. I finally know I can have it all. *I want it all.* I'm sorry, but I don't believe I can have it with you. It's better this way for both of us."

This time she was the one to walk away.

Chapter 24

The next morning, head aching and dry-mouthed from crying all night, Rebecca staggered to the door when someone seemed to be leaning on the buzzer. She squinted through the peephole and saw Malcolm's craggy face.

When she opened the door, he sighed. "There you are, miss. Phone must be out. Mr. Sumner is downstairs. Says he's been trying to reach you all night."

The heavy throb of despair in her chest rose to fill her throat. "I unhooked the phone," she whispered. "I need to rest. Thank you, Malcolm." She closed the door before he saw the tears soaking her hot cheeks.

She hadn't yet mastered her confident face for the world. She'd never felt so fragile, so torn between what she knew was the only path for survival and the ache at her core for David and everything she once believed they could share.

Two hours later, she wasn't any closer to putting on her fake face when there was a timid knock on the door.

Malcolm again. This time carrying a rosebush. "Mr. Sumner brought it for you."

David delivered the second one at two p.m. Malcolm brought up the third, a larger yellow rosebush, at five o'clock. Each rosebush had a small card with David's handwriting.

This rosebush is called Amore.

She turned her phone back on, sobbing each time it rang and the caller ID told her it was David.

On Monday, she wasn't surprised to find Harry on her doorstep, holding two rosebushes in his arms. "David is downstairs, leaving these for you."

"So far that makes eight! Since flowers helped win Jasmine over, obviously David thinks it will work with me. The masseur will probably be next."

"Do you need a massage?" Harry sounded amused.

Rebecca rolled her shoulders, trying to relieve some of the stress. She desperately wanted to talk to David, but the fear she might start believing him again kept her strong. "Yes! I'm getting a pain in my neck."

"Probably from dragging all those rosebushes around the house. Where's the rest of them?"

"I had them picked up and delivered to the nursing home at Irving Park and Lake Shore Drive."

"Lovely idea, sweet pea. But why don't you see David and tell him yourself to stop sending you rosebushes?"

She stuck up her chin. "Absolutely not!"

Harry sighed. "If you won't talk to him, then what do you suggest I tell him? He's asked me to intervene on his behalf."

She flicked a tear out of the corner of her eye. "Whose side are you on, Harry?"

"Yours, sweet pea. Always yours."

At nine a.m. Tuesday morning, Malcolm called from the lobby. "Mr. Sumner delivered another rosebush and brought Olga from Healing Fingers Spa to give you a massage."

She laughed despite her determination not to be swayed. "Please thank Olga and tell her I won't be needing any massages."

By Wednesday evening she had sent fifteen rosebushes to the nursing home but kept the fifteen cards in David's neat handwriting. She spread them across her kitchen counter and read them over and over.

Amore.

Funny how when something is repeated often enough, somehow it becomes tangible, almost rock solid. But if she'd learned nothing else in her life, she knew actions spoke louder than words. David had rejected her, and that was one action she could never forgive.

Thursday, Kate arrived with the morning's rosebush delivery. She thrust the small bush into Rebecca's hands.

"Why don't you talk to David and tell him to send these directly to the nursing home?"

Surprised, Rebecca blinked at her. "Not you, too?"

"Yes. You are contagious. I've come to mother you." Kate took off her heavy wool winter coat and hung it up in the foyer closet. "We need to talk."

Dreading listening to more attacks on her crumbling defenses against David, Rebecca tried to think of a new tack to take with her friends. "Would you like some tea? Coffee? Diet Coke? Champagne, maybe?" she asked hopefully.

"Sit down, Rebecca," Kate said sternly.

Resigned, Rebecca placed the small rosebush on the coffee table. The phone rang and, seeing it was Pauline, she picked it up. "Hi, sweetheart."

"Is Kate there yet?" Pauline asked.

"Yes, she's here." Rebecca glanced at Kate, who didn't look surprised. "Do you want to talk to her?"

"No. I want you to listen to her. Poor Mr. Sumner. Oh, he looks so . . . haggard. Really he does. He's getting white hair at his temples," she said, lowering her voice dramatically.

More amused than angry, Rebecca smiled. "No problem. He'll look even more dashing."

"Oh, Rebecca, it's Christmas! You always have such generosity of spirit. You should be . . . kind to Mr. Sumner. Promise me . . . you'll listen to Kate."

She could hear the worry in Pauline's voice, and old habits kicked in. "Of course I'll listen to Kate. I'll see you tomorrow at Harry's for Christmas Eve dinner."

Rebecca met Kate's determined gaze. "This is a conspiracy, right?"

"Yes. You've taught us well. The people who love you have joined together to help you. The way you have always done for us. However, we need more information, which I have come to retrieve. Now, I don't want you to try to charm me, or try to make me stop worrying like you did Pauline. I want you to tell me honestly why you won't give David another chance."

Rebecca dropped down on the coach. "I'm afraid," she said simply.

Kate nodded. "I see. Now let me give you some advice a very brave, wise woman once gave me. You have this second chance. There are new, exciting opportunities right around the corner for you."

Hearing her own words come back, Rebecca knew they weren't true for her. "A few months ago I wrote about the 'social brain.' How scientists are able to map the invisible connection when two people are attracted.

The brain releases dopamine, which delivers a dollop of real pleasure. I felt it the first time I saw David. Science has proven the opposite happens with rejection. His rejection that day I left the paper hurt the same as a blow. Not just emotionally." She placed her hands across her heart. "I felt honest-to-goodness physical pain. I felt the same pain with my parents. With Peter. But *never* with the same intensity as I felt with David."

"I understand pain, Rebecca. I experienced social and professional rejection after my breakdown. Because of you I've been able to face my fears of feeling that pain again. I've contacted my old publisher. I'm writing my book on women and finance," Kate stated abruptly. "I'm trying to seize back my power. So can you."

"I'm happy for you, Kate. And I understand what you're trying to tell me." A huge lump of regret filled her throat. "I just can't do it."

Kate stood up and pulled down on her dark green fitted jacket. She'd accessorized perfectly with a topaz brooch and earrings she'd bought at LuLu's. "I understand, Rebecca. Let me ask you one last question. After that, I promise I will never say another word about your choice. Do you love David?"

She'd known what was coming and had steeled herself. "Heaven help me. I do," she confessed. As much as she wanted to deny it, it was one lie she couldn't bring herself to tell.

Kate nodded. "That's all I wanted to know."

After Kate left, Rebecca shuffled through the sixteen cards from David.

Amore.

She so wanted to give him another chance. But want-

ing to and actually *seizing* the courage to jump again were
not the same thing.

Christmas Eve morning dawned with another rosebush. The delivery was followed by a call from the nursing home.

"David had every patient's room filled with flowers.
Plus the lobby. And the lounges. The director called to
tell me they can't accept any more rosebushes. There's
no space," Rebecca complained to Harry on the phone,
charmed despite her best intentions.

"You could call David and stop all this. If not, I plan to
call my broker and tell him to buy rosebush futures."

"Very funny!" she laughed, feeling almost happy for
some reason. "Wait! Let me get the door. It's my afternoon delivery."

Malcolm smiled at her over the top of a long, lush
arrangement of dusty antique pink roses with holly
branches.

"Mr. Sumner just delivered it. Different today, huh,
Miss Covington."

"Yes." She pulled out the tiny white card on the top.
These roses are called Kisses. Memories flooded over
her in a tidal wave of warmth. She leaned against the
door. "Malcolm, would you mind carrying the arrangement back downstairs for me? I'll be taking it with me
this evening."

"Sure thing."

"Wait!" From the pile of gifts lined up along her foyer
wall, she lifted off a long, narrow box wrapped in green
paper with a white card taped beneath the red ribbon.
"Here's your Christmas present. Can you carry it now?"

"Sure thing." He tucked it under his arm. "What time should I have the cab for you?"

"Five o'clock. Thanks!" Remembering Harry was waiting, she hurried back to the phone. "Have you got your centerpiece for the table yet?"

"I'm putting something together this afternoon."

"Forget it. I'm bringing an arrangement of dusty pink roses David just delivered. Forget about rosebush futures. Obviously, he's run out of them."

It took her two trips down in the elevator to carry out all her packages for Pauline and the girls. Next came Kate's and Harry's.

Malcolm helped her take everything to the cab. Around his neck, he'd wrapped the gray and black plaid cashmere scarf from Burberry. She'd bought it thinking it would keep him warm on jaunts out into the cold to help the residents of the condo building.

"This scarf is sure warm," he said, holding the cab door open for her. "Thanks, Miss Covington. And that nice check sure will help with our expenses."

"Happy holidays, Malcolm." She smiled and stepped into the waiting cab. It had Shannon's picture advertising "Shannon Shares with Her Friends" in the *Chicago Daily Mail* plastered across the back of the front seat. It was a terrible picture. Shannon really should have it redone.

"Didn't you used to be Rebecca Covington?" shouted the cabbie.

She met his dark eyes in the rearview mirror. "I still am Rebecca Covington. Next week you can read me in the *Chicago Journal and Courier*."

When she got out in front of Harry's brownstone, she

gave the cabbie such a huge tip, he helped her carry the flowers and all the presents up onto the porch.

Harry opened the door dressed in a white chef's hat and apron. "You look wonderful, sweet pea. Look, it's beginning to snow. A perfect Christmas Eve."

She turned her head and saw snowflakes swirling through the air. She smiled. "Love it. Here, see if this arrangement will work on your table."

They moved the gifts into the foyer before they walked into the dining room. The flowers fit perfectly between the Waterford crystal goblets and the gold-rimmed Tiffany china.

She stepped back to admire how beautiful it looked. "Wow! It's like it was made for this table setting."

"Imagine that. Now go into the living room and fuss with the presents and tree like you do every year."

"Can I help you in the kitchen?"

He hugged her. "You are the most divine woman on the planet. But the kitchen is not your milieu. In fact, no one must enter my domain today. Genius demands privacy."

The zeal in Harry's eyes was contagious. Well, he might be king of the kitchen, but she was the Christmas maven. Rebecca placed all the presents under the tree, rearranged some of his ornaments for maximum effect, and plugged in the lights. She could see the tree reflected in the window. With the background of falling snow, it reminded her of that old movie about miracles at Christmas.

Everyone else arrived together. While Kate hung up coats, Pauline put more presents under the tree. Patty and Polly, dressed in matching green velvet skirts and frilly white blouses, jumped up and down, trying to figure out which presents belonged to them.

"We're not opening presents until after dinner," Pauline reminded them for the fifth time.

"When are we going to eat?" Polly asked again for the sixth time.

"Dinner is served," Harry announced from the doorway. He'd removed his hat and apron. Impeccably dressed in sharply creased charcoal gray trousers and a gray cashmere sweater that hung perfectly on his broad shoulders, he ushered them all into the dining room.

"Sorry for that short cocktail hour. The little angels would have driven us mad," he whispered out of the side of his mouth.

This year, Harry sat at one end of the table and Kate at the other. Rebecca was on Harry's right. Pauline on his left. With the girls on either side of Kate. It was perfect. All of them together for the holidays.

The wild mushroom soup was already on the table. As soon as everyone finished, Harry whisked the bowls away and brought out frisée salad with Stilton and grapes. He passed around a basket of popovers.

"Boy, you're quick in that kitchen," Patty said, grabbing a popover.

Harry gave her a little smile. "I have little elves, like Santa's helpers, in the kitchen cooking for me."

"Really?" Polly eyed the closed kitchen door.

"No, girls, Dr. Grant is trying to be amusing." Kate shot him a look, and he sat down good-naturedly.

Through the contre filet in Perigourdine sauce, wild rice, and puree of broccoli, plus several refills of apple juice served in crystal flutes for the girls and champagne for everyone else, Harry remained true to his word and allowed no one near the kitchen.

When he came back into the dining room carrying a

tray with bowls of grot laced with cream and sprinkled with cinnamon, Rebecca groaned.

"Harry, it's too much."

"Nonsense. We're continuing the tradition your granny began. Whoever gets the ring will be the next to wed." He winked at Pauline.

Polly saw it and stuck her spoon in the grot. "I want the ring! I want the ring!" She scraped the spoon around in her bowl.

"Stop." Pauline took the spoon out of her hand. "Wait until everyone is served. You're too young to think about boys."

"Ugh, I hate boys!" Polly said in disgust. "I want the prize."

Something large came up in Rebecca's first spoonful of grot. A huge square-cut diamond ring winked at her through a thin layer of cream.

"Very funny, Harry." She wiped the stone clean with her napkin. "My God, it's gorgeous. At least five carats." As she slipped it on, she laughed up into his beaming face. "Where did you get it? A Cracker Jack box?"

"No. It came from Van Cleef and Arpels," David answered softly from the open kitchen door.

He didn't look the slightest bit haggard with his hair mussed up and his shirtsleeves rolled up to his elbows. His eyes, bright and clear, leveled on Rebecca's face. She felt a sense of inevitability, as if she'd expected, *wanted,* this moment someplace deep inside from the moment they met.

David watched his willing accomplices leave the room one by one.

A little weepy, Pauline hustled the girls out. He heard Polly ask, "Why is Aunt Becky so red and glowy?"

Kate touched Rebecca's shoulder. "You have a royal flush. I couldn't let you fold."

Harry lifted Rebecca's chin. "Be good to yourself, sweet pea. David is a whiz in the kitchen," he whispered, and kissed her cheek.

At last David was alone with her.

In three strides he reached her, pulled her chair away from the table, and dropped to his knees in front of her.

He looked up at her, holding nothing back, wanting her to see how much he needed and loved her. "I couldn't believe my good fortune. I fought against it. I kept thinking, this can't be happening. This can't be real. I looked for a reason not to be happy with you so I could keep my promise to myself. And Shannon allowed me to find one. I couldn't see how I could be true to both of us at the same time. Now I do."

He took her hands and kissed each palm. "Accepting I love you, I've surrendered to living life to the fullest, the way we all should. I'm luckier than I deserve to have had two great loves in my life. To have found you is the greatest gift of my life.

"Don't you think I'm afraid to jump, too? Please catch me." He gazed into her eyes and saw his life come full circle, back to happiness.

❧

She looked straight into his eyes, and her brain released so much dopamine she thought she'd die of the pleasure rush.

She closed her eyes and slid to the floor, pressing

her soft thighs to his harder ones, her breasts against his chest. She felt his arms encircle her, and she lifted hers around his neck. She opened her eyes and there was no pain. Only joy.

"We'll catch each other," she whispered.

"Always?" he said, his voice a little gruff around the edges from emotion.

"I promise." She smiled, so full of love she might burst, but she needed to tell him *everything*.

"Marry me," he demanded, pulling her closer.

She put her palms against his chest, holding him at bay a moment longer. "There is something you should know first. I'm marrying you, but I'm working for the *Journal and Courier*."

A mischievous grin curled his mouth. "A whole new twist on the legendary rivalry. This could be interesting."

"I'm betting on it. I'm planning for it to be *extremely* interesting. Especially for my readers." Slowly she outlined his lips with the tips of her fingers. "Still want to marry me? We'll be the talk of the town."

"The jet is fueled and ready to go. We can be married in Vegas tomorrow." He nodded toward the living room. "They all have their bags packed, ready to come with us."

She sighed and replaced her fingertips with her lips, brushing his ever so slowly. "Then I see no reason to spoil my granny's devout belief in the grot ring and happy endings."

Epilogue

Even on Christmas Day the casino at the Bellagio was packed with hopeful players. But here, floors above the clamor, in the changing room of the chapel, there was only serene silence.

Rebecca wondered how many others who began their journey to "happily ever after" in this wedding chapel felt the same raw rush of emotion. *I'm marrying the love of my life.*

Clasping her small bouquet of red roses to her breasts, she stepped to the door of the chapel, festooned with more roses. Everyone she loved turned to look at her.

Her family. Old and new.

David rushed up the aisle and clasped her hand. His gaze swept over her gold Luca Luca gown, and he grinned.

"I love you in that dress. I can't wait to take it off you."

He tried to pull her forward, but she resisted, digging in her stilettos.

He kissed her hand. "Nerves?"

"Confession. You should know I'm really not a very good cook."

He kissed her nose. "I am."

"Do you have any last words?" she whispered, dangerously close to tears of joy.

He took a deep breath. "Are you all right with being a grandmother so soon?"

She glanced past him to Jasmine, who glowed with impending motherhood. "Are you kidding? *That* was the deciding vote to marry you. Everyone I know says if they'd known what fun grandchildren are, they would have had them first. I am."

He tilted her chin up and gazed into her eyes. "Then what are we waiting for?"

Hand in hand, they walked into the glorious future.

DON'T MISS SHERRILL BODINE'S NEXT BOOK!

CHICAGO JOURNAL AND COURIER
SUNDAY

Talk of the Town
by Rebecca Covington-Sumner

Darlings, tongues are wagging about the grand opening of Pandora's Box. Athena Smith is opening the vintage couture bazaar with her sisters in honor of their late mother. After all, it was she who taught them that when you enter a woman's closet, you get a glimpse into her life: who she is, who she has been, and who she has hoped to be.

But their mother never dreamed that her beloved oldest daughter, Athena, would have the opportunity to get a glimpse into the closet of Chicago's most famous family: the Clayworth's top-secret fallout shelter built beneath a farmer's field during the cold war. And she certainly never dreamed that Athena would be battling the Clayworth heirs of our iconic Chicago Store to salvage her father's once pristine reputation. In this battle of wits and wills between Athena and Dr. Drew Clayworth, the most enigmatic of the devastatingly handsome cousins, enough sparks will fly to light up our long, hot summer nights.

Sherrill Bodine's next book promises to open up the secrets of Chicago's finest closets to all of us. Don't miss it! And check out her Web site at www.sherrillbodine.com.

THE DISH

Where authors give you the inside scoop!

♥ ♥ ♥ ♥ ♥ ♥ ♥ ♥ ♥ ♥ ♥ ♥ ♥ ♥ ♥

From the desk of Eve Silver

Dear Reader,

The best part about writing a series is falling in love with the characters and having the chance to visit them again. The tough part is writing a book that can be read as part of an ongoing story and read as a stand-alone. Those are the series I enjoy most as a reader, and in DEMON'S HUNGER (on sale now), I was determined to create a unique and independent story within the larger framework of the Compact of Sorcerers series.

I wanted Dain Hawkins, the sexy, seductive mage of illusion first introduced in DEMON'S KISS, to have a chance at his happily-ever-after. But I needed a heroine who was his true match, someone strong and smart and independent, someone who could hold her own. Someone who could help him overcome the shadows of his past. I'm such a sucker for a tortured hero.

In DEMON'S HUNGER, Vivien Cairn is a forensic anthropologist who fears she's losing her mind. She's been suffering from blackouts, with no memory of where she's been or what she's done.

When Dain asks for her help in hunting a super-natural serial killer, she agrees, and as they delve deeper into the mysterious deaths, they are forced to confront the horrific possibility that Vivien is somehow connected to the crimes. But is Vivien the killer . . . or the next intended victim?

Bones play an important role in the hunt for the killer, and the study of bones happens to be near and dear to my heart. I'm an instructor of human anatomy, so the unfolding connection between the killer and the bespelled bones in the story held a particular fascination for me. The research for this story was great fun, and I almost forgot to draw the line and not dig deeper than I absolutely had to. Oh, and the urge to include pages of scientific explanation was powerful, but I wrestled it into submission and included only the tidbits that the story absolutely required. Temptation, temptation. LOL!

For more info on the Compact of Sorcerers, check out my Web site at www.evesilver.net.

Happy reading!

Eve Silver

♥ ♥   ♥ ♥ ♥ ♥   ♥   ♥

From the desk of Sherrill Bodine

Darling Reader,

As my heroine Rebecca Covington would say, *I promise to tell you everything!*

Renowned as Chicago's most notorious gossip columnist and real spitfire to boot, Rebecca certainly isn't shy about keeping her word in TALK OF THE TOWN (on sale now). She *reveals all*, especially how she feels when the new owner of the *Chicago Daily Mail* tosses her off her gossip guru throne and into the lowly Home and Food section to write a biweekly recipe column. The best part is what she plans to do to regain her lofty position and convince the new boss he's made a dreadful error in judgment . . . but I'm not going to tell you *all* of Rebecca's secrets. You'll have to pick up a copy of TALK OF THE TOWN and read them for yourself!

I will say *anyone's* best laid plans would go awry when confronted by her boss, David Alan Sumner. Not only is he impossibly handsome, intriguingly arrogant, and wealthy, he also possesses a nobility of spirit that is impossible to resist—although she gives it her best shot. After all, she is no longer a naïve young woman who is looking for prince charming. She's been through the divorce wars, so she no longer believes in "happily ever after." But then why does David inspire such powerful, passionate, *torrid* emotions, bringing her to wish for the impossible?

Much of TALK OF THE TOWN is based on my life and friends in Chicago, so research is a joy—I'm living it and loving it. I *especially* love sharing some of my favorite haunts, like Lulu's—truly the finest vintage couture anywhere—and a few of *my* favorite recipes from when I cooked. Don't miss the *Not Low Cal Triple Orgasmic Fudge Pie*. I promise it is worth every calorie. It actually won a bake-off, and my friend Ann has the first-place copper pan to prove it. *She* is truly Chicago's most famous gossip columnist, and at her knee, I learned to always change names to protect the guilty. Lucky for the innocent, they have nothing to hide.

I hope you enjoy this peek beneath society's glitter and into its heart. I'd love to hear *your* secrets, so please visit me at www.sherrillbodine.com!

Sherrill Bodine

Want more contemporary romance?
You'll love these titles!

Jane Graves

"Sassy, sexy and fun. Jane Graves will win your heart."
—LORI FOSTER, *New York Times* bestselling author

TALL TALES AND WEDDING VEILS
0-446-61787-3

HOT WHEELS AND HIGH HEELS
0-446-61786-5

Diana Holquist

"A writer to watch."
—DEIRDRE MARTIN, *USA Today* bestselling author

HUNGRY FOR MORE
0-446-19704-1

SEXIEST MAN ALIVE
0-446-61798-9

MAKE ME A MATCH
0-446-61797-0

Wendy Markham

"A fun, yet unique voice which we'll enjoy
for a long time."
—*Rendezvous*

THAT'S AMORE
0-446-61844-6

LOVE, SUBURBAN STYLE
0-446-61843-8

BRIDE NEEDS GROOM
0-446-61454-8

HELLO, IT'S ME
0-446-61453-X

ONCE UPON A BLIND DATE
0-446-61176-X

THE NINE MONTH PLAN
0-446-61175-1

Want to know more about romances at
Grand Central Publishing and Forever?
Get the scoop online!

GRAND CENTRAL PUBLISHING'S
ROMANCE HOME PAGE

Visit us at www.hachettebookgroup.com/romance
for all the latest news, reviews, and chapter excerpts!

NEW AND UPCOMING TITLES

Each month we feature our new titles
and reader favorites.

CONTESTS AND GIVEAWAYS

We give away galleys, autographed copies,
and all kinds of fun stuff.

AUTHOR INFO

You'll find bios, articles, and links to personal
Web sites for all your favorite authors—and
so much more!

THE BUZZ

Sign up for our monthly romance newsletter,
and be the first to read all about it!

VISIT US ONLINE
@ WWW.HACHETTEBOOKGROUP.COM.

AT THE HACHETTE BOOK GROUP WEB SITE YOU'LL FIND:

CHAPTER EXCERPTS FROM SELECTED NEW RELEASES
•
ORIGINAL AUTHOR AND EDITOR ARTICLES
•
AUDIO EXCERPTS
•
BESTSELLER NEWS
•
ELECTRONIC NEWSLETTERS
•
AUTHOR TOUR INFORMATION
•
CONTESTS, QUIZZES, AND POLLS
•
FUN, QUIRKY RECOMMENDATION CENTER
•
PLUS MUCH MORE!

BOOKMARK HACHETTE BOOK GROUP
@ WWW.HACHETTEBOOKGROUP.COM.